P9-DUV-721

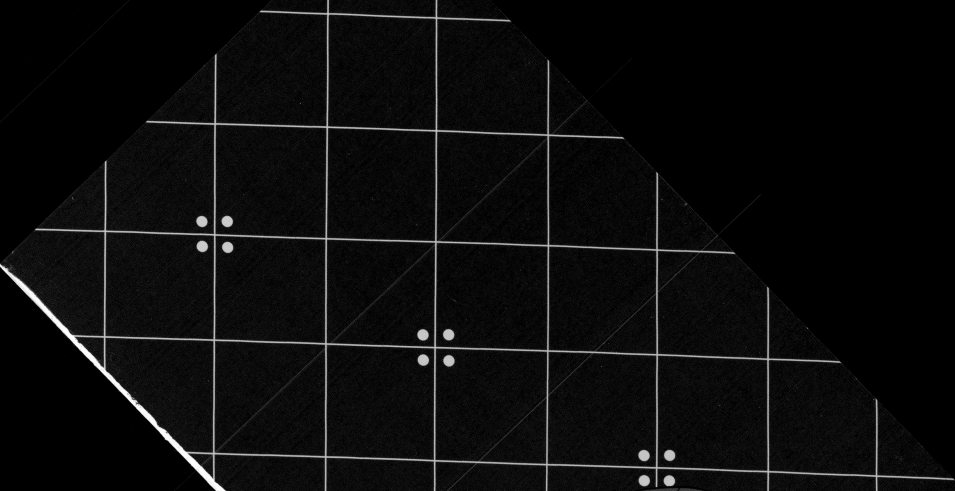

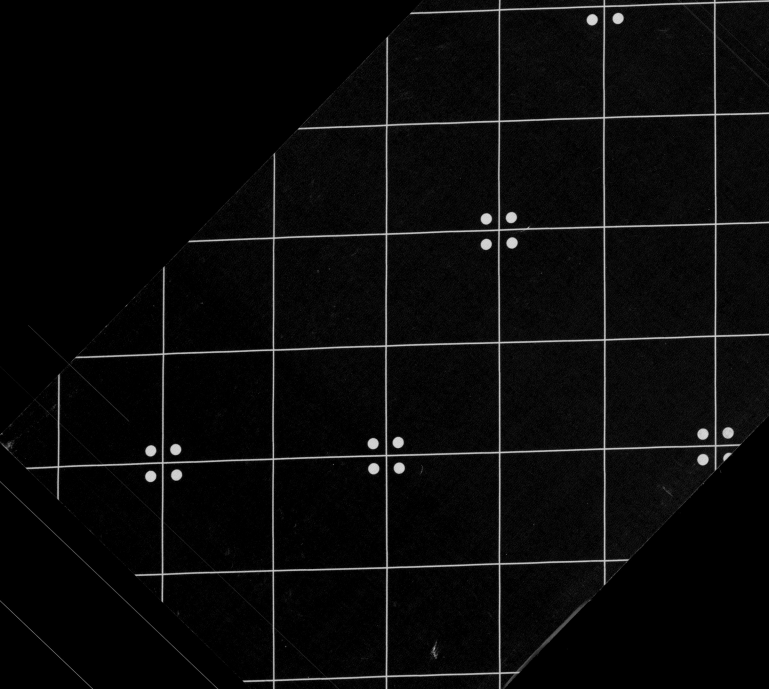

33305250485301
ca   07/29/22

DRAGON KINGDOM

of Wrenly

GHOST ISLAND

By Jordan Quinn

Illustrated by Ornella Greco at Glass House Graphics

LITTLE SIMON

New York   London   Toronto   Sydney   New Delhi

This book is a work of fiction. Any references to historical events, real people, or real places are used fictitiously. Other names, characters, places, and events are products of the author's imagination, and any resemblance to actual events or places or persons, living or dead, is entirely coincidental.

LITTLE SIMON

An imprint of Simon & Schuster Children's Publishing Division
1230 Avenue of the Americas, New York, New York 10020
First Little Simon edition July 2021
Copyright © 2021 by Simon & Schuster, Inc.
All rights reserved, including the right of reproduction in whole or in part in any form.
LITTLE SIMON is a registered trademark of Simon & Schuster, Inc., and associated colophon is a
trademark of Simon & Schuster, Inc. For information about special discounts for bulk purchases, please
contact Simon & Schuster Special Sales at 1-866-506-1949 or business@simonandschuster.com.
The Simon & Schuster Speakers Bureau can bring authors to your live event. For more information or
to book an event, contact the Simon & Schuster Speakers Bureau at 1-866-248-3049 or visit our website
at www.simonspeakers.com.
Designed by Kayla Wasil
Text by Matthew J. Gilbert
GLASS HOUSE GRAPHICS Creative Services
Art and cover by ORNELLA GRECO
Colors by ORNELLA GRECO and GABRIELE CRACOLICI
Lettering by GIOVANNI SPATARO/Grafimated Cartoon
Supervision by SALVATORE DI MARCO/Grafimated Cartoon
Manufactured in China 0421 SCP
2 4 6 8 10 9 7 5 3 1
Library of Congress Cataloging-in-Publication Data
Names: Quinn, Jordan, author. | Glass House Graphics, illustrator.
Title: Ghost island / by Jordan Quinn ; illustrated by Glass House Graphics.
Description: First Little Simon edition. | New York : Little Simon, 2021. | Series: Dragon kingdom of Wrenly; 4
| Audience: Ages 5–9 | Audience: Grades K–1 | Summary: "Fresh off the excitement of the Night Hunt, Ruskin,
Cinder, Groth, and Roke set out for a camping trip on Ghost Island, which, according to Groth, is definitely not
haunted despite its name"–Provided by publisher.
Identifiers: LCCN 2020027675 (print) | LCCN 2020027676 (ebook) | ISBN 9781534478664 (paperback) |
ISBN 9781534478671 (hardcover) | ISBN 9781534478688 (ebook)
Subjects: LCSH: Graphic novels. | Graphic novels. | CYAC: Dragons–Fiction. | Fantasy.
Classification: LCC PZ7.7.Q55 Gh 2021 (print) | LCC PZ7.7.Q55 (ebook) | DDC 741.5/973–dc23
LC record available at https://lccn.loc.gov/2020027675
LC ebook record available at https://lccn.loc.gov/2020027676

Contents

Chapter 1

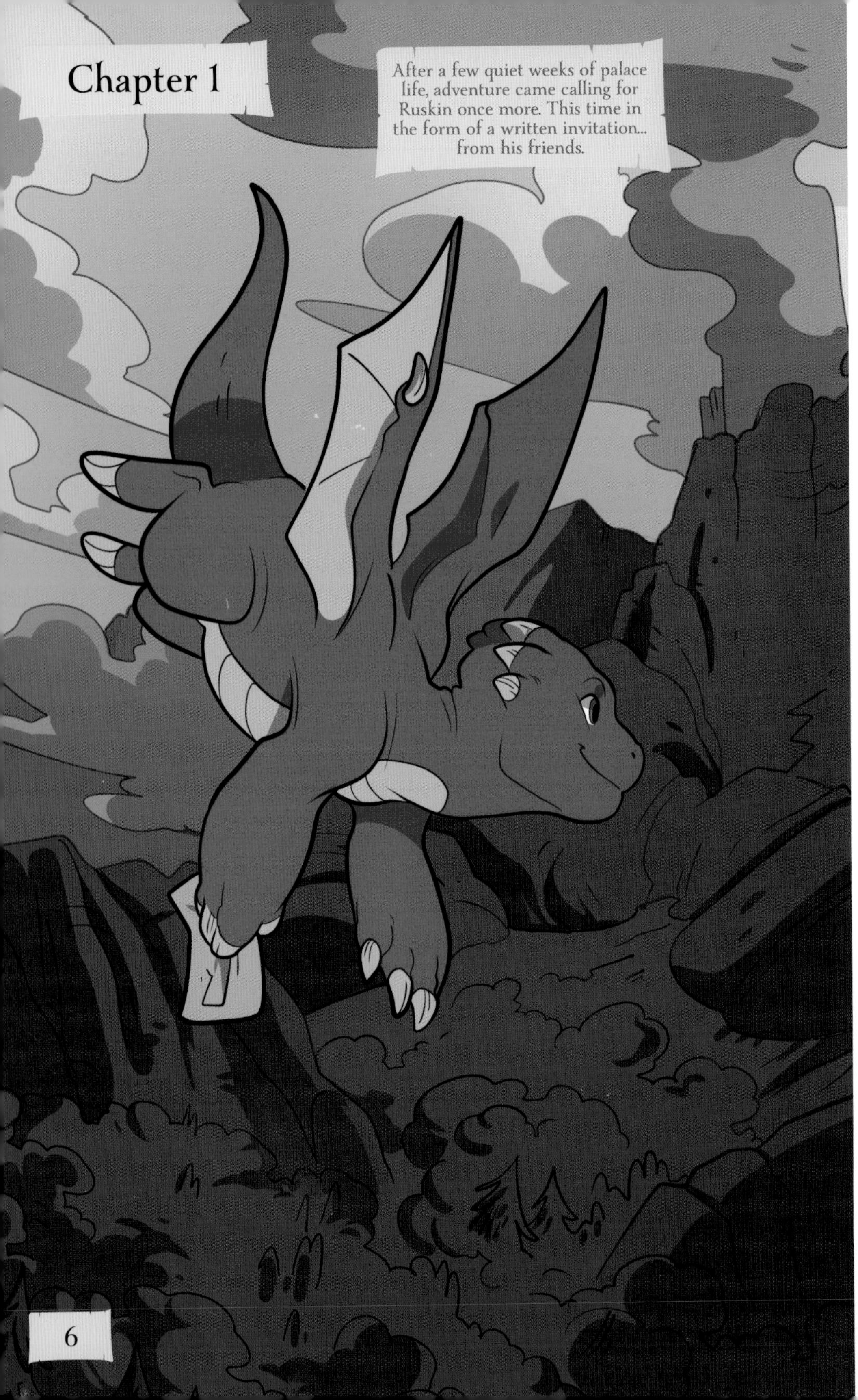
After a few quiet weeks of palace life, adventure came calling for Ruskin once more. This time in the form of a written invitation... from his friends.

Best buddy!

It seems I've been invited to an overnight camping adventure...

...and "adventure" is underlined, like, eighteen times.

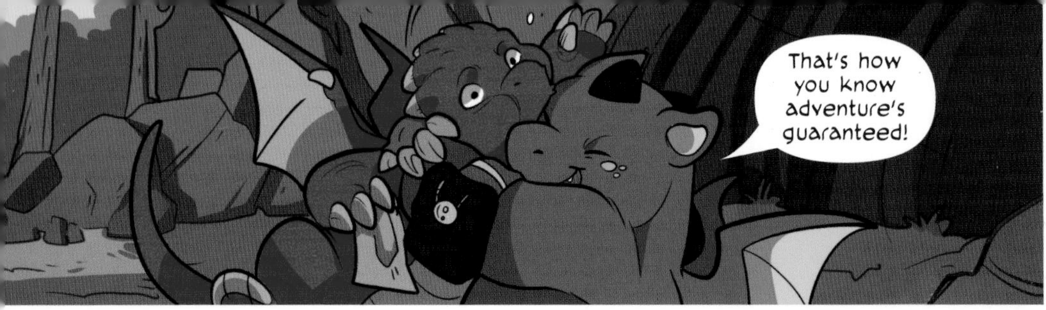
That's how you know adventure's guaranteed!

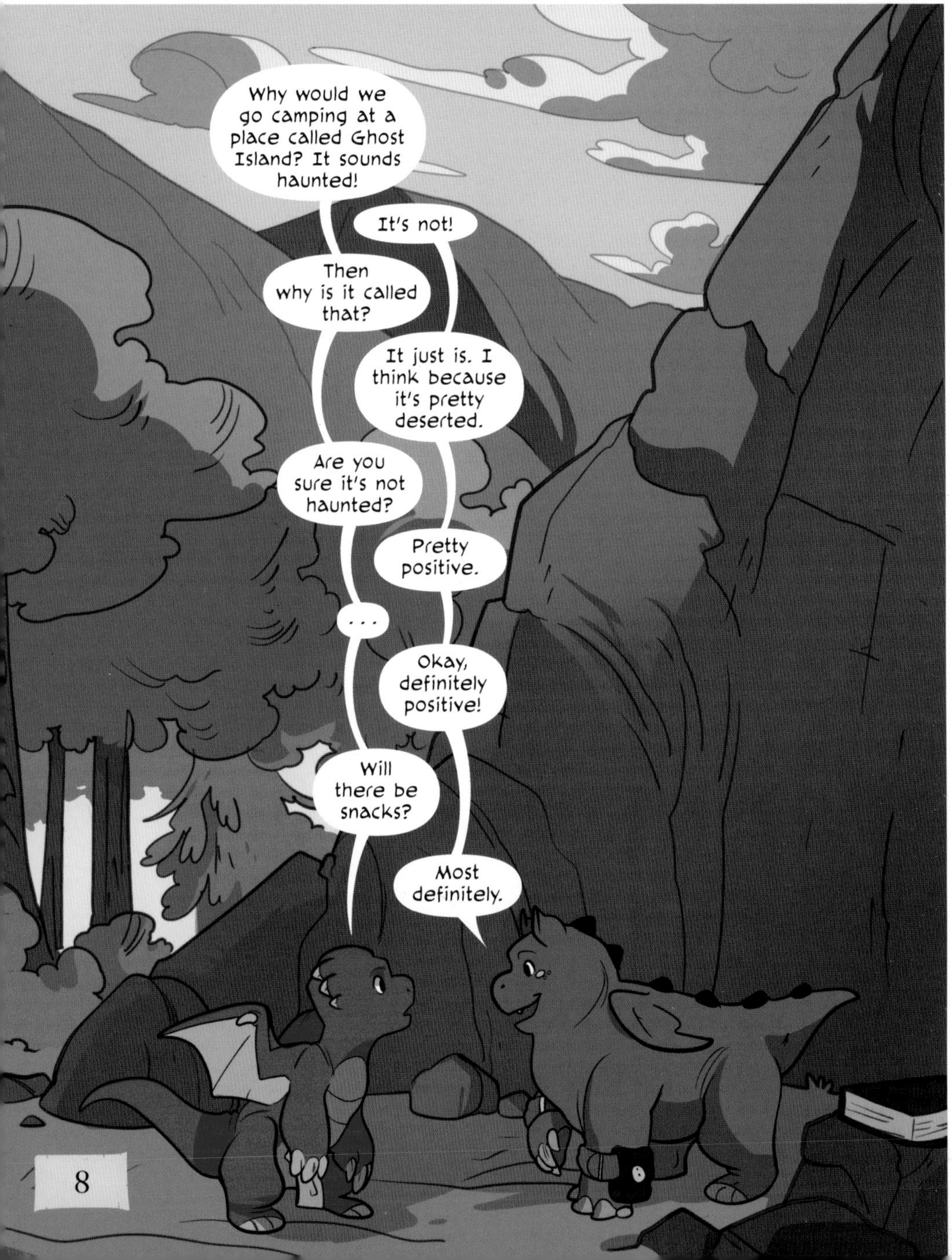
Why would we go camping at a place called Ghost Island? It sounds haunted!
It's not!
Then why is it called that?
It just is. I think because it's pretty deserted.
Are you sure it's not haunted?
Pretty positive.
. . .
Okay, definitely positive!
Will there be snacks?
Most definitely.

9

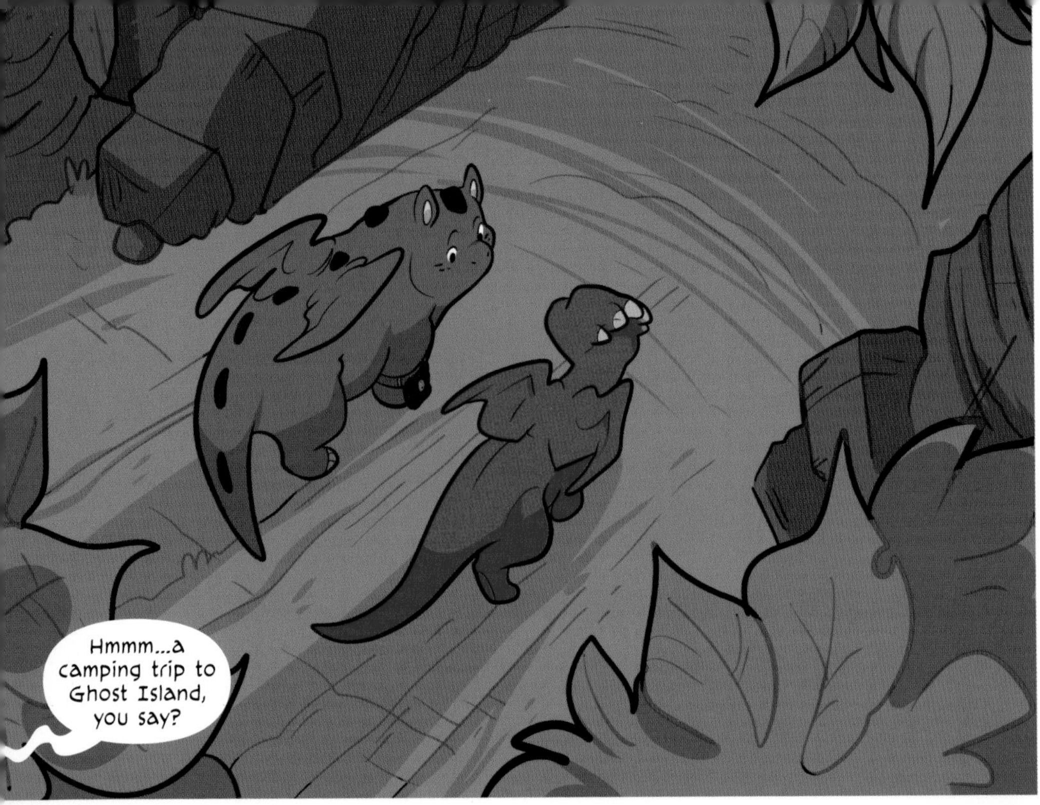
Hmmm...a camping trip to Ghost Island, you say?

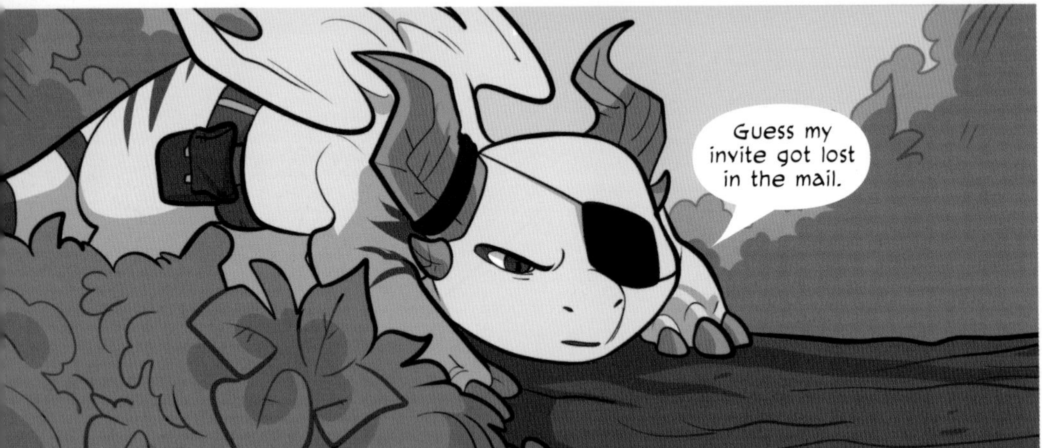
Guess my invite got lost in the mail.

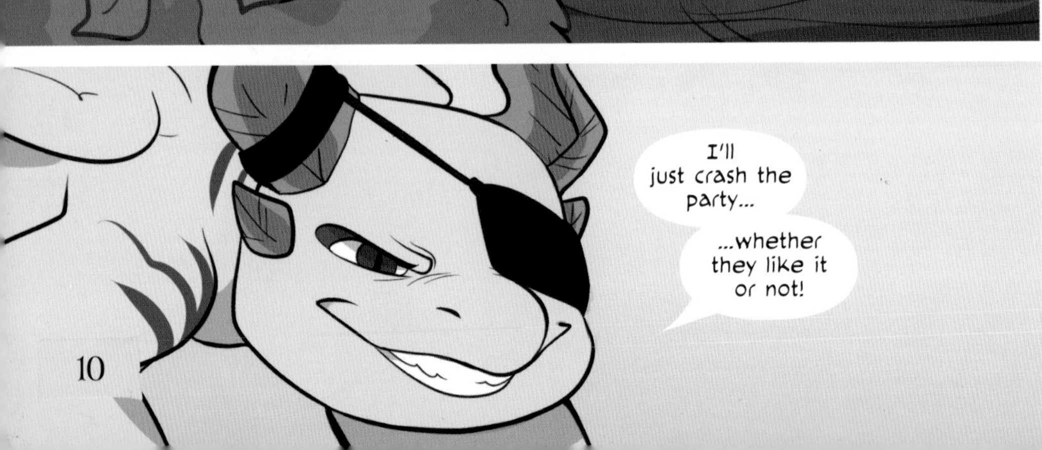
I'll just crash the party...
...whether they like it or not!

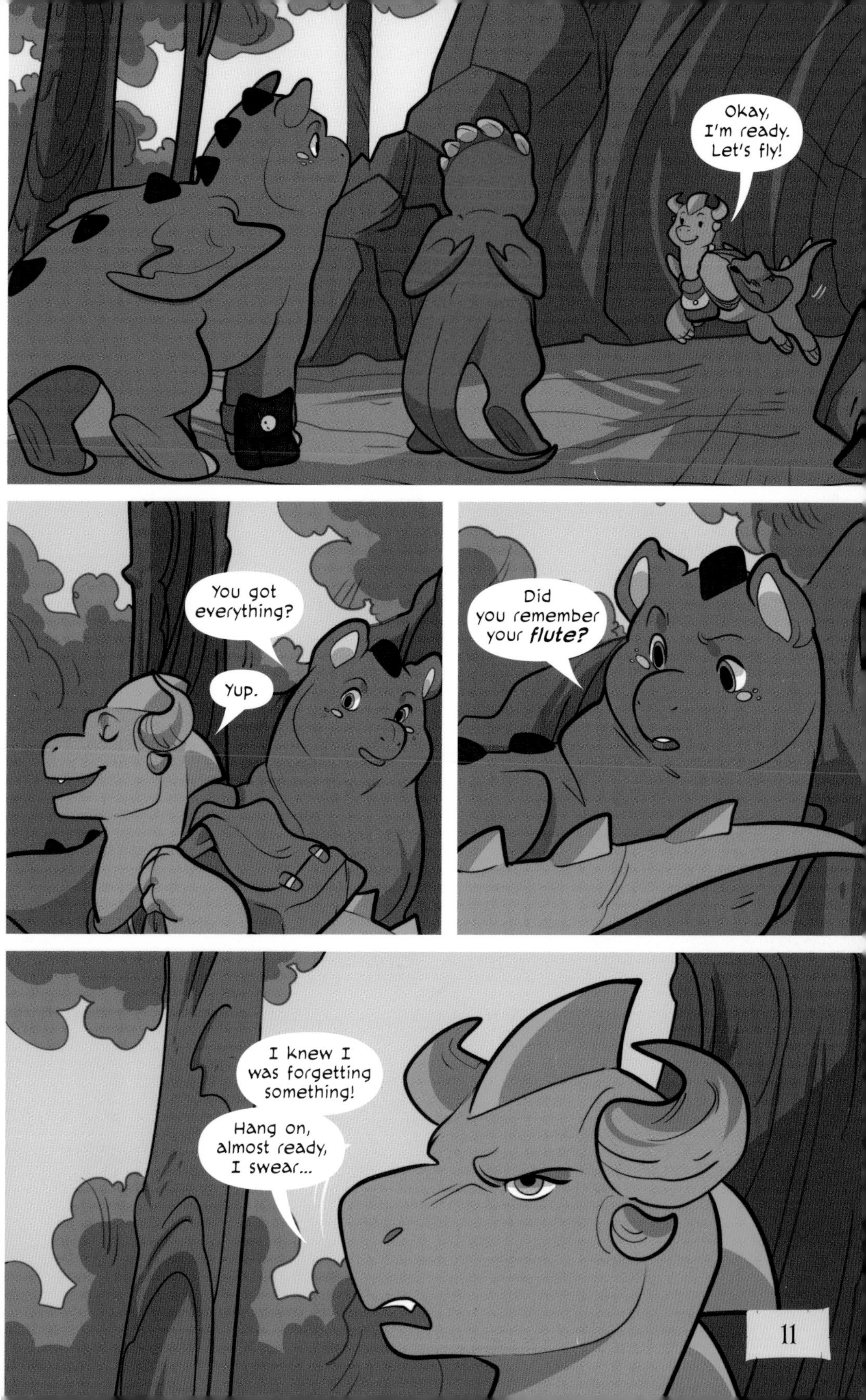
Okay, I'm ready. Let's fly!
You got everything?
Yup.
Did you remember your ***flute?***
I knew I was forgetting something!
Hang on, almost ready, I swear...

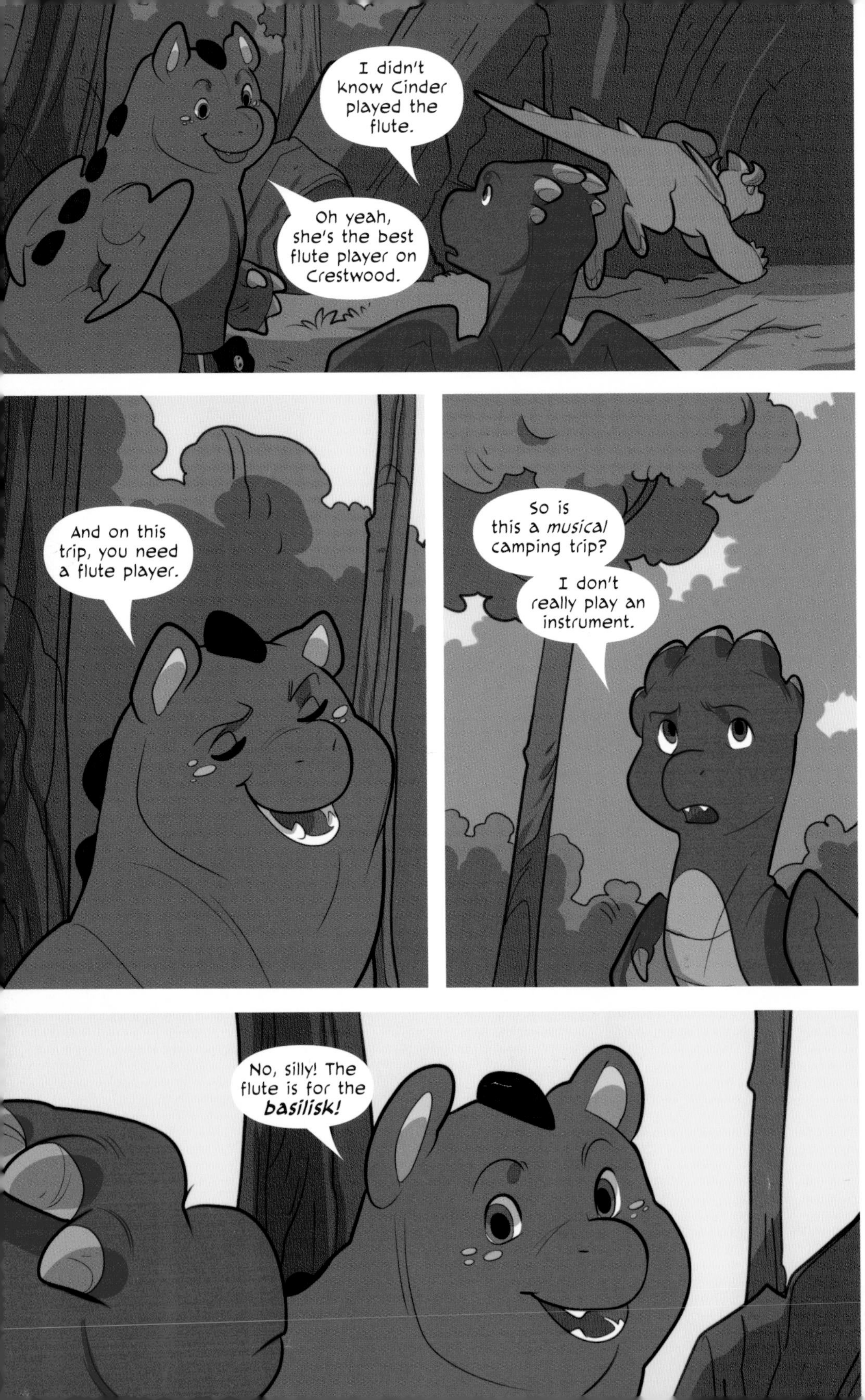
I didn't know Cinder played the flute.
Oh yeah, she's the best flute player on Crestwood.
And on this trip, you need a flute player.
So is this a *musical* camping trip?
I don't really play an instrument.
No, silly! The flute is for the ***basilisk!***

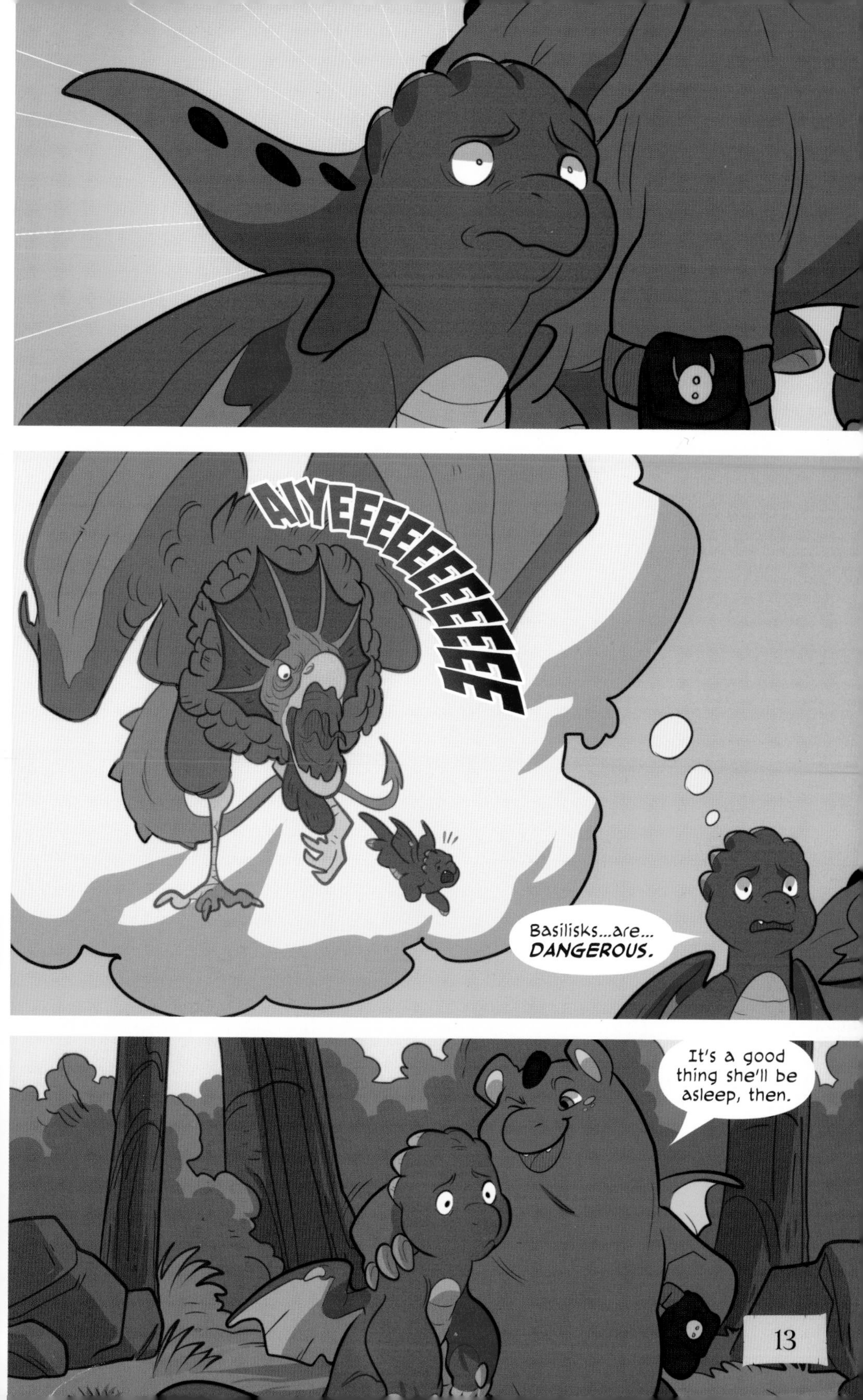
AIYEEEEEEEEEEEE
Basilisks...are...
DANGEROUS.
It's a good thing she'll be asleep, then.

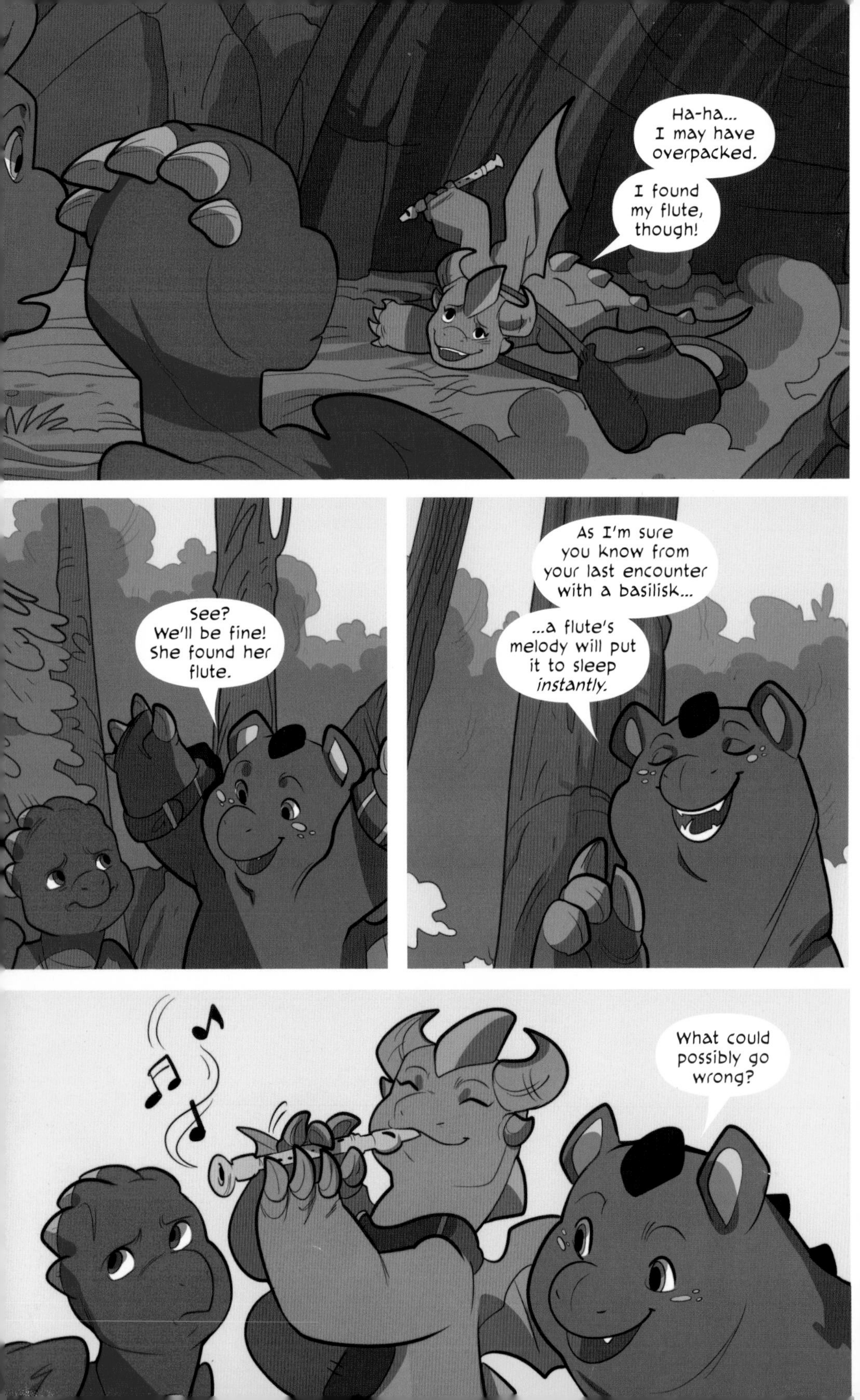
Ha-ha... I may have overpacked.
I found my flute, though!
See? We'll be fine! She found her flute.
As I'm sure you know from your last encounter with a basilisk...
...a flute's melody will put it to sleep *instantly.*
What could possibly go wrong?

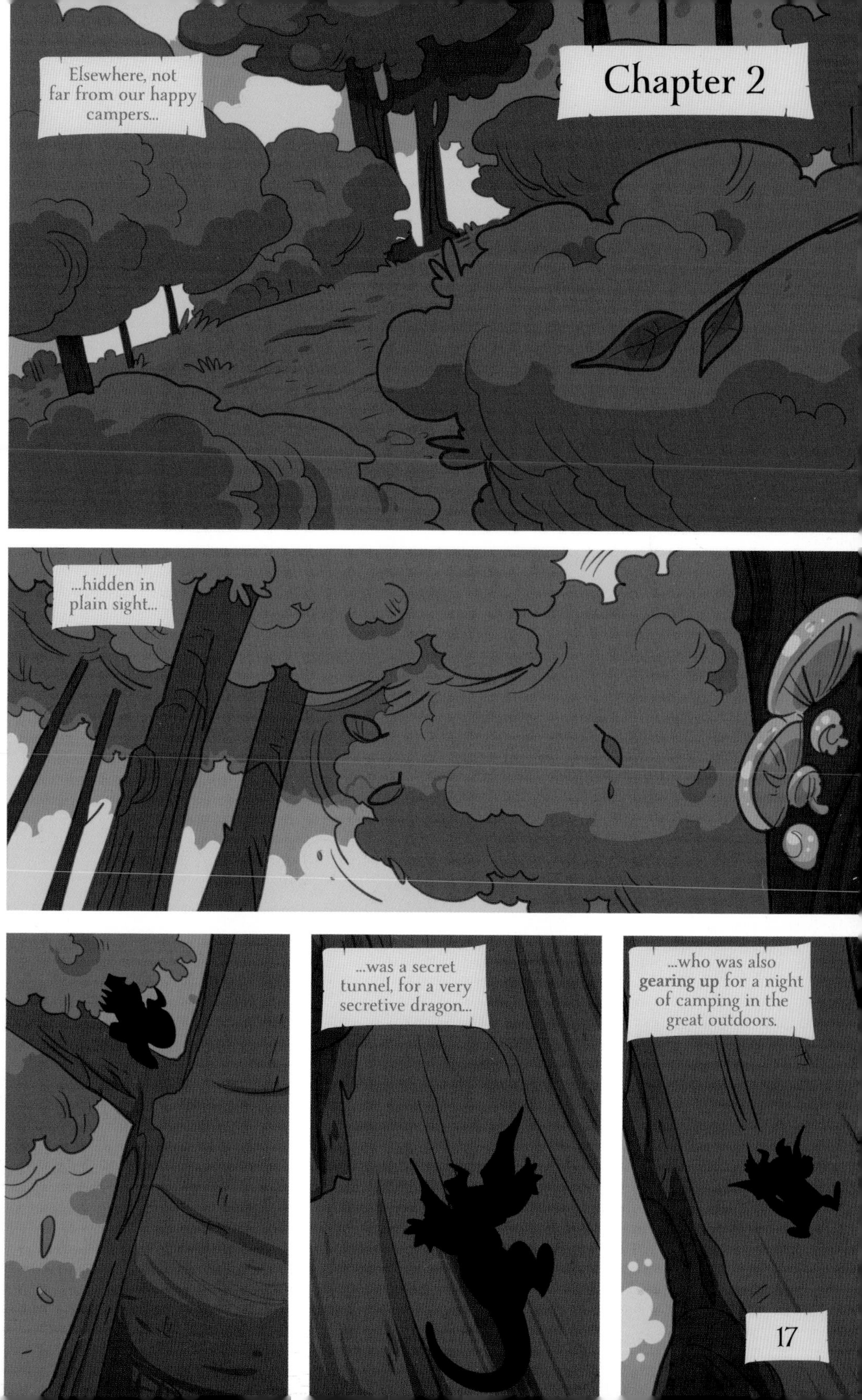
Chapter 2
Elsewhere, not far from our happy campers...
...hidden in plain sight...
...was a secret tunnel, for a very secretive dragon...
...who was also **gearing up** for a night of camping in the great outdoors.

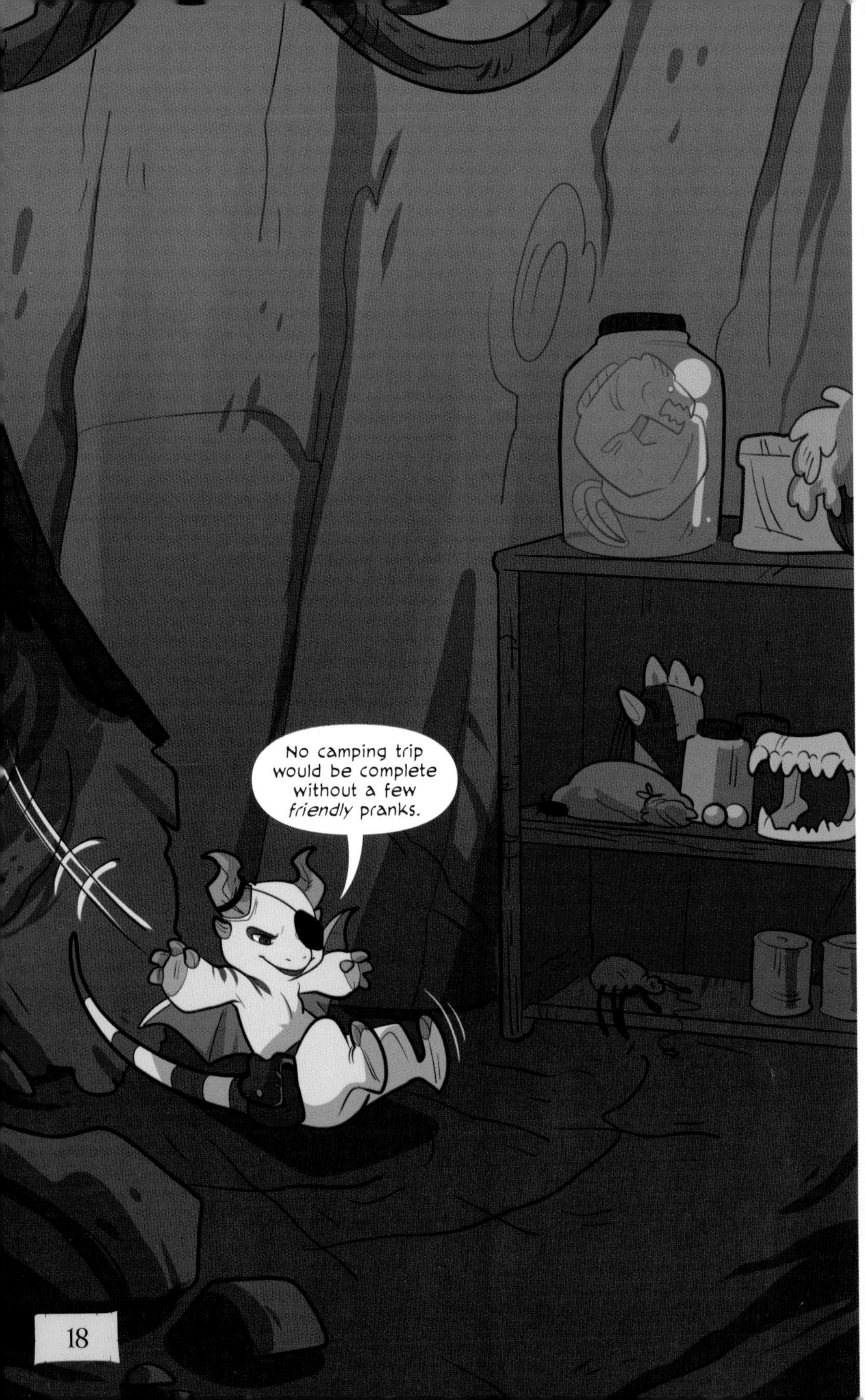
No camping trip would be complete without a few *friendly* pranks.

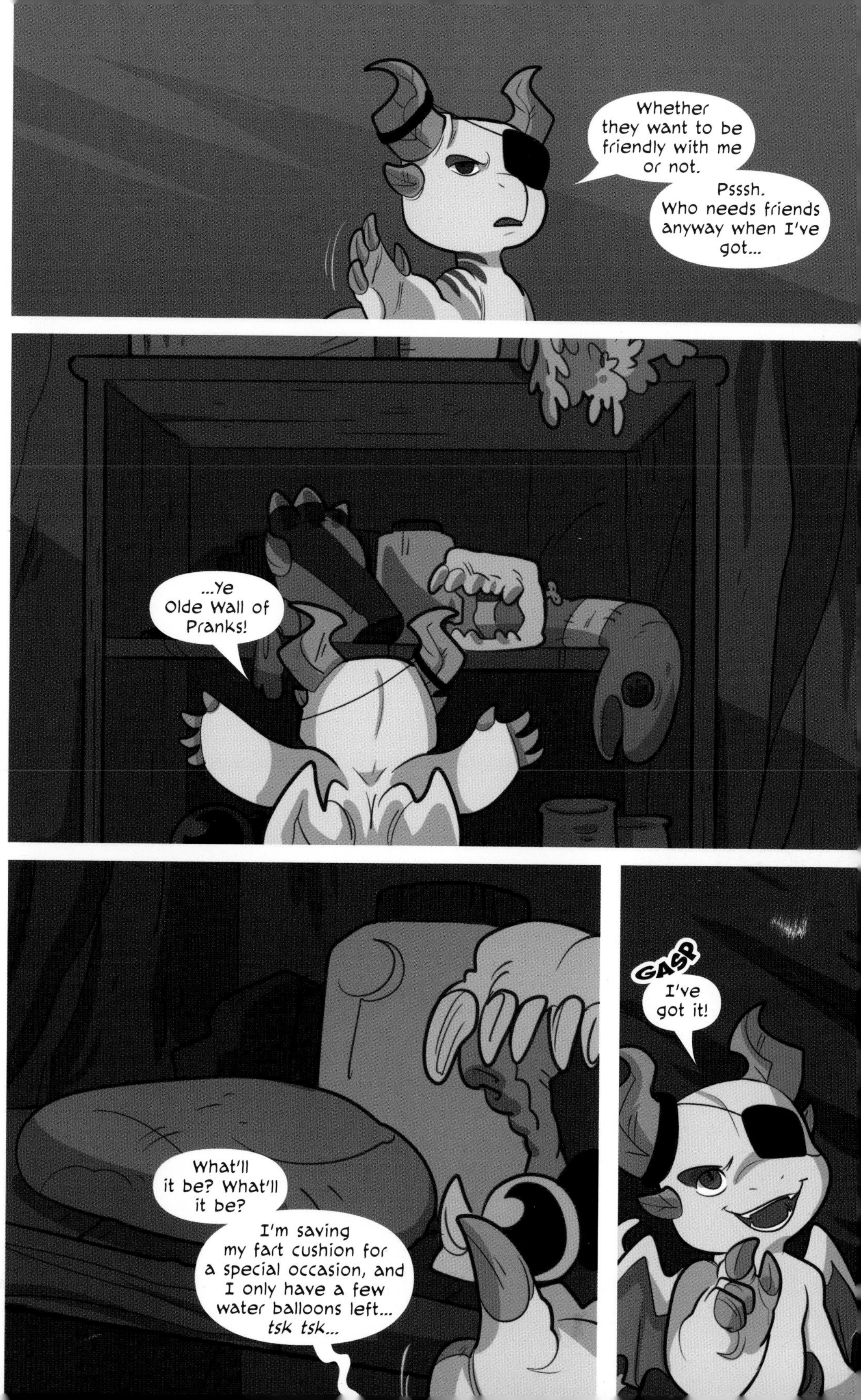
Whether they want to be friendly with me or not.
Psssh. Who needs friends anyway when I've got...
...Ye Olde Wall of Pranks!
What'll it be? What'll it be?
I'm saving my fart cushion for a special occasion, and I only have a few water balloons left... *tsk tsk...*
GASP
I've got it!

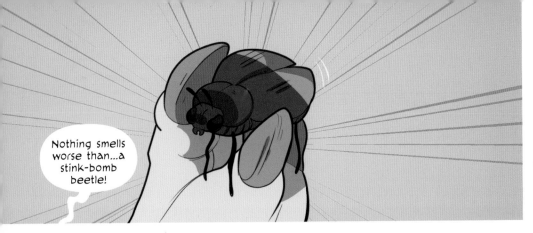

Nothing smells worse than...a stink-bomb beetle!

SNIFF SNIFF SNIFF

Still has that "just died" smell.

They're EXACTLY what I need!

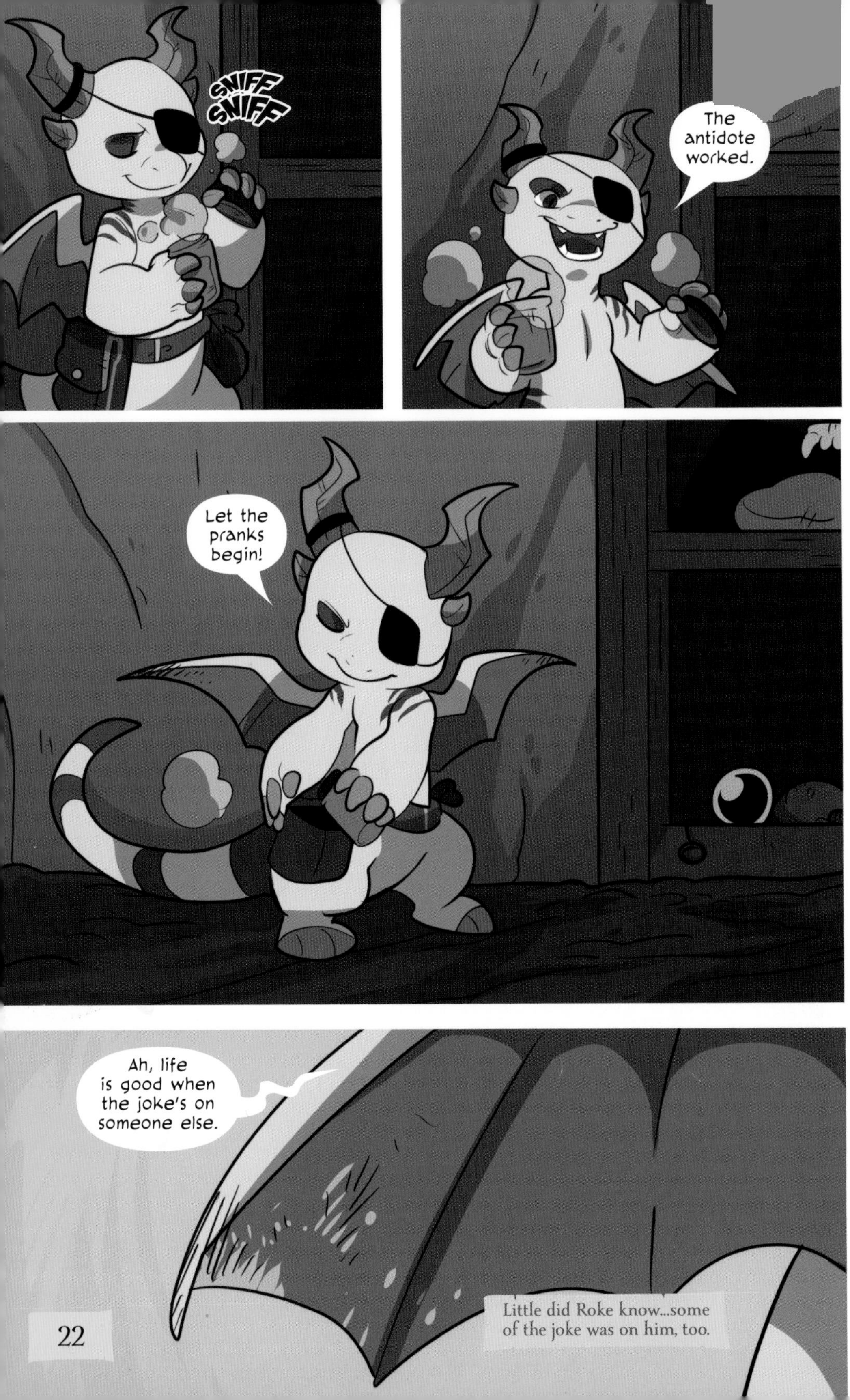
SNIFF SNIFF
The antidote worked.
Let the pranks begin!
Ah, life is good when the joke's on someone else.
Little did Roke know...some of the joke was on him, too.

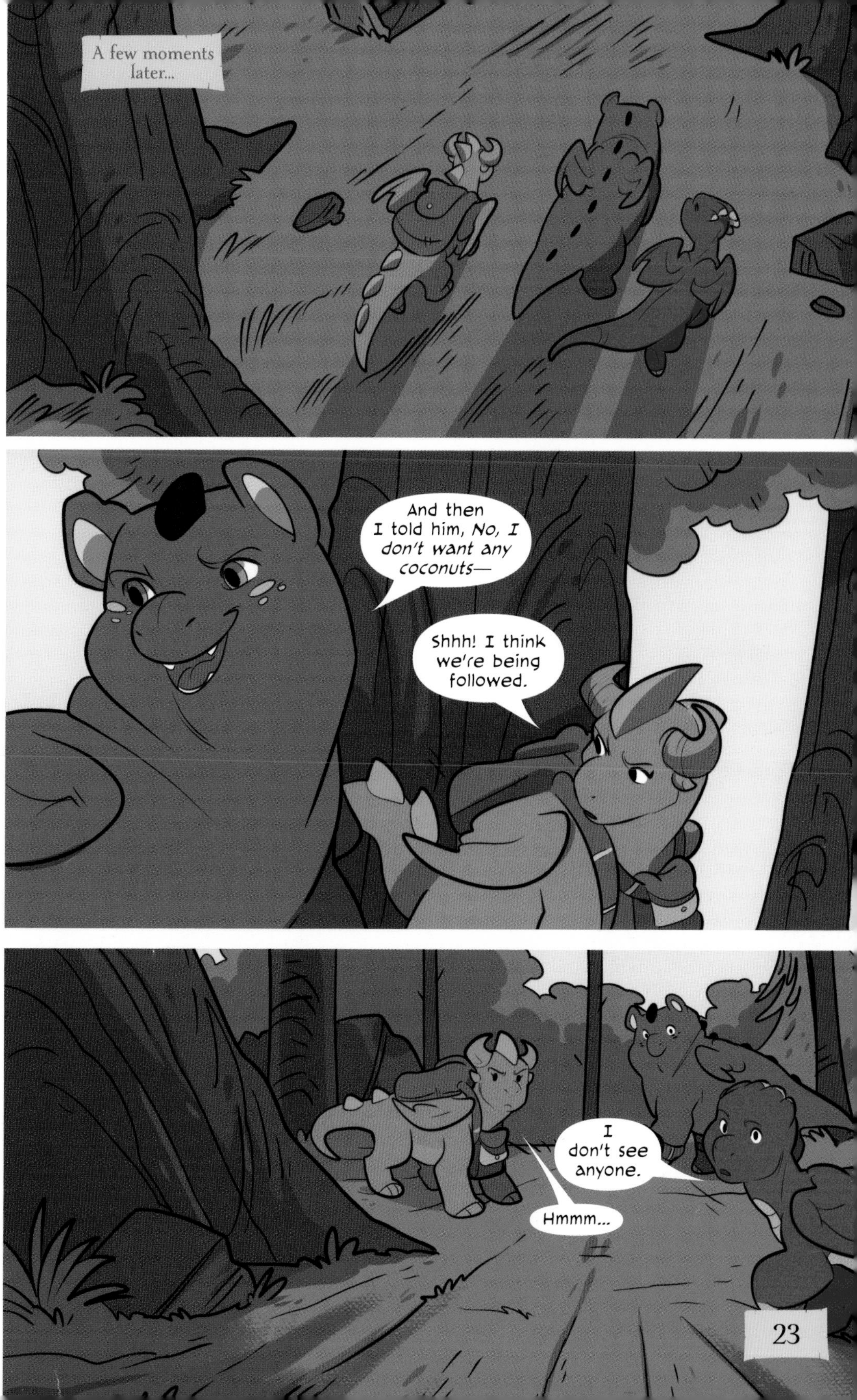
A few moments later...
And then I told him, *No, I don't want any coconuts*—
Shhh! I think we're being followed.
I don't see anyone.
Hmmm...

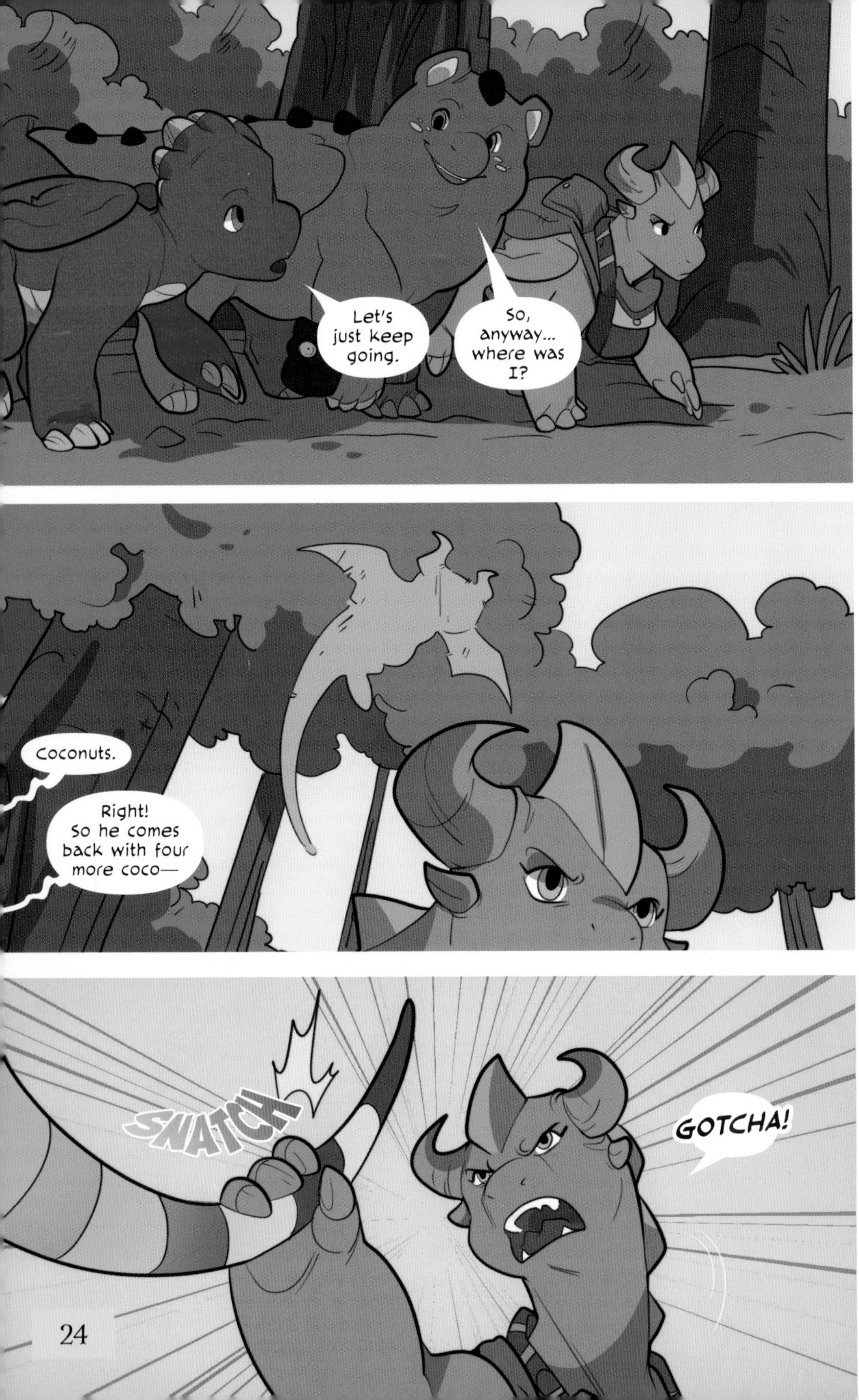
Let's just keep going.
So, anyway... where was I?
Coconuts.
Right! So he comes back with four more coco—
SNATCH
GOTCHA!

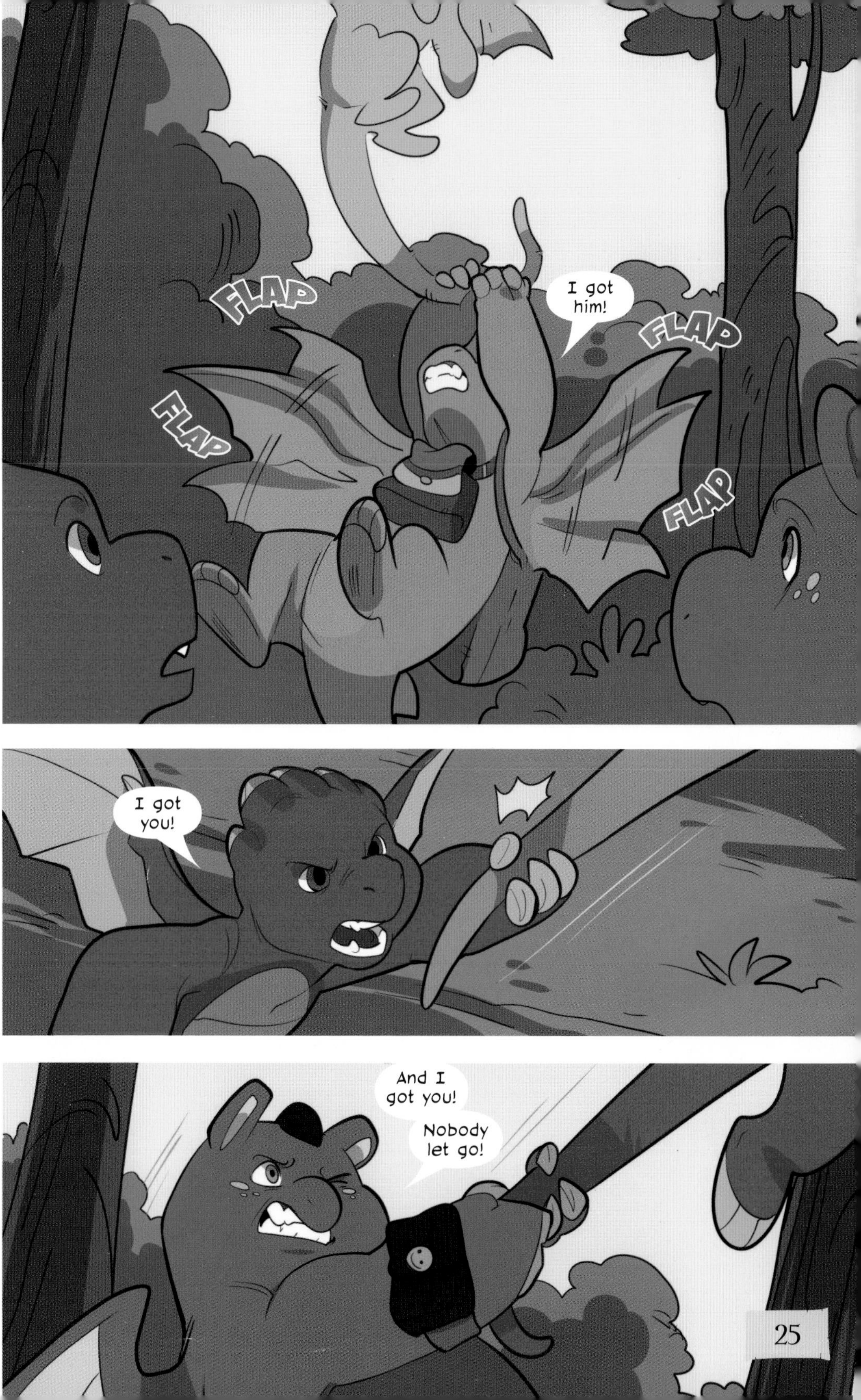
FLAP
FLAP
I got him!
FLAP
FLAP
I got you!
And I got you!
Nobody let go!

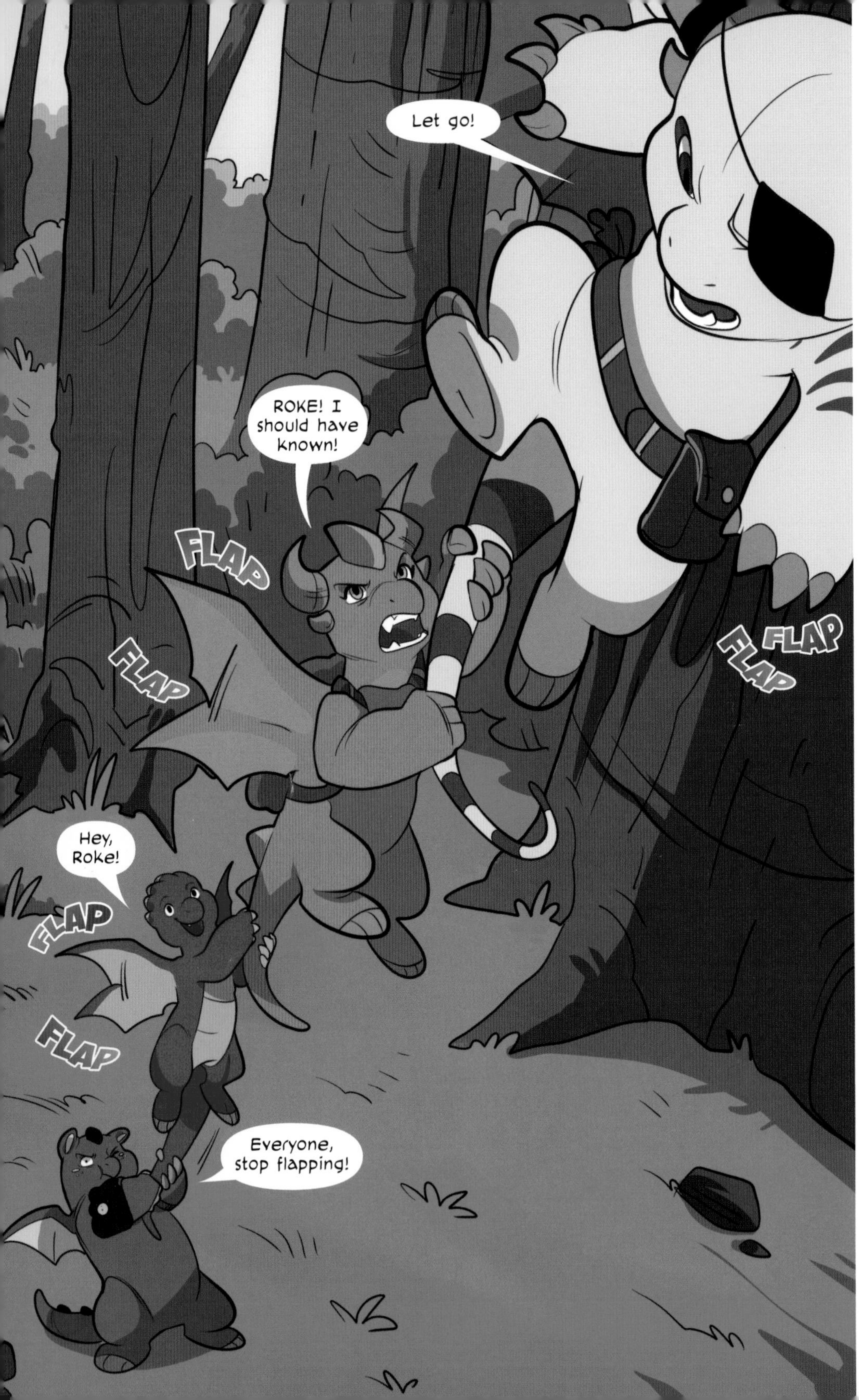

Let go!
ROKE! I should have known!
FLAP
FLAP
FLAP
FLAP
Hey, Roke!
FLAP
FLAP
Everyone, stop flapping!

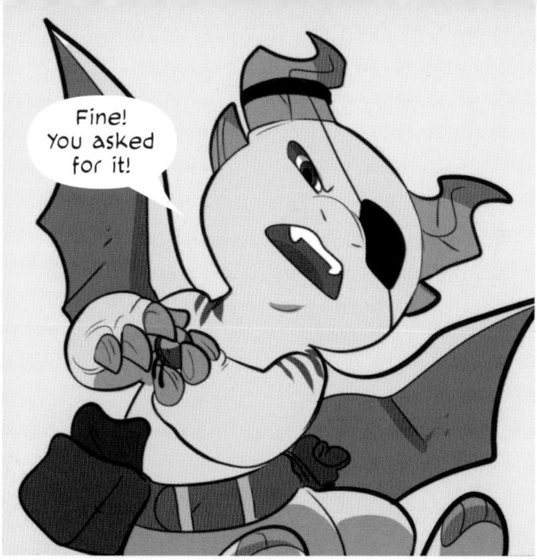
Fine! You asked for it!

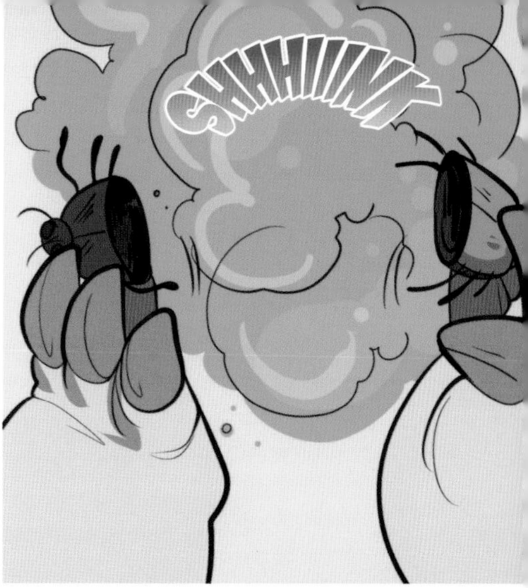
SHHHIIINK

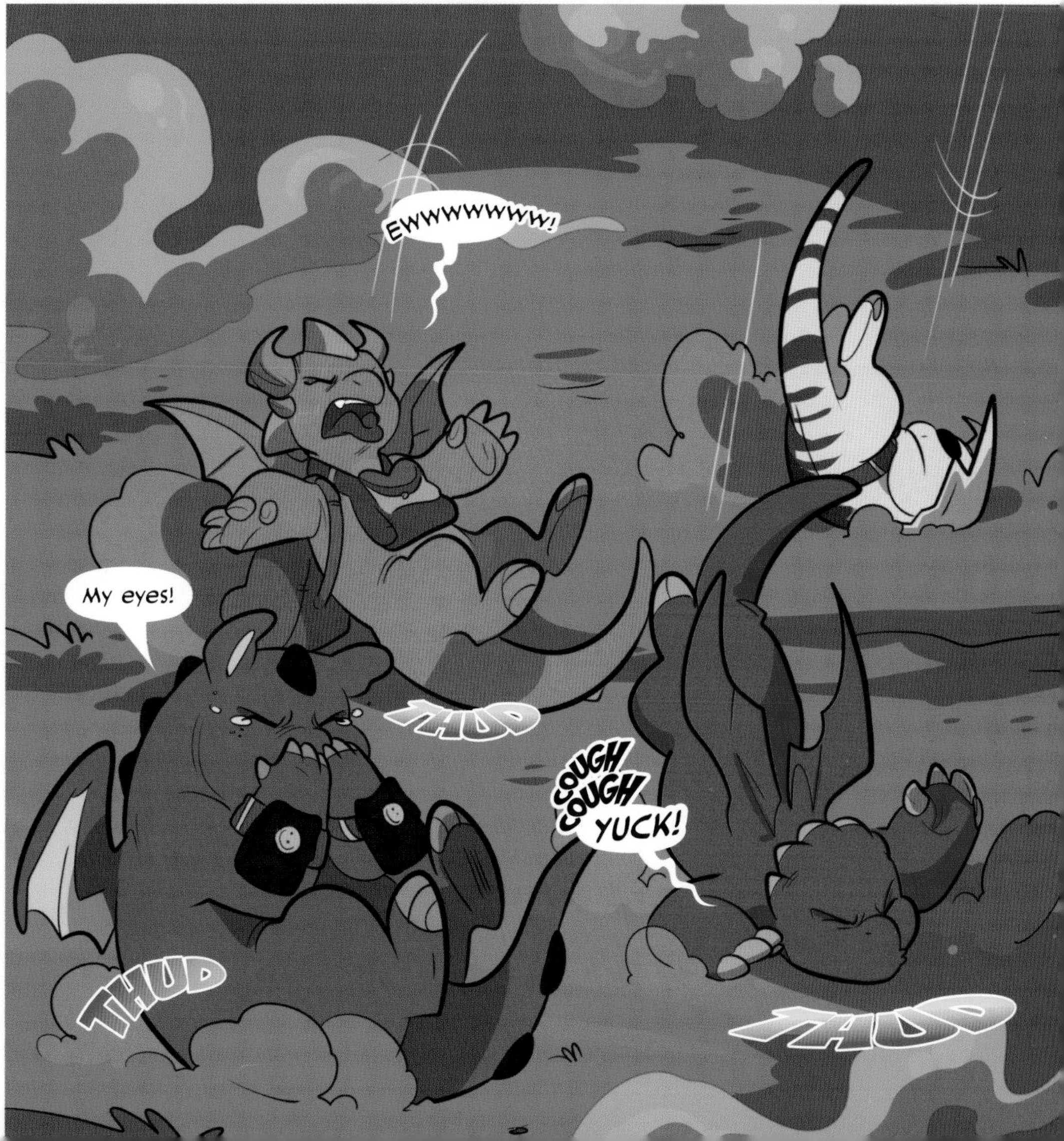
EWWWWWWW!
My eyes!
THUD
COUGH COUGH
YUCK!
THUD
THUD

29

30

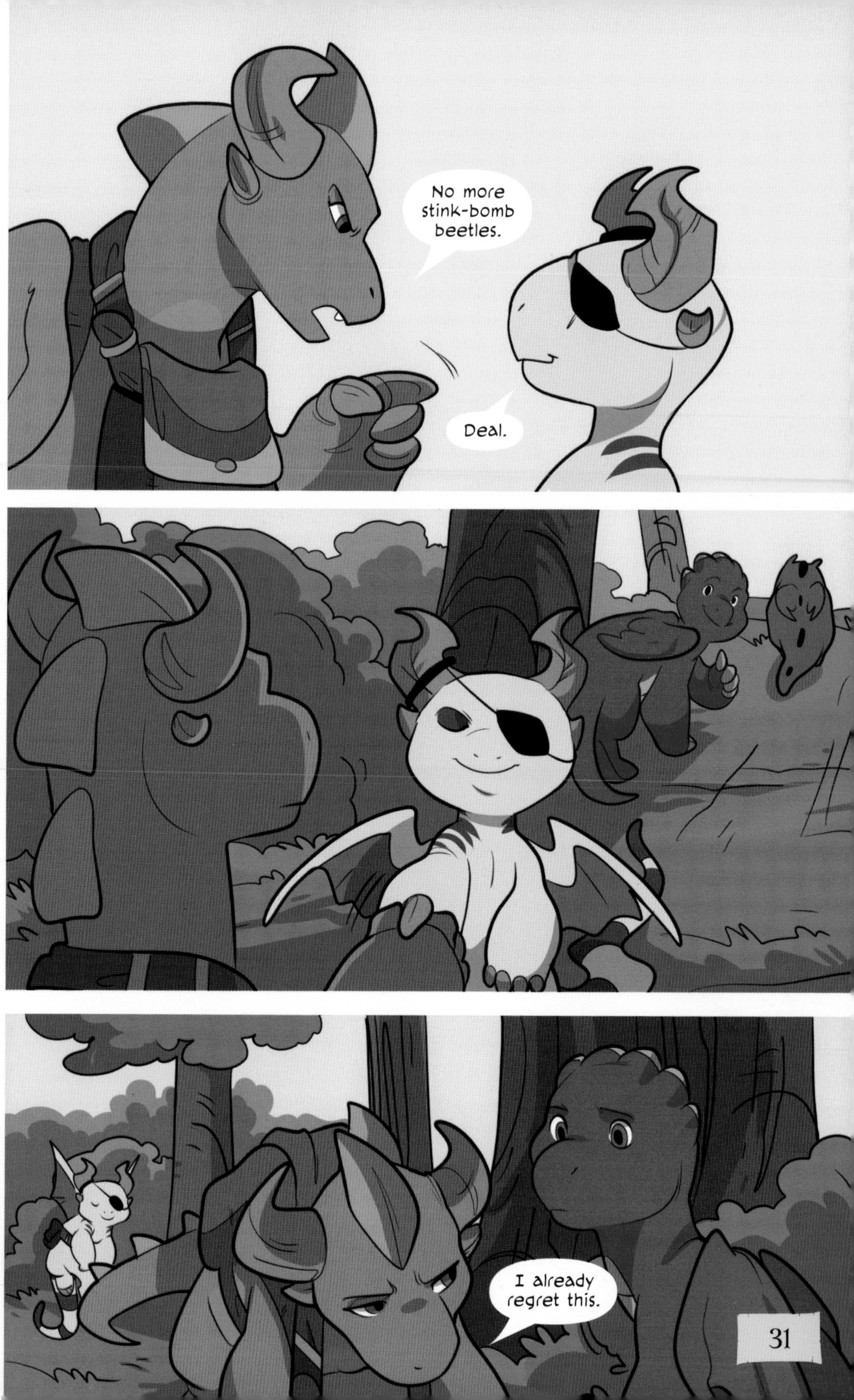
No more stink-bomb beetles.
Deal.
I already regret this.

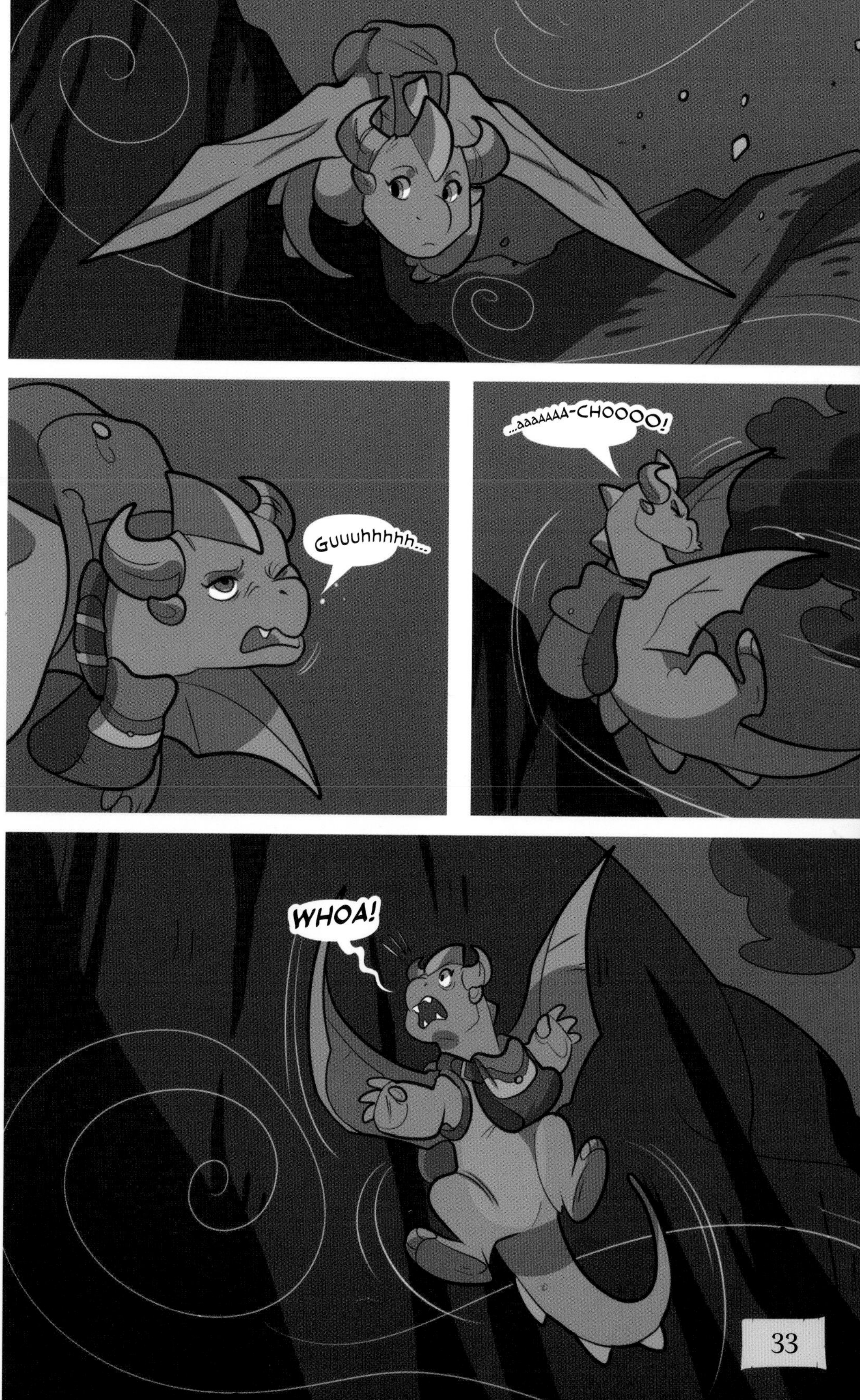
Guuuhhhhh...
...aaaaaaA-CHOOOO!
WHOA!

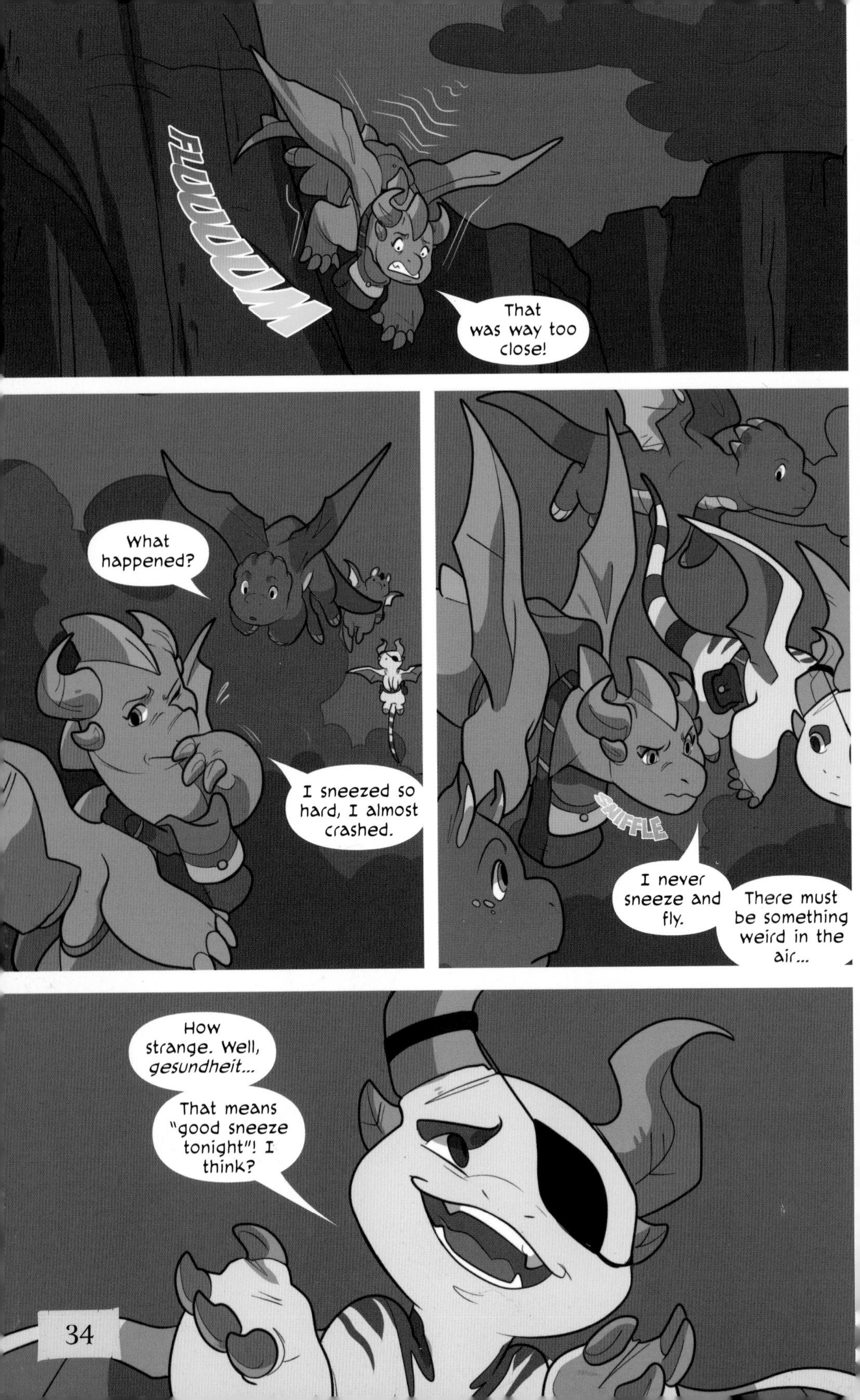
FLUUUUUM
That was way too close!
What happened?
I sneezed so hard, I almost crashed.
SNIFFLE
I never sneeze and fly.
There must be something weird in the air...
How strange. Well, *gesundheit*...
That means "good sneeze tonight"! I think?

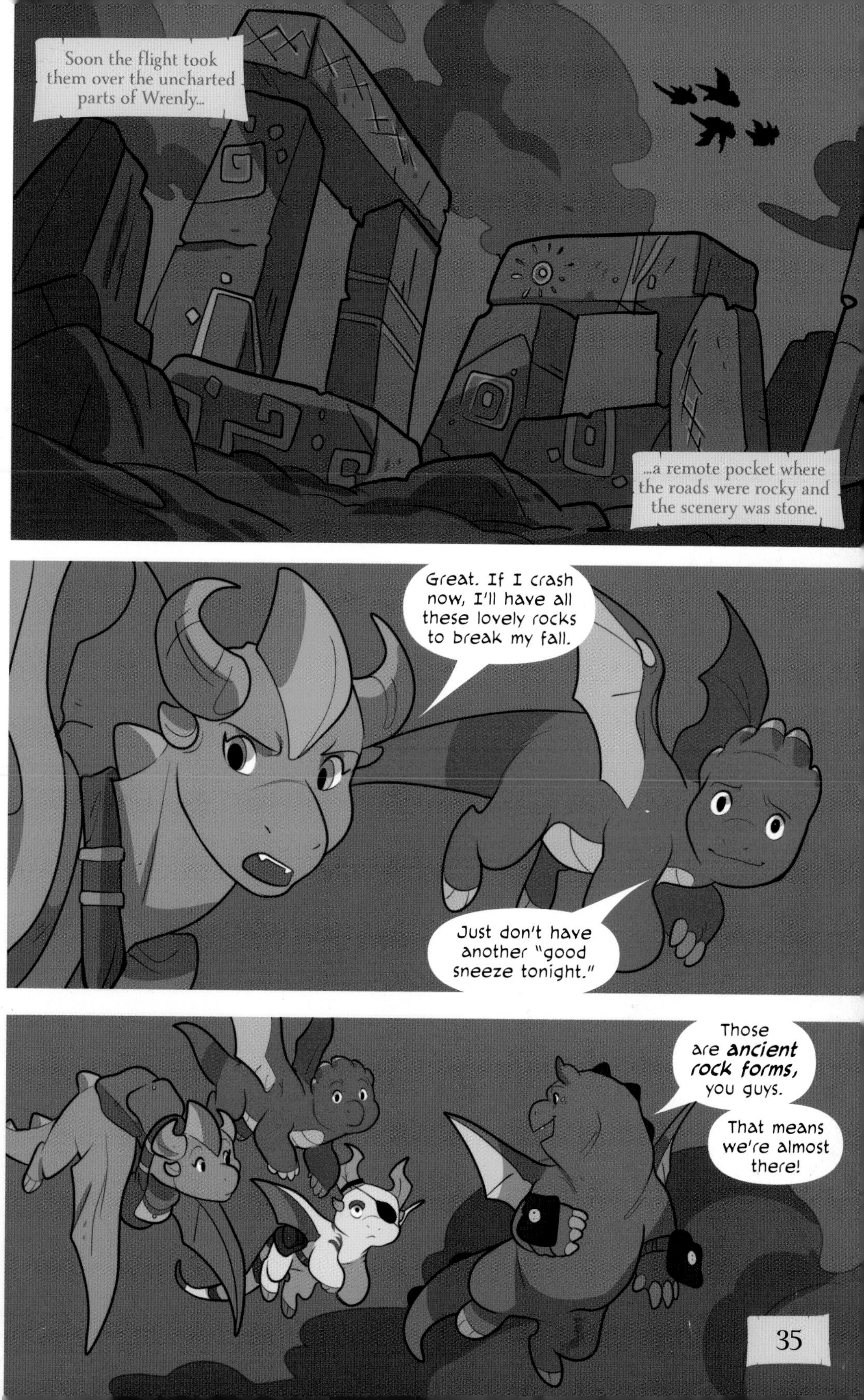
Soon the flight took them over the uncharted parts of Wrenly...
...a remote pocket where the roads were rocky and the scenery was stone.
Great. If I crash now, I'll have all these lovely rocks to break my fall.
Just don't have another "good sneeze tonight."
Those are ***ancient rock forms,*** you guys.
That means we're almost there!

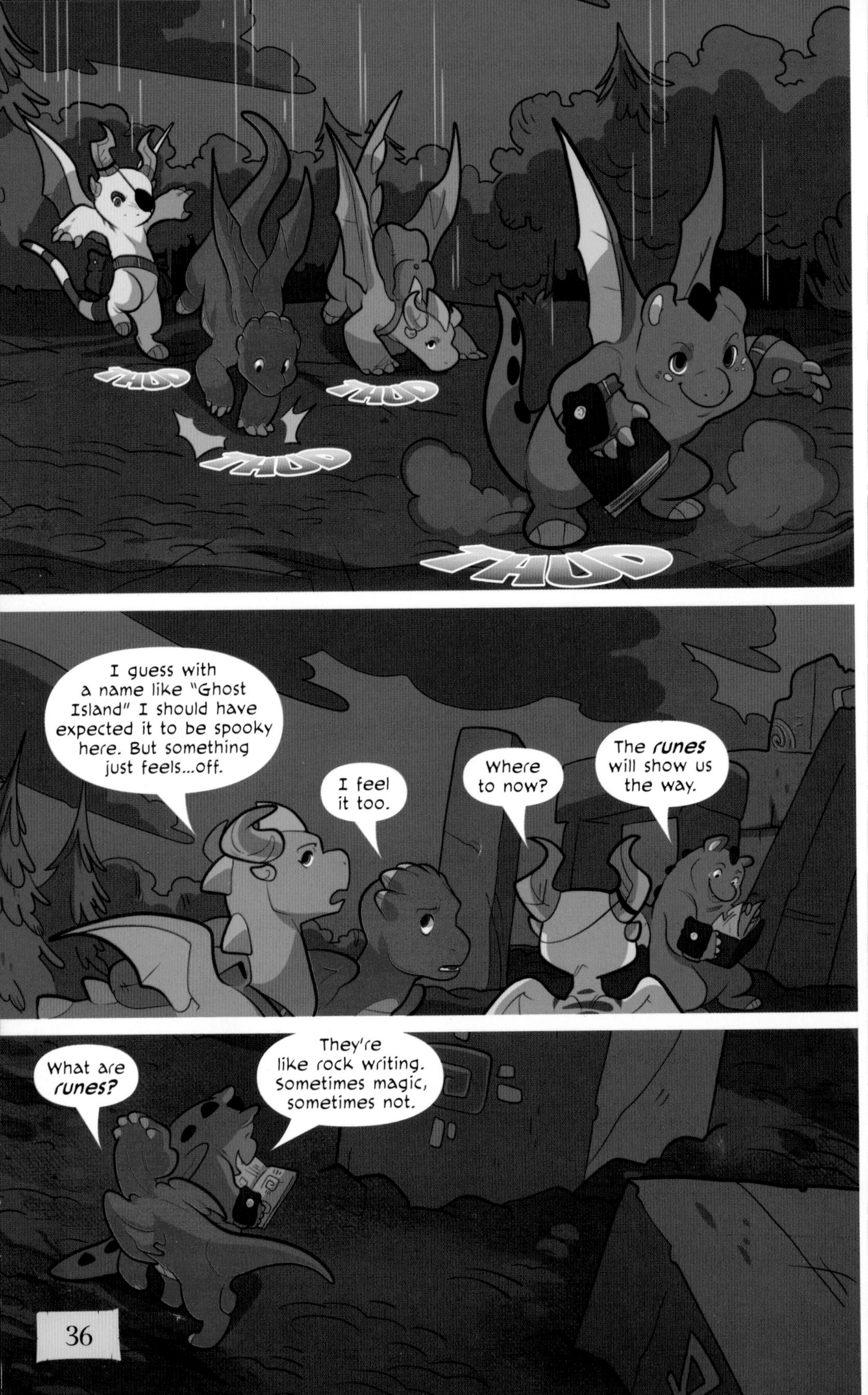
THUD
THUD
THUD
THUD
I guess with a name like "Ghost Island" I should have expected it to be spooky here. But something just feels...off.
I feel it too.
Where to now?
The *runes* will show us the way.
What are *runes?*
They're like rock writing. Sometimes magic, sometimes not.

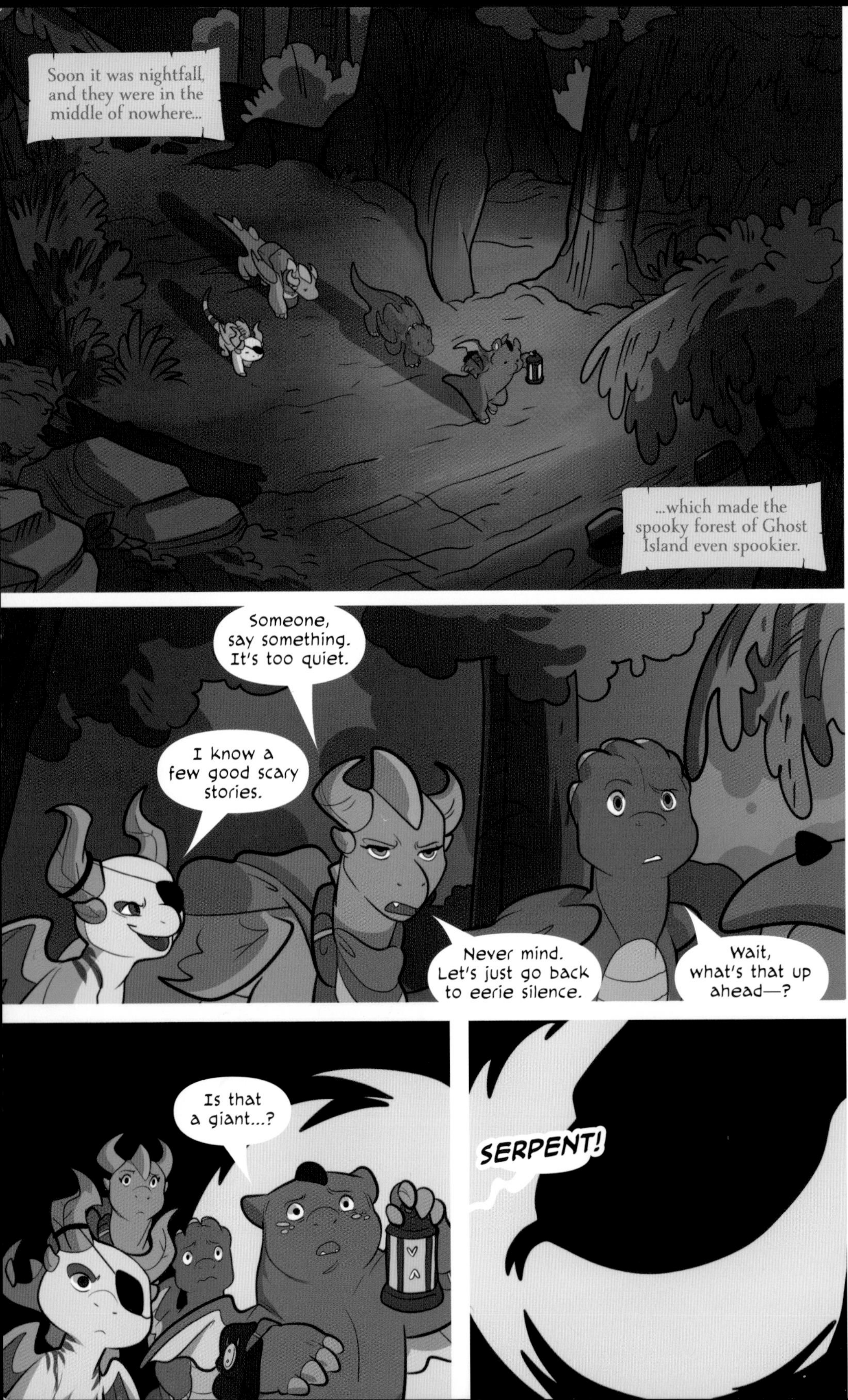
Soon it was nightfall, and they were in the middle of nowhere...
...which made the spooky forest of Ghost Island even spookier.
Someone, say something. It's too quiet.
I know a few good scary stories.
Never mind. Let's just go back to eerie silence.
Wait, what's that up ahead—?
Is that a giant...?
SERPENT!

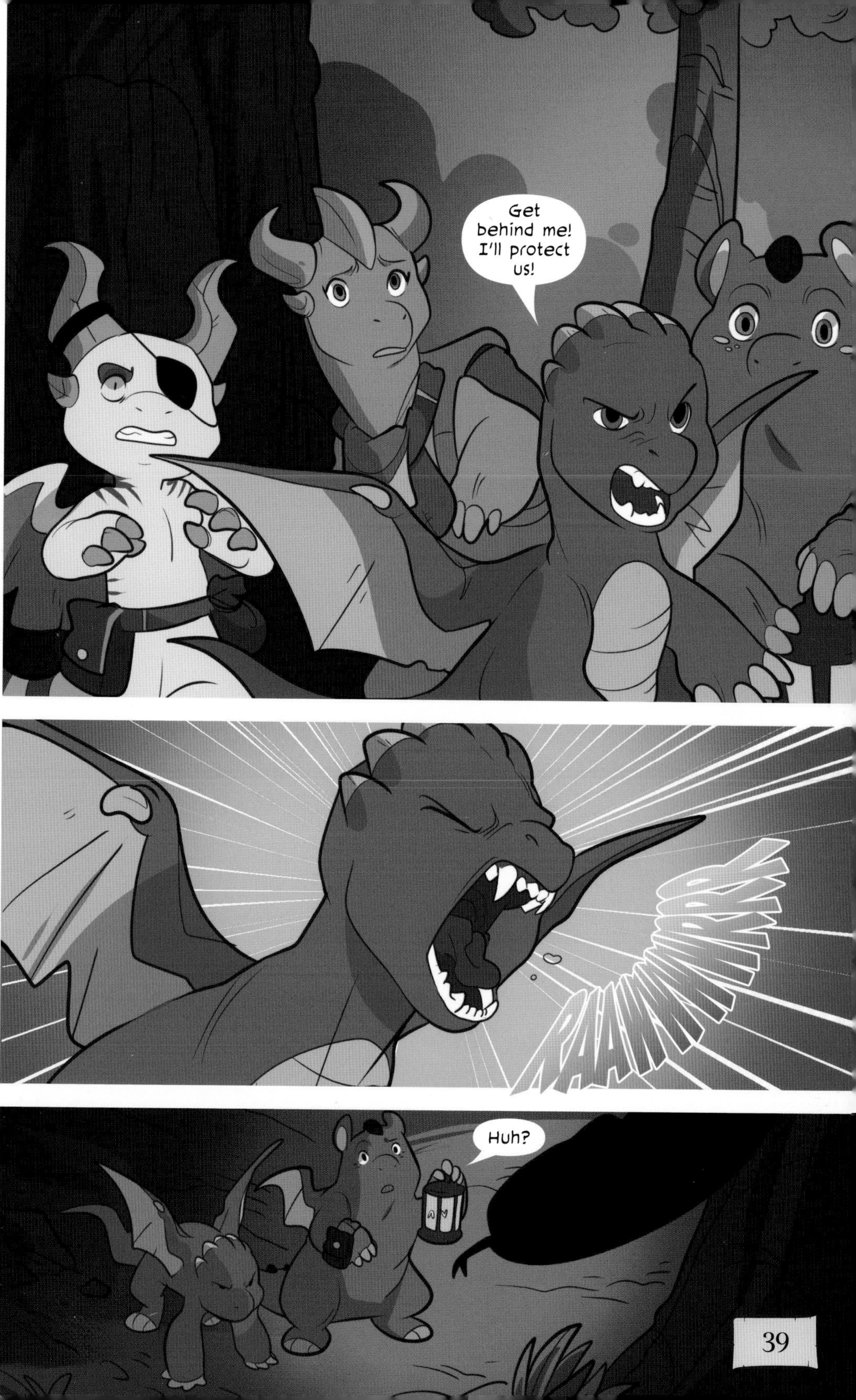
Get behind me! I'll protect us!
Huh?

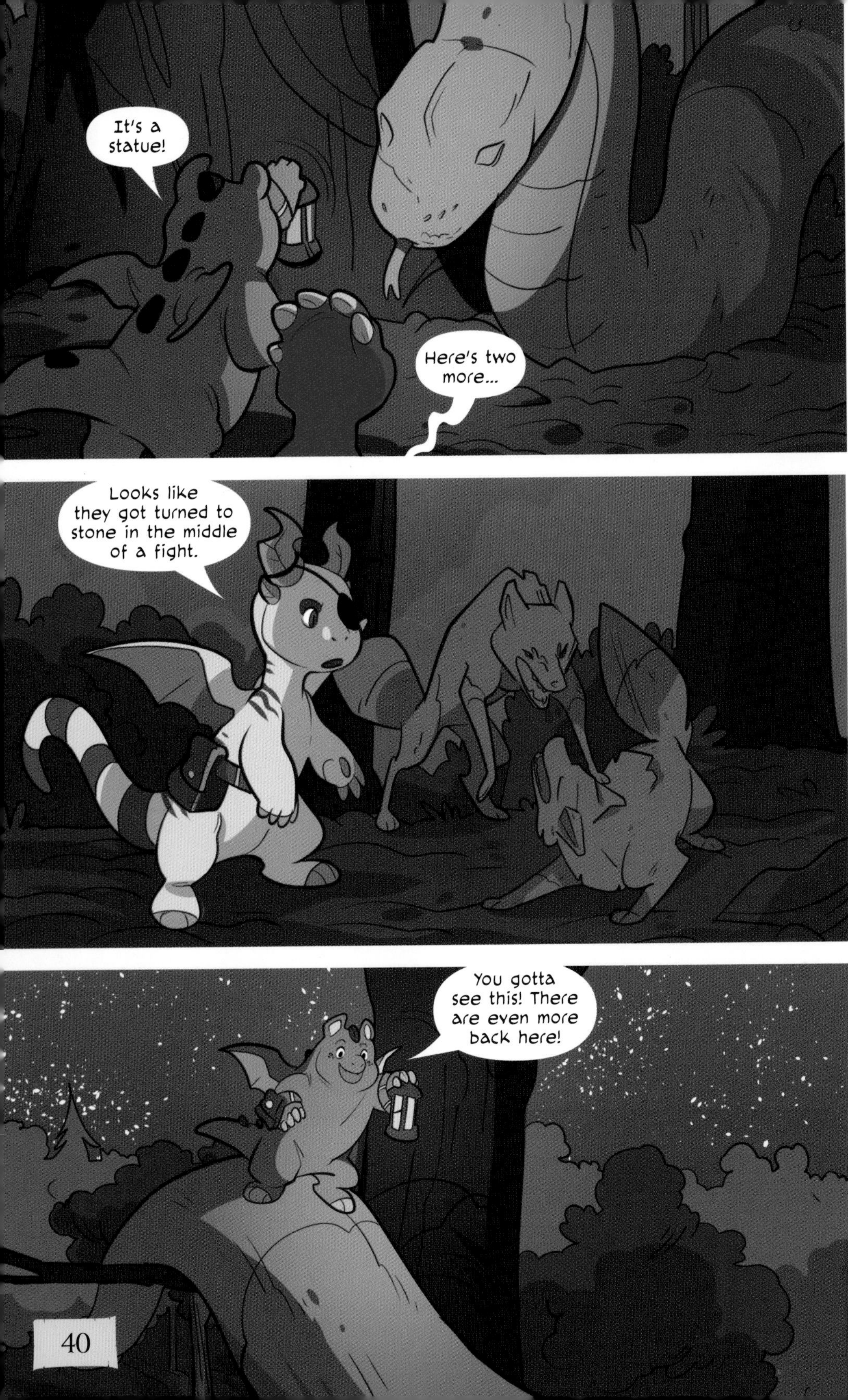
It's a statue!
Here's two more...
Looks like they got turned to stone in the middle of a fight.
You gotta see this! There are even more back here!

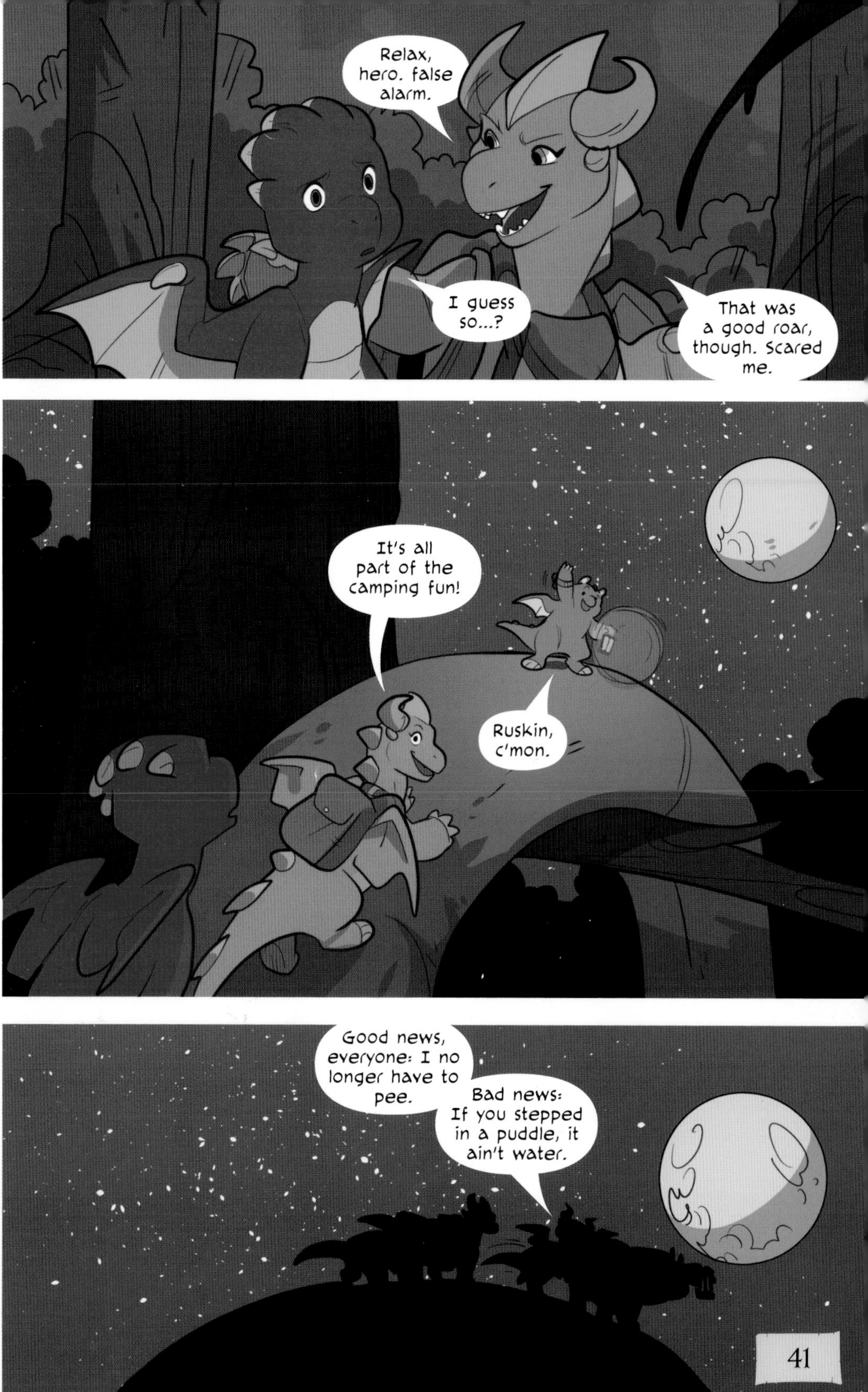
Relax, hero. false alarm.
I guess so...?
That was a good roar, though. Scared me.
It's all part of the camping fun!
Ruskin, c'mon.
Good news, everyone: I no longer have to pee.
Bad news: If you stepped in a puddle, it ain't water.

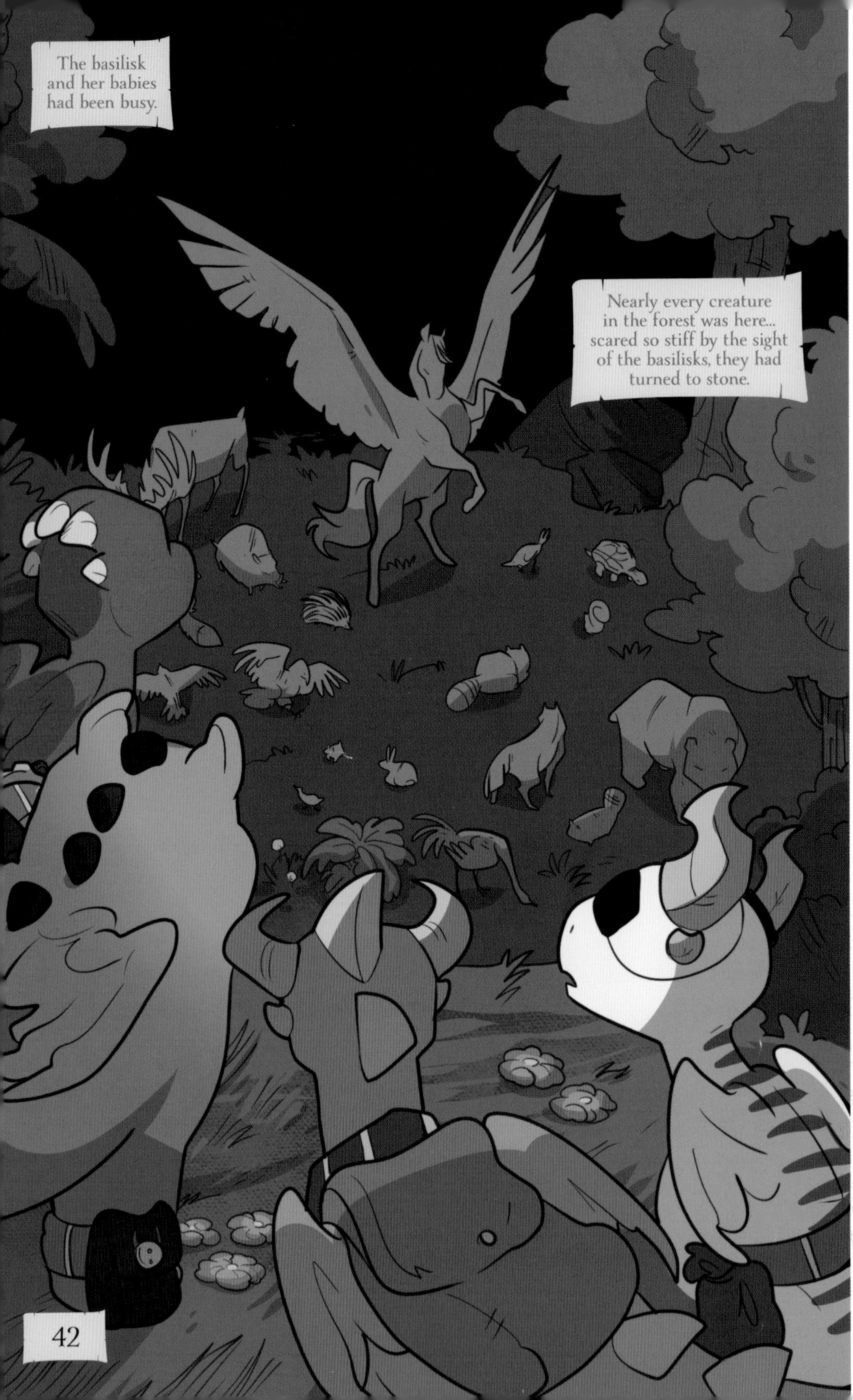
The basilisk and her babies had been busy.
Nearly every creature in the forest was here... scared so stiff by the sight of the basilisks, they had turned to stone.

43

45

Chapter 4

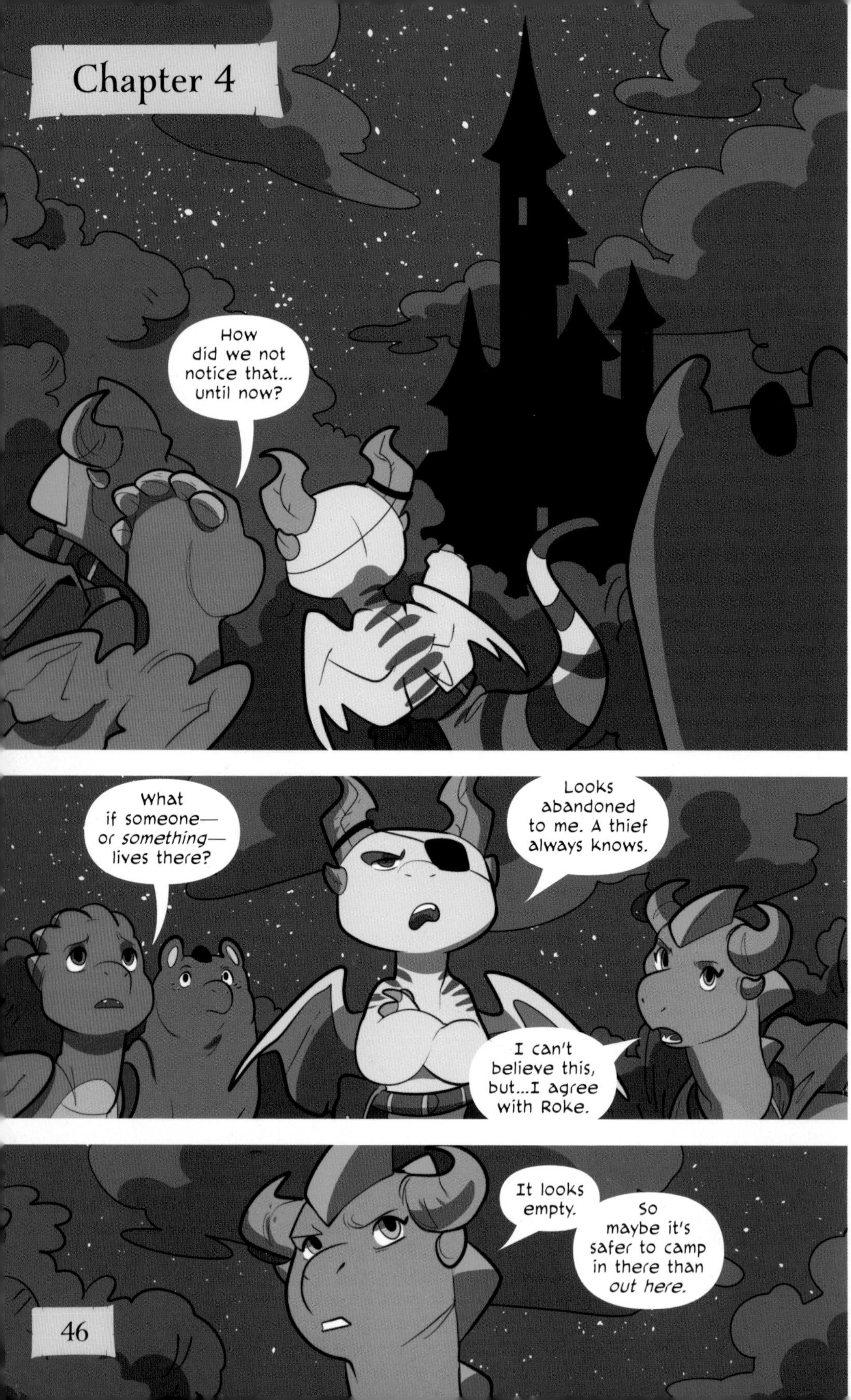
How did we not notice that... until now?
What if someone— or *something*— lives there?
Looks abandoned to me. A thief always knows.
I can't believe this, but...I agree with Roke.
It looks empty.
So maybe it's safer to camp in there than *out here*.

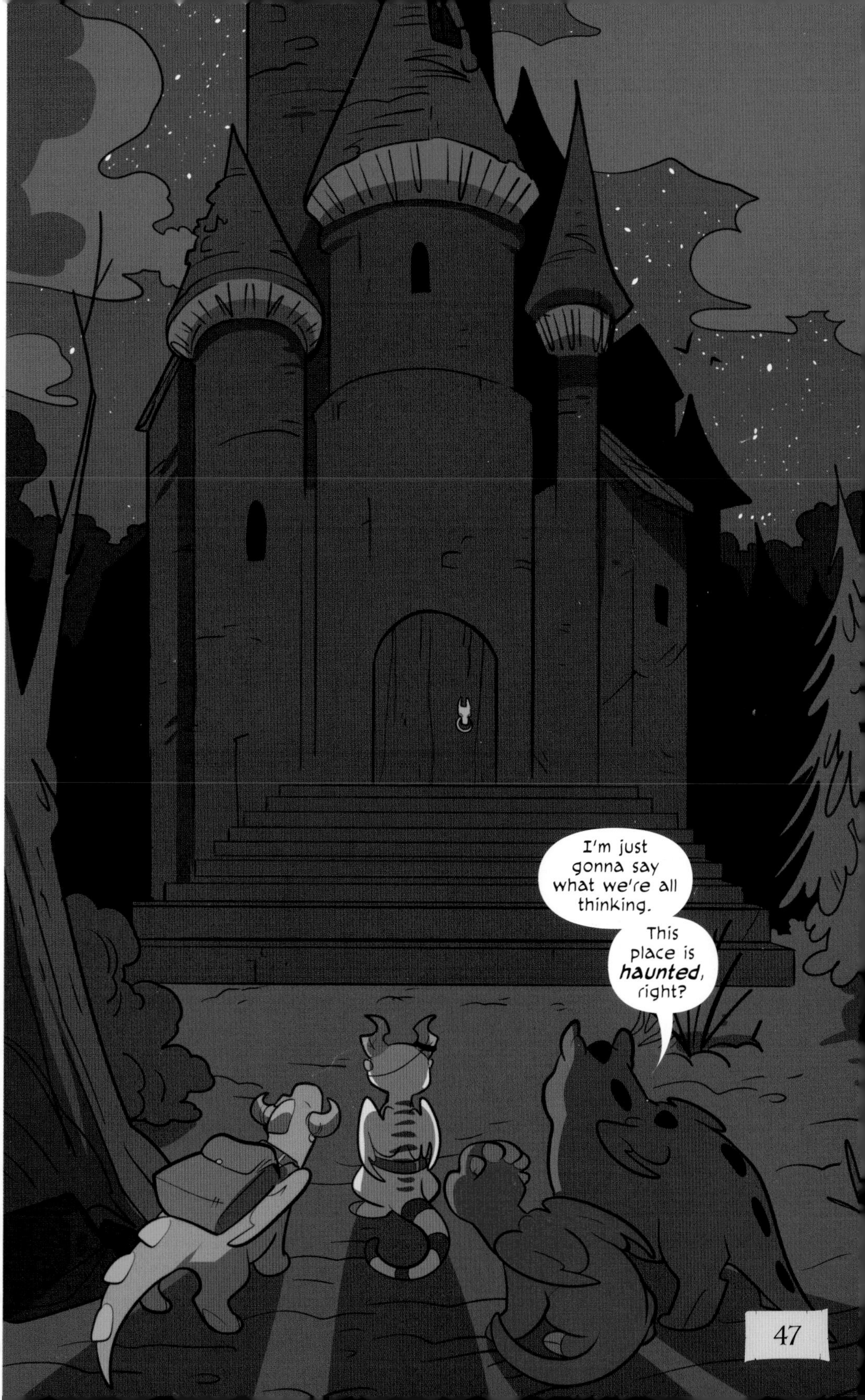
I'm just gonna say what we're all thinking.
This place is ***haunted***, right?

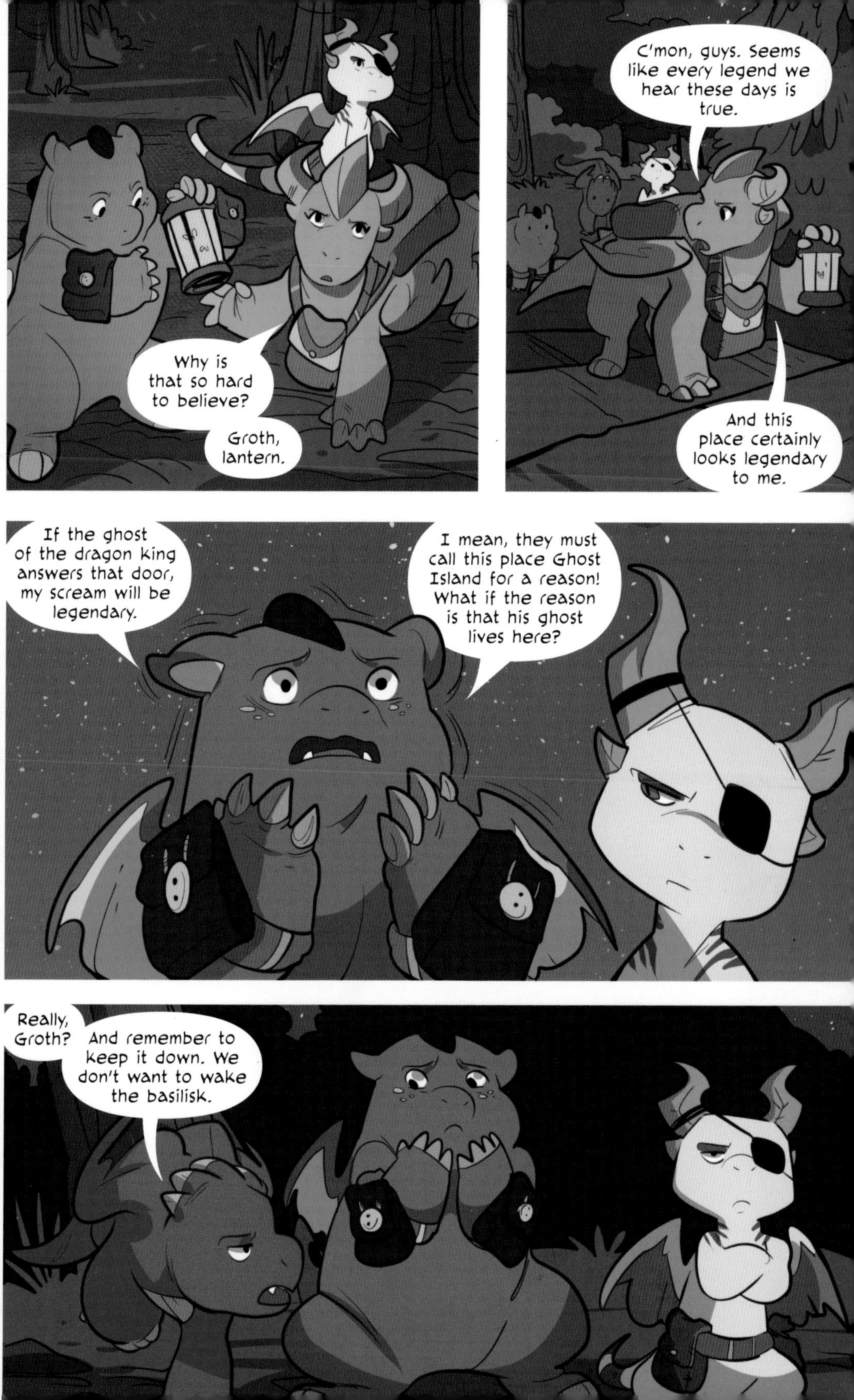
Why is that so hard to believe?
Groth, lantern.
C'mon, guys. Seems like every legend we hear these days is true.
And this place certainly looks legendary to me.
If the ghost of the dragon king answers that door, my scream will be legendary.
I mean, they must call this place Ghost Island for a reason! What if the reason is that his ghost lives here?
Really, Groth?
And remember to keep it down. We don't want to wake the basilisk.

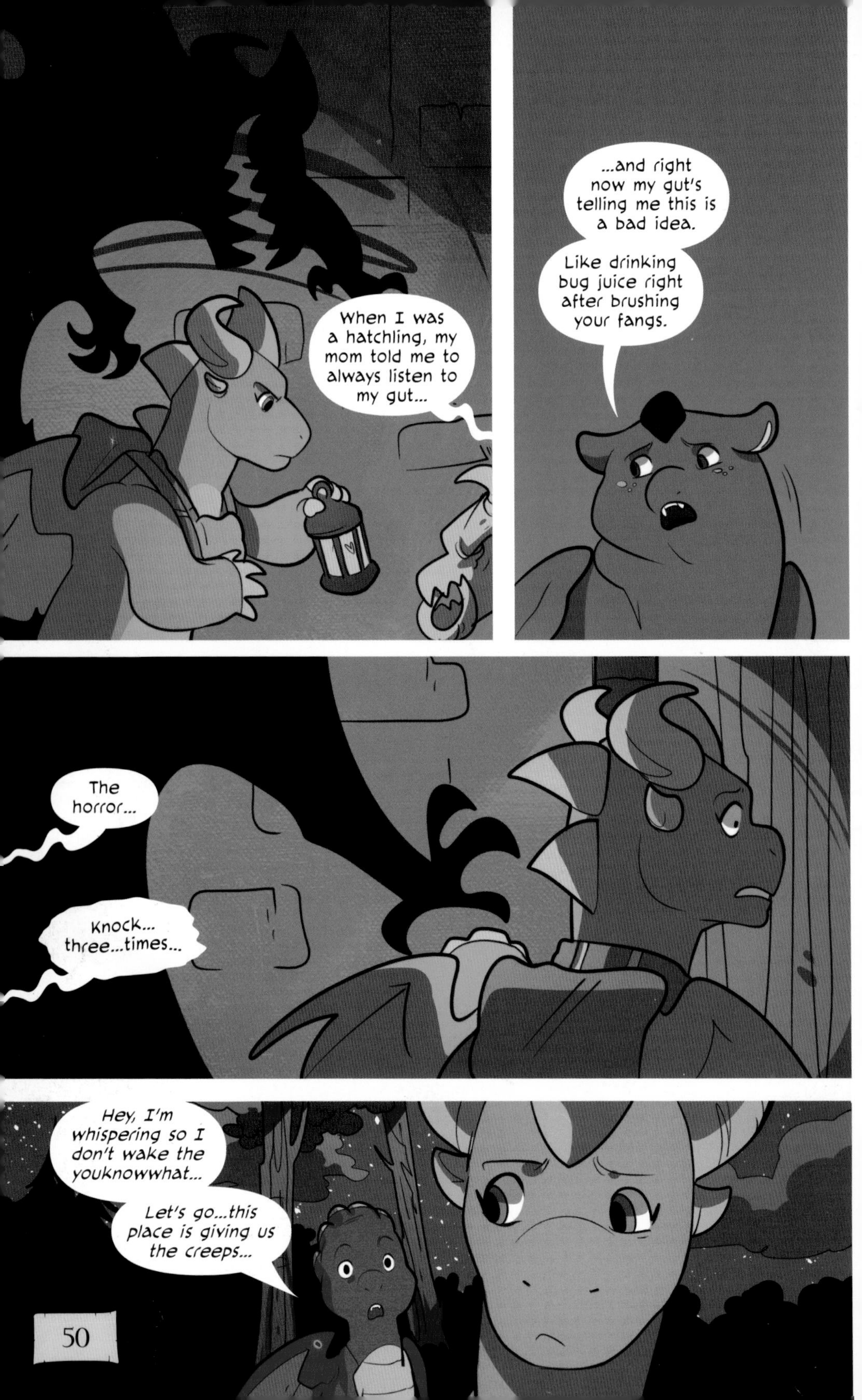
When I was a hatchling, my mom told me to always listen to my gut...
...and right now my gut's telling me this is a bad idea.
Like drinking bug juice right after brushing your fangs.
The horror...
Knock... three...times...
Hey, I'm whispering so I don't wake the youknowwhat...
Let's go...this place is giving us the creeps...

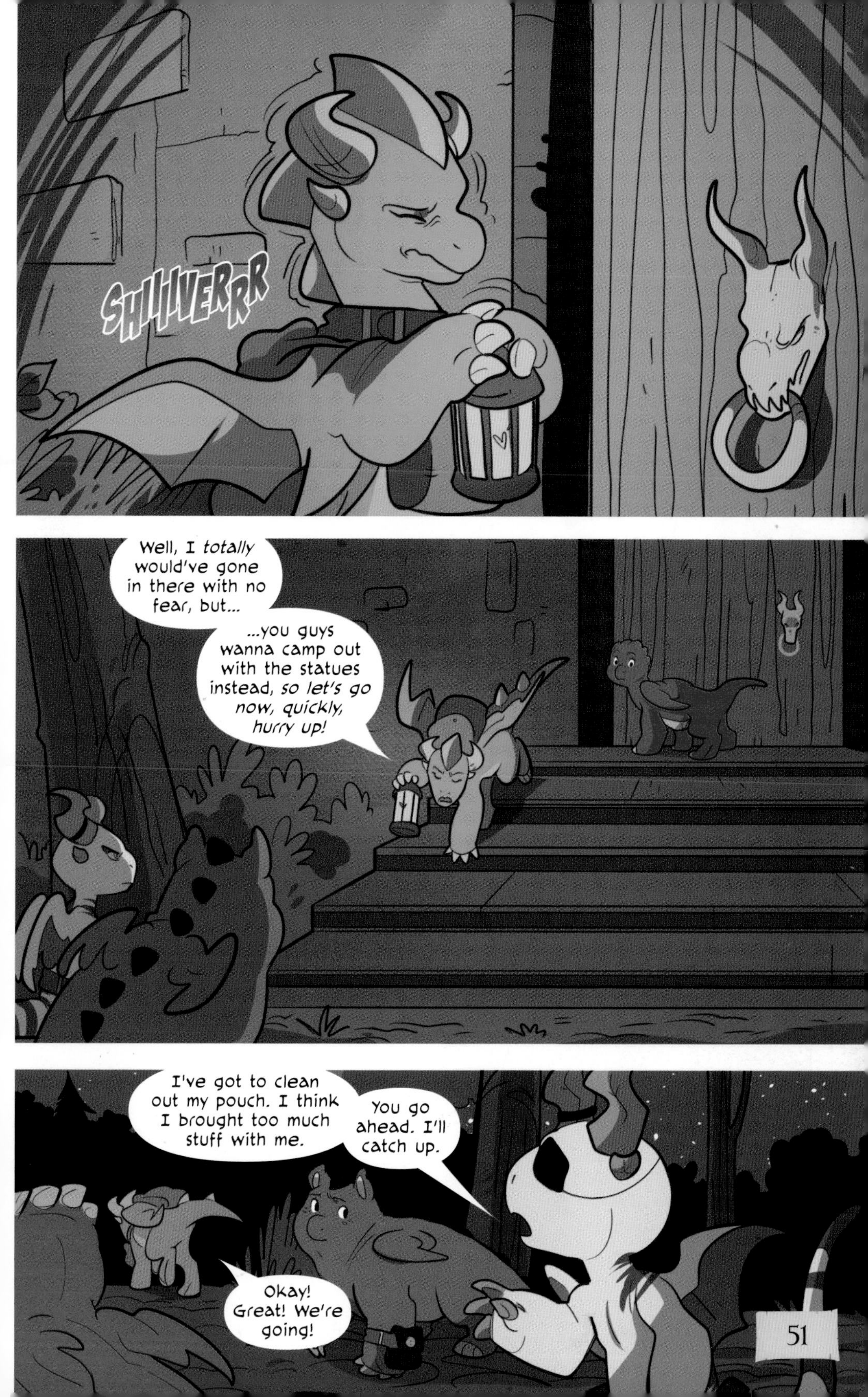
SHIIIIVERRR
Well, I *totally* would've gone in there with no fear, but...
...you guys wanna camp out with the statues instead, *so let's go now, quickly, hurry up!*
I've got to clean out my pouch. I think I brought too much stuff with me.
You go ahead. I'll catch up.
Okay! Great! We're going!

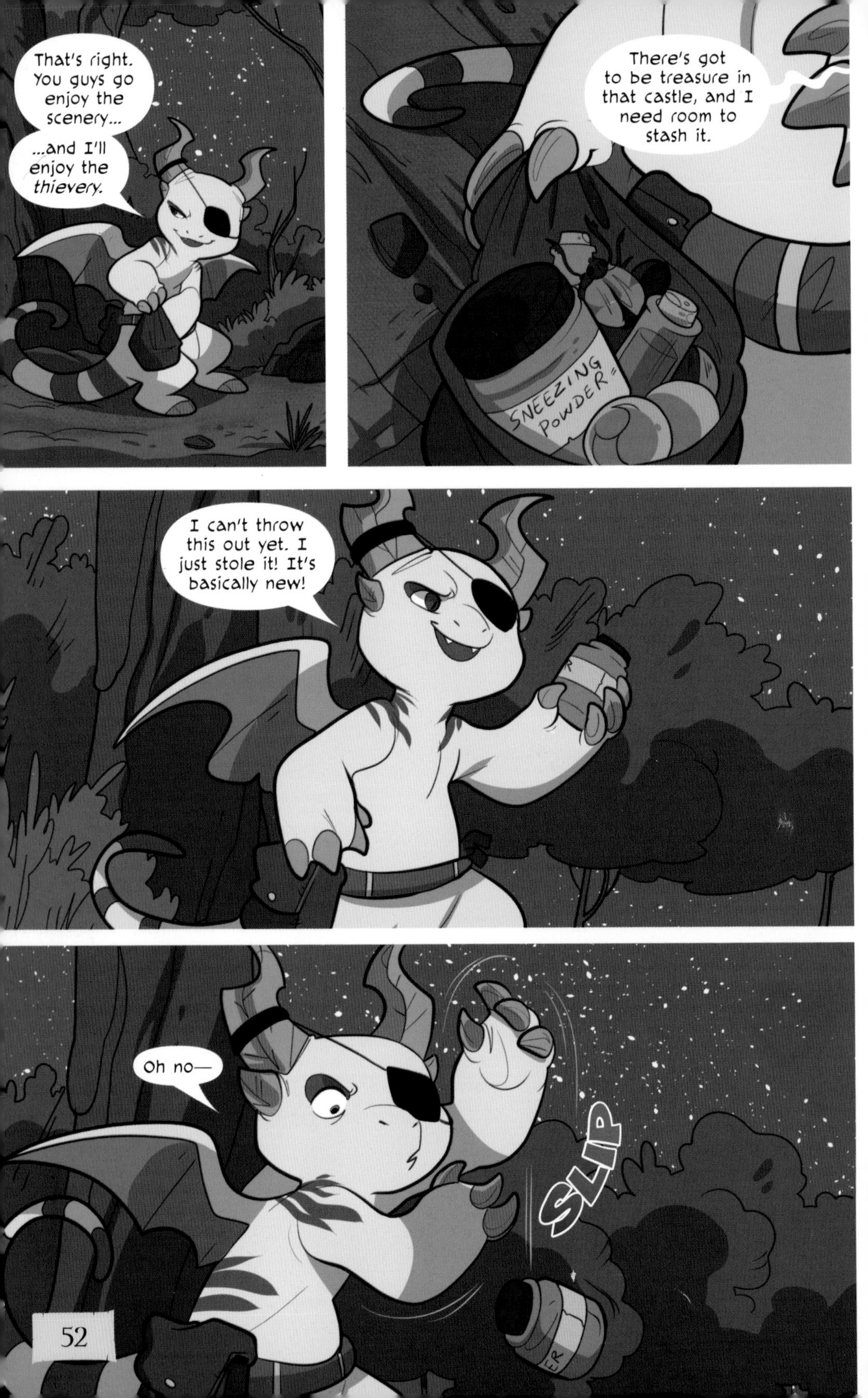
That's right. You guys go enjoy the scenery...
...and I'll enjoy the *thievery.*
There's got to be treasure in that castle, and I need room to stash it.
SNEEZING POWDER
I can't throw this out yet. I just stole it! It's basically new!
Oh no—
SLIP

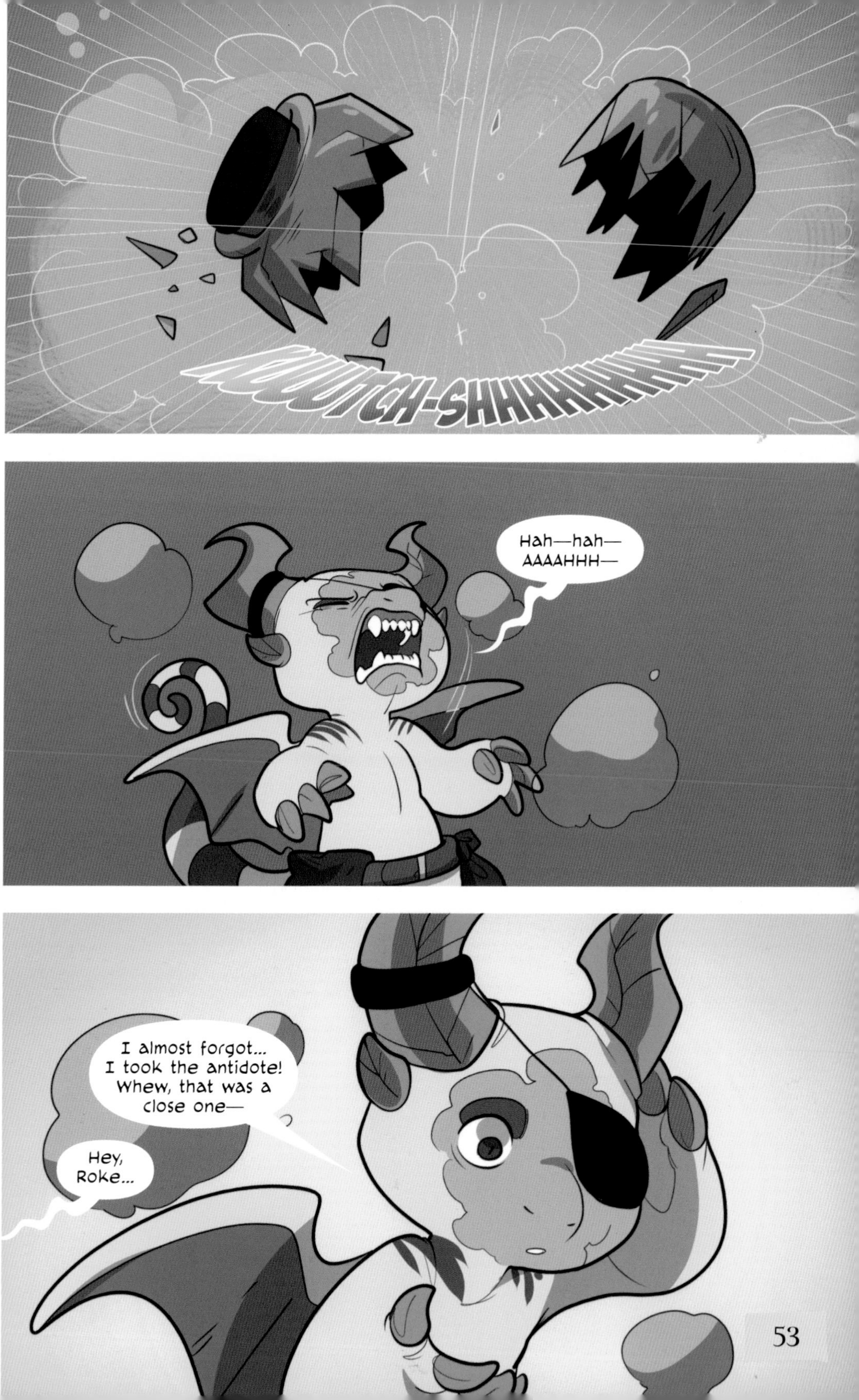
Hah—hah—
AAAAHHH—
I almost forgot... I took the antidote! Whew, that was a close one—
Hey, Roke...

Ruskin, no! Why are you back?

I heard something break, and I wanted to make sure you were—

What's all over your face...?

PFFF

Something... happening...

...nose tickling...

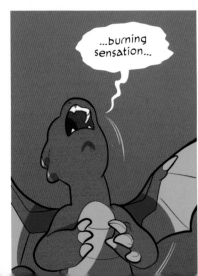

...burning sensation...

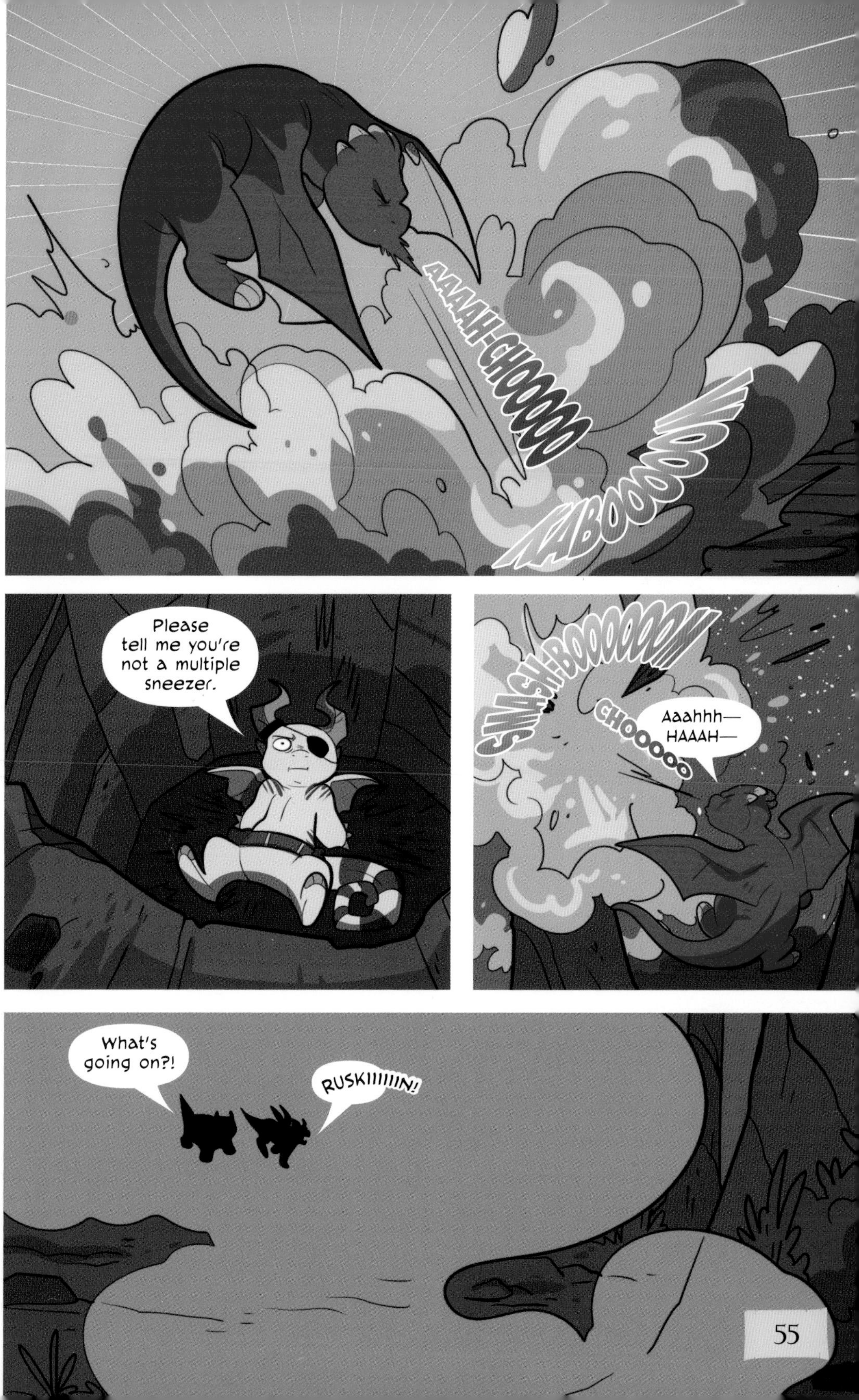
AAAAH-CHOOOOO
KABOOOOOM
Please tell me you're not a multiple sneezer.
SMASH-BOOOOOOM
Aaahhh— HAAAH—
CHOOOOOO
What's going on?!
RUSKIIIIIIIN!

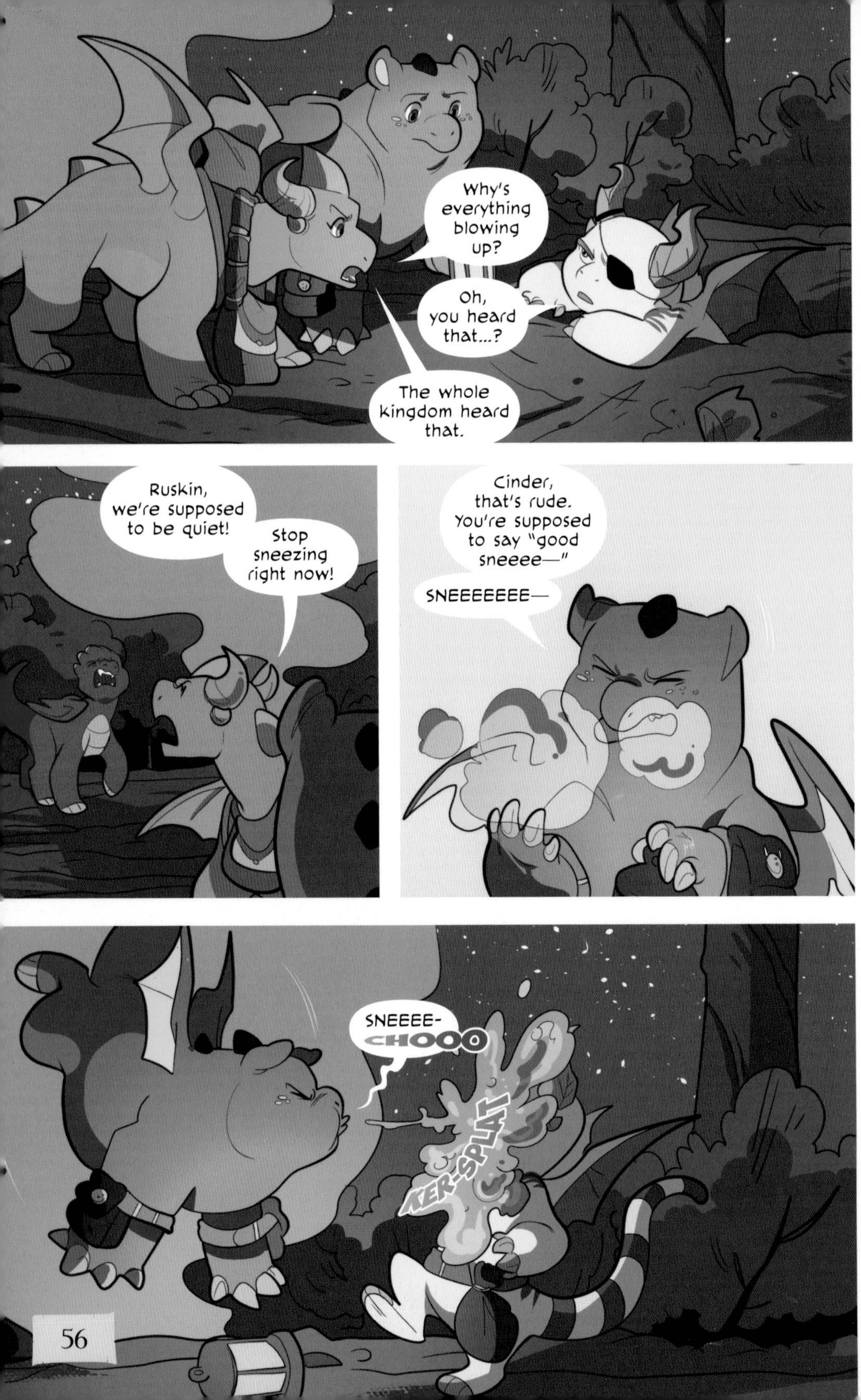
Why's everything blowing up?
Oh, you heard that...?
The whole kingdom heard that.
Ruskin, we're supposed to be quiet!
Stop sneezing right now!
Cinder, that's rude. You're supposed to say "good sneeee—"
SNEEEEEEE—
SNEEEE-CHOOO
KER-SPLAT

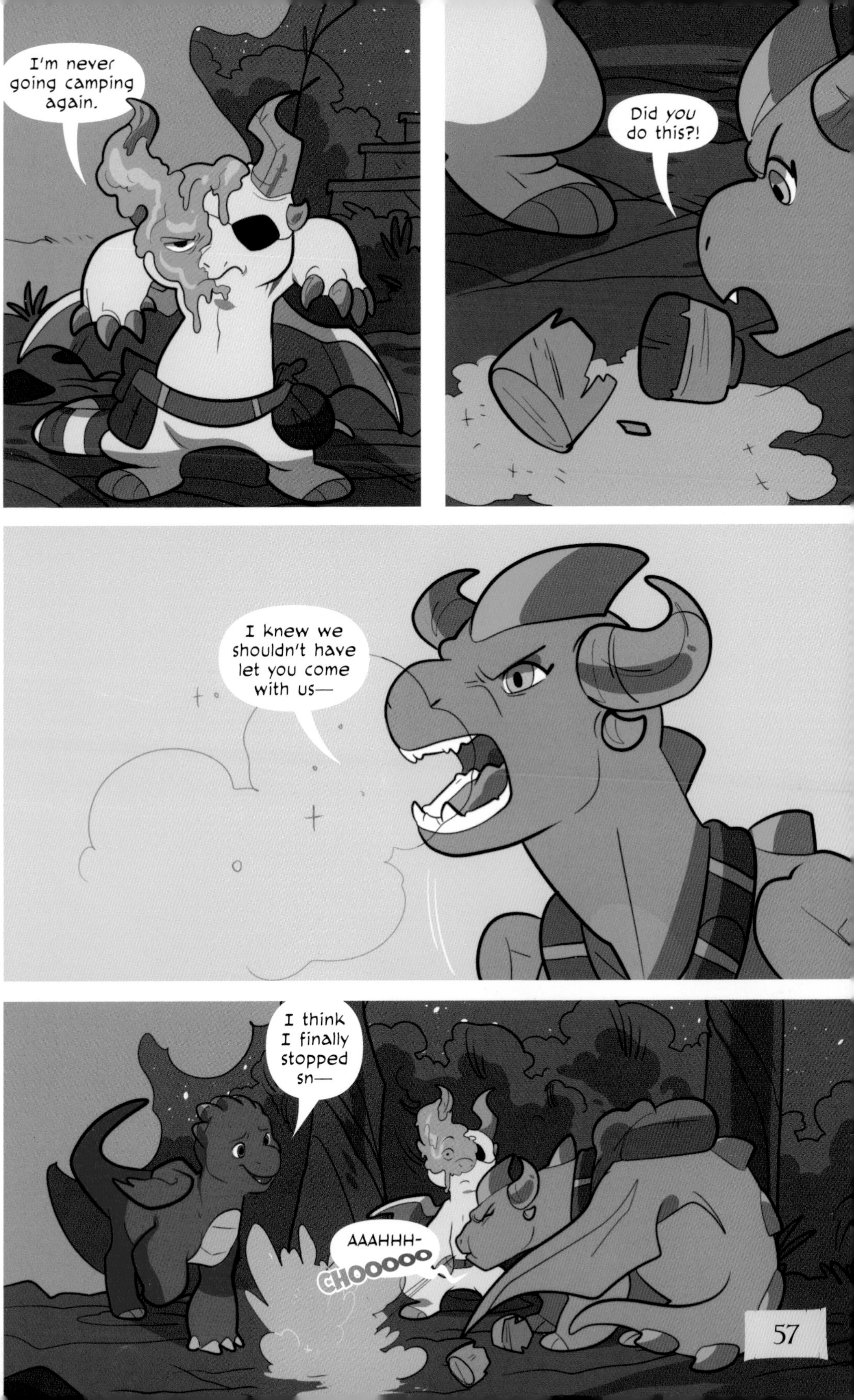
I'm never going camping again.
Did *you* do this?!
I knew we shouldn't have let you come with us—
I think I finally stopped sn—
AAAHHH-
CHOOOOO

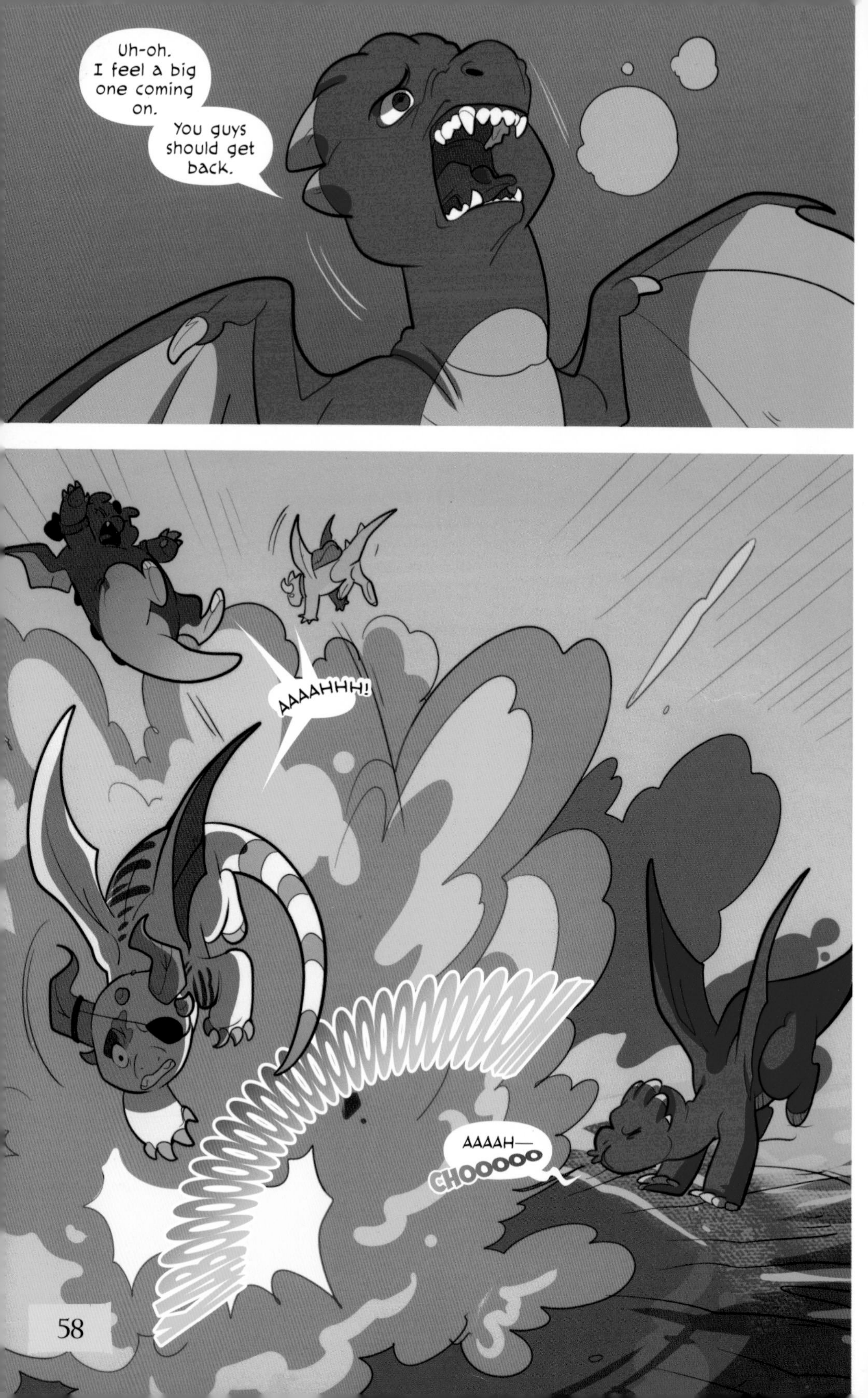
Uh-oh. I feel a big one coming on.
You guys should get back.
AAAAHHH!
AAAAH—CHOOOOO

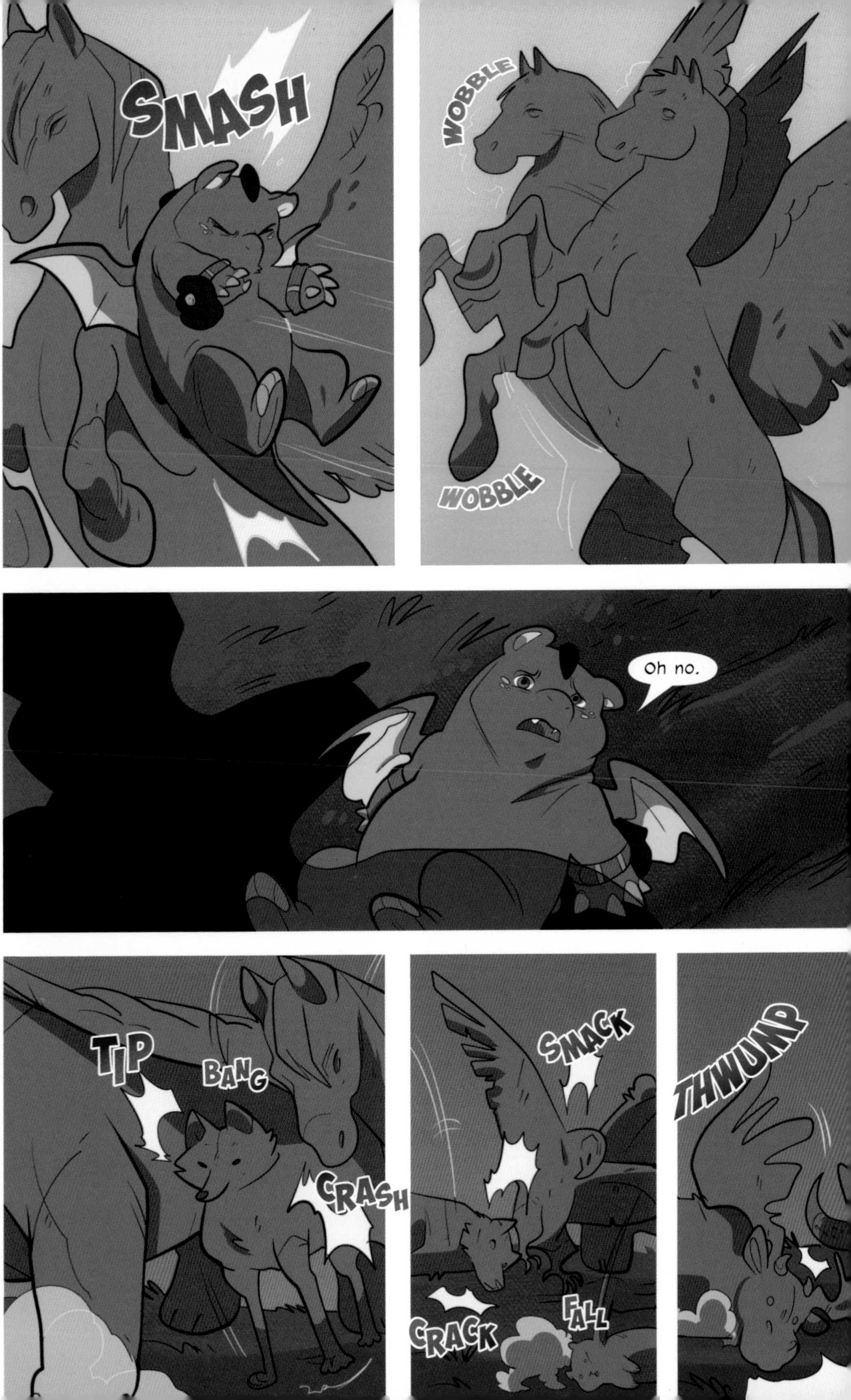
SMASH
WOBBLE
WOBBLE
Oh no.
TIP
BANG
CRASH
SMACK
CRACK
FALL
THWUMP

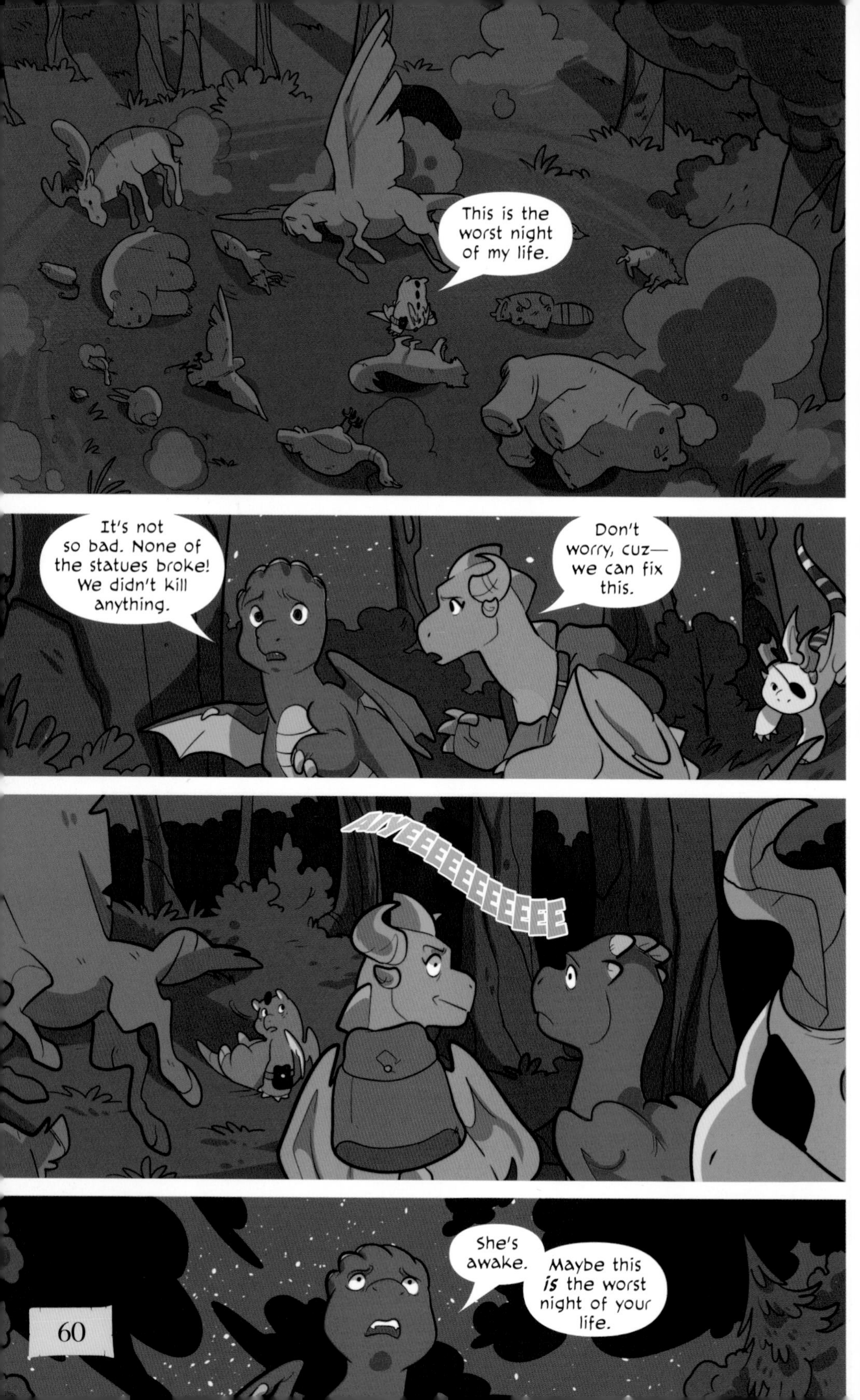
This is the worst night of my life.
It's not so bad. None of the statues broke! We didn't kill anything.
Don't worry, cuz— we can fix this.
AIIYEEEEEEEEEEEE
She's awake.
Maybe this *is* the worst night of your life.

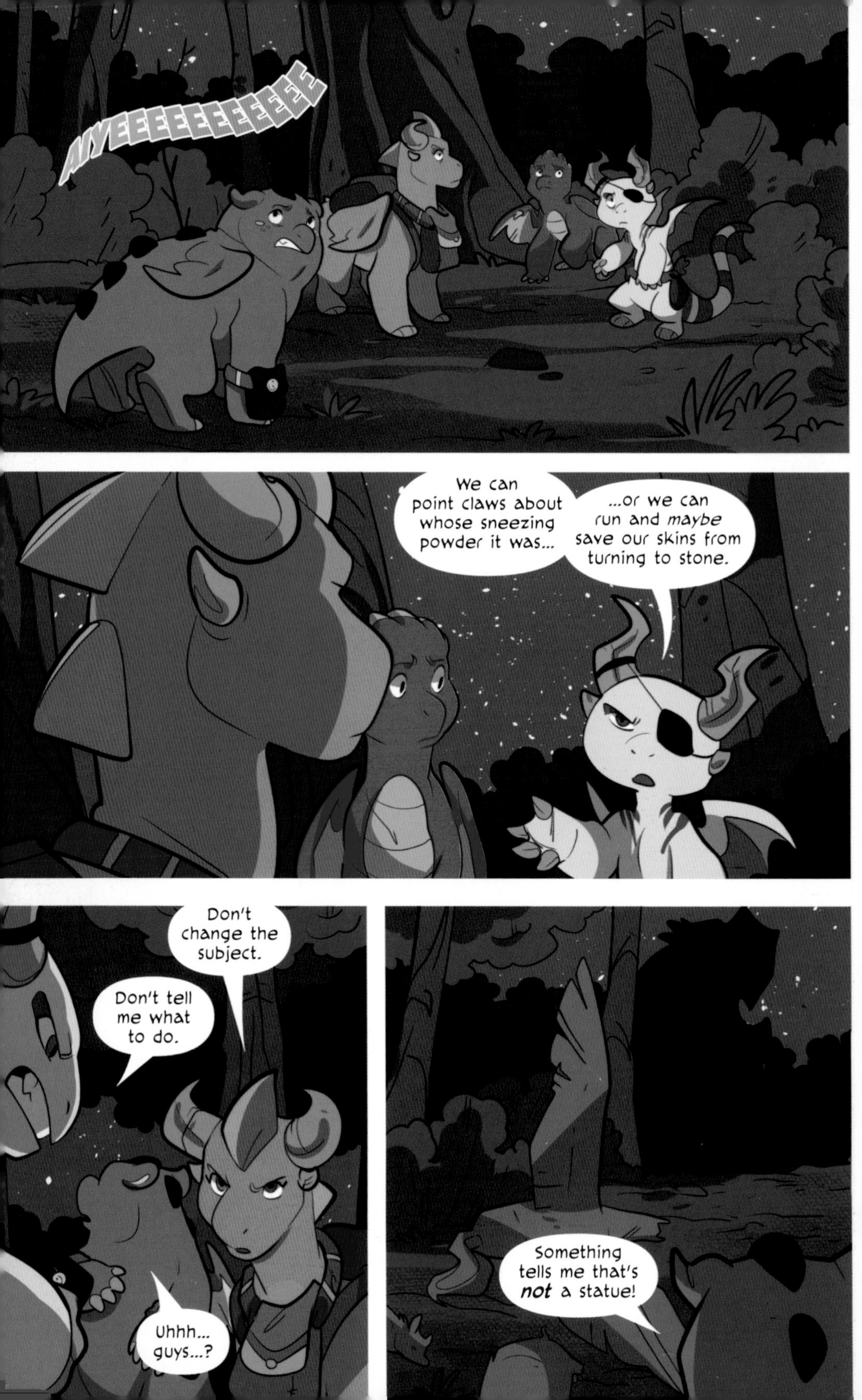
AIYEEEEEEEEEEEE
We can point claws about whose sneezing powder it was...
...or we can run and *maybe* save our skins from turning to stone.
Don't change the subject.
Don't tell me what to do.
Uhhh... guys...?
Something tells me that's *not* a statue!

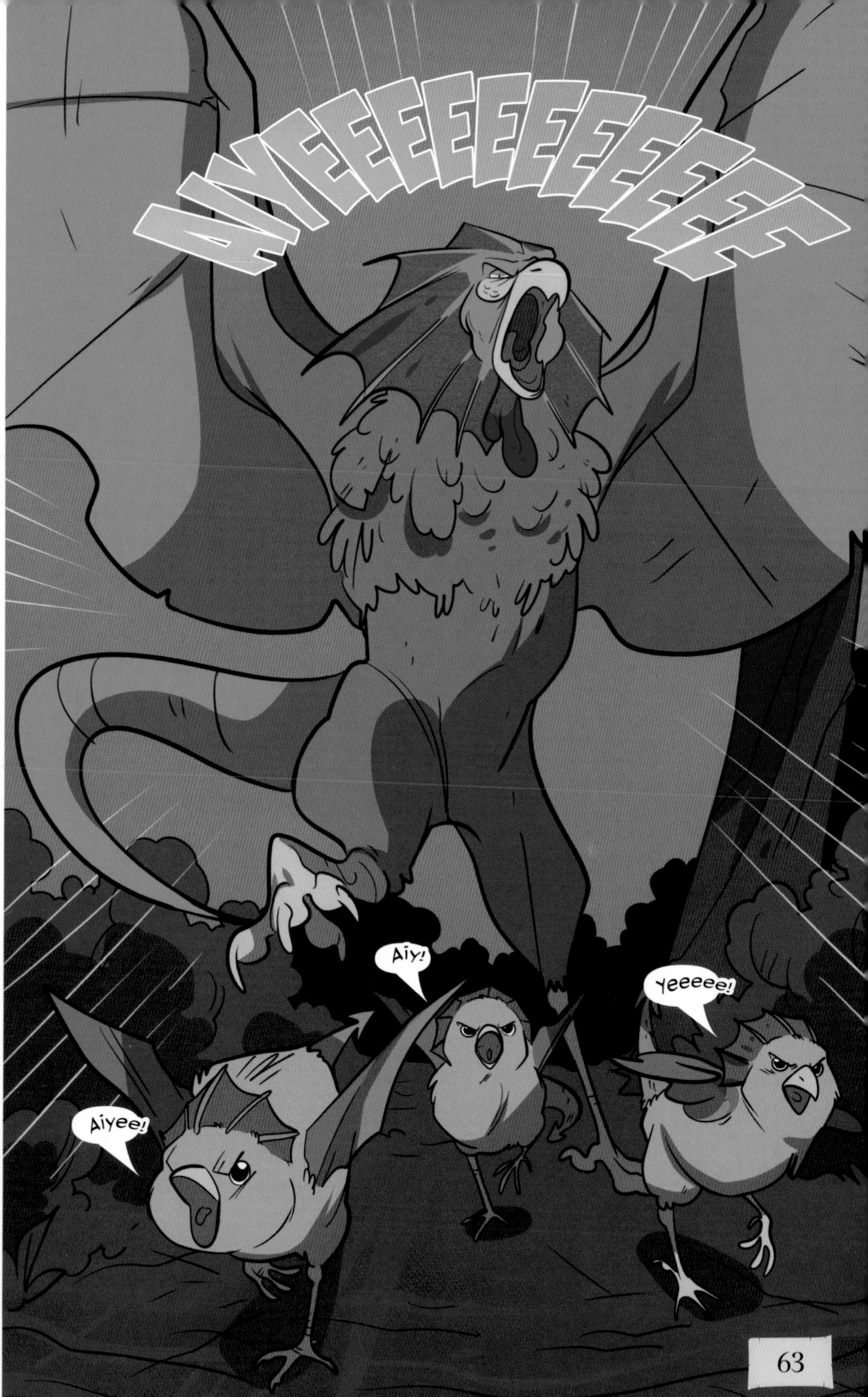
AIYEEEEEEEEEEEEE
Aiy!
Yeeeee!
Aiyee!

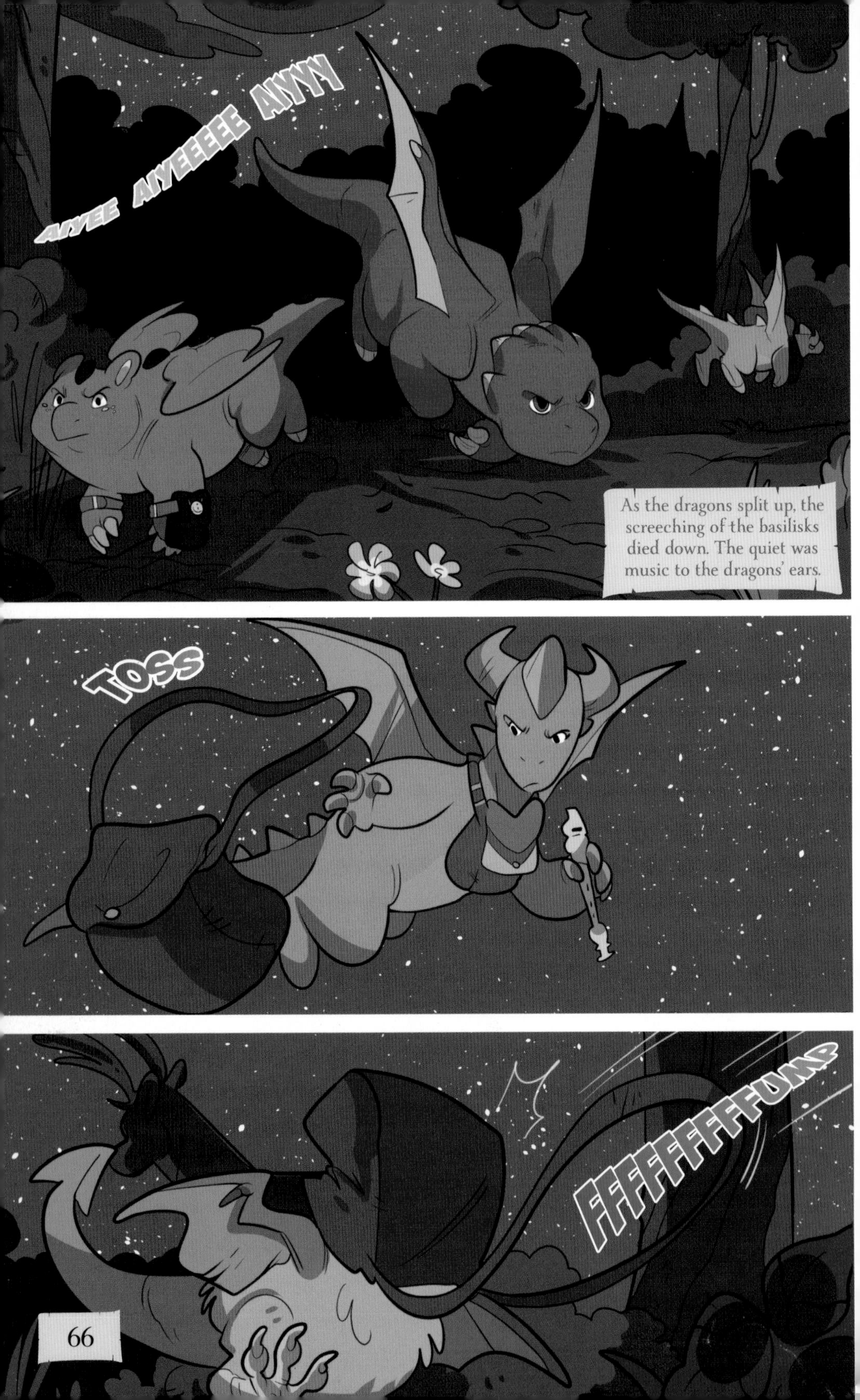
AIYEE AIYEEEEE AIYYY
As the dragons split up, the screeching of the basilisks died down. The quiet was music to the dragons' ears.
TOSS
FFFFFFFFFUMP

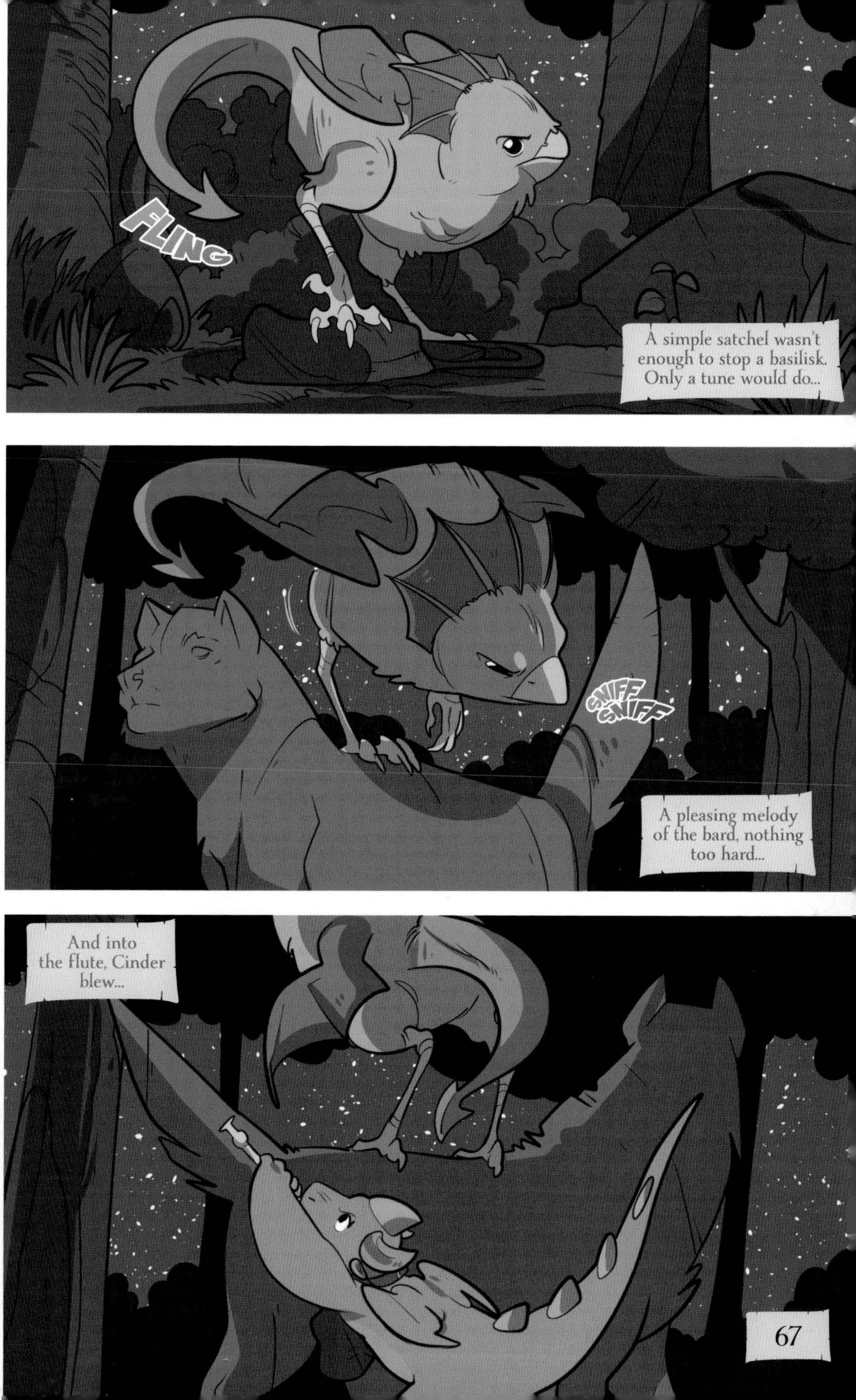
FLING
A simple satchel wasn't enough to stop a basilisk. Only a tune would do...
SNIFF SNIFF
A pleasing melody of the bard, nothing too hard...
And into the flute, Cinder blew...

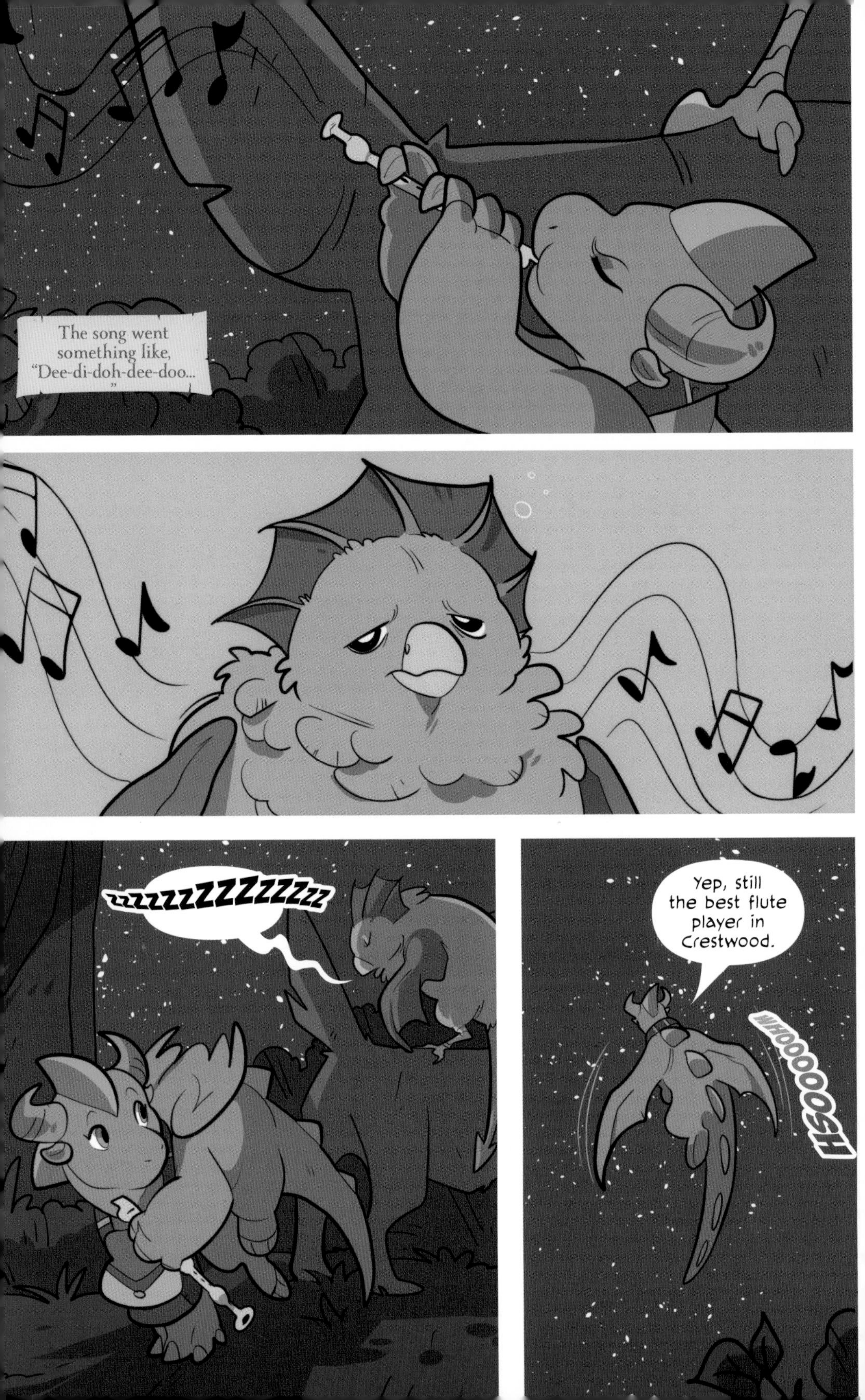

The song went something like, "Dee-di-doh-dee-doo..."
zzzzzzzZZZZzzzzz
Yep, still the best flute player in Crestwood.
WHOOOOOSH!

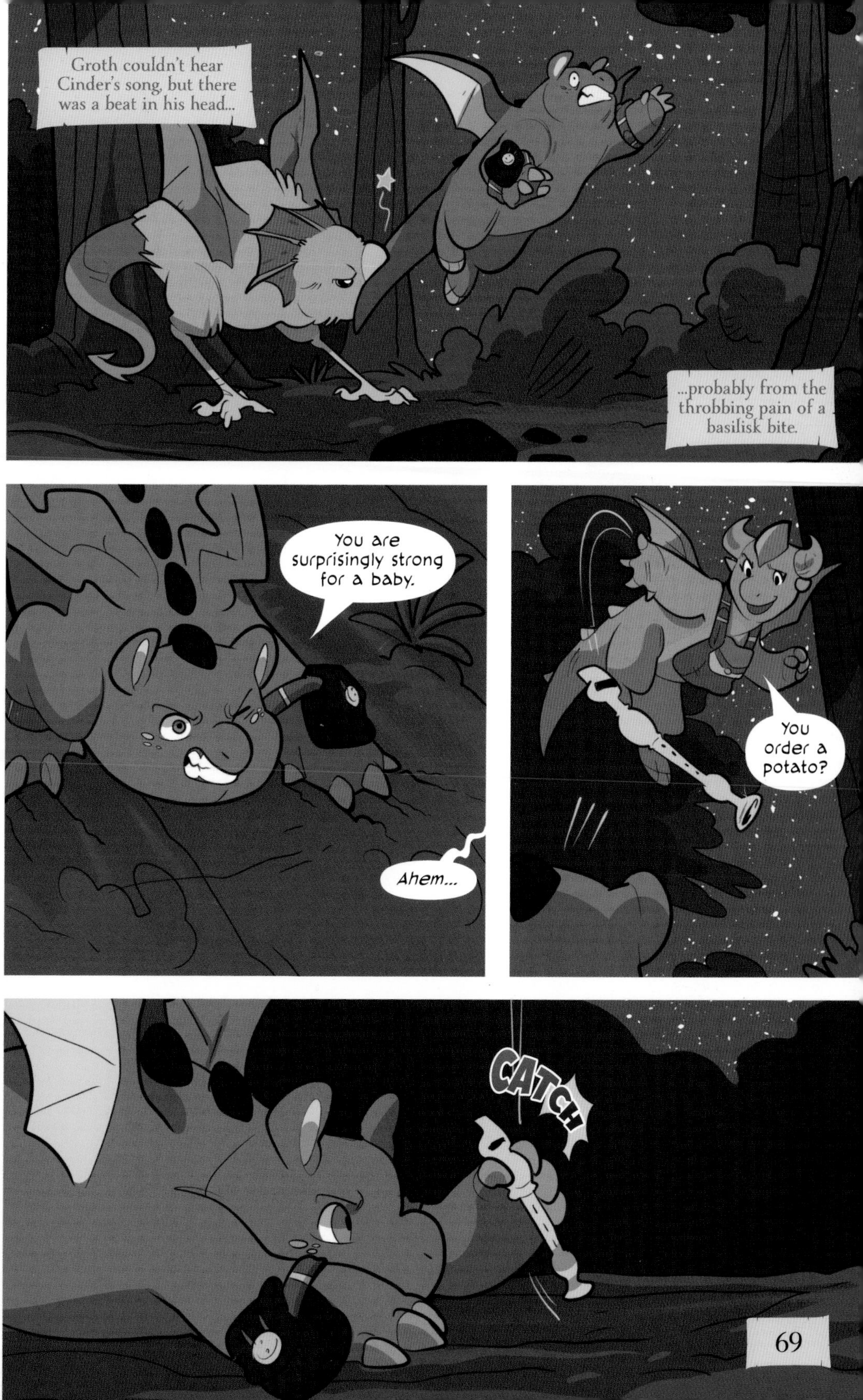
Groth couldn't hear Cinder's song, but there was a beat in his head...
...probably from the throbbing pain of a basilisk bite.
You are surprisingly strong for a baby.
Ahem...
You order a potato?
CATCH

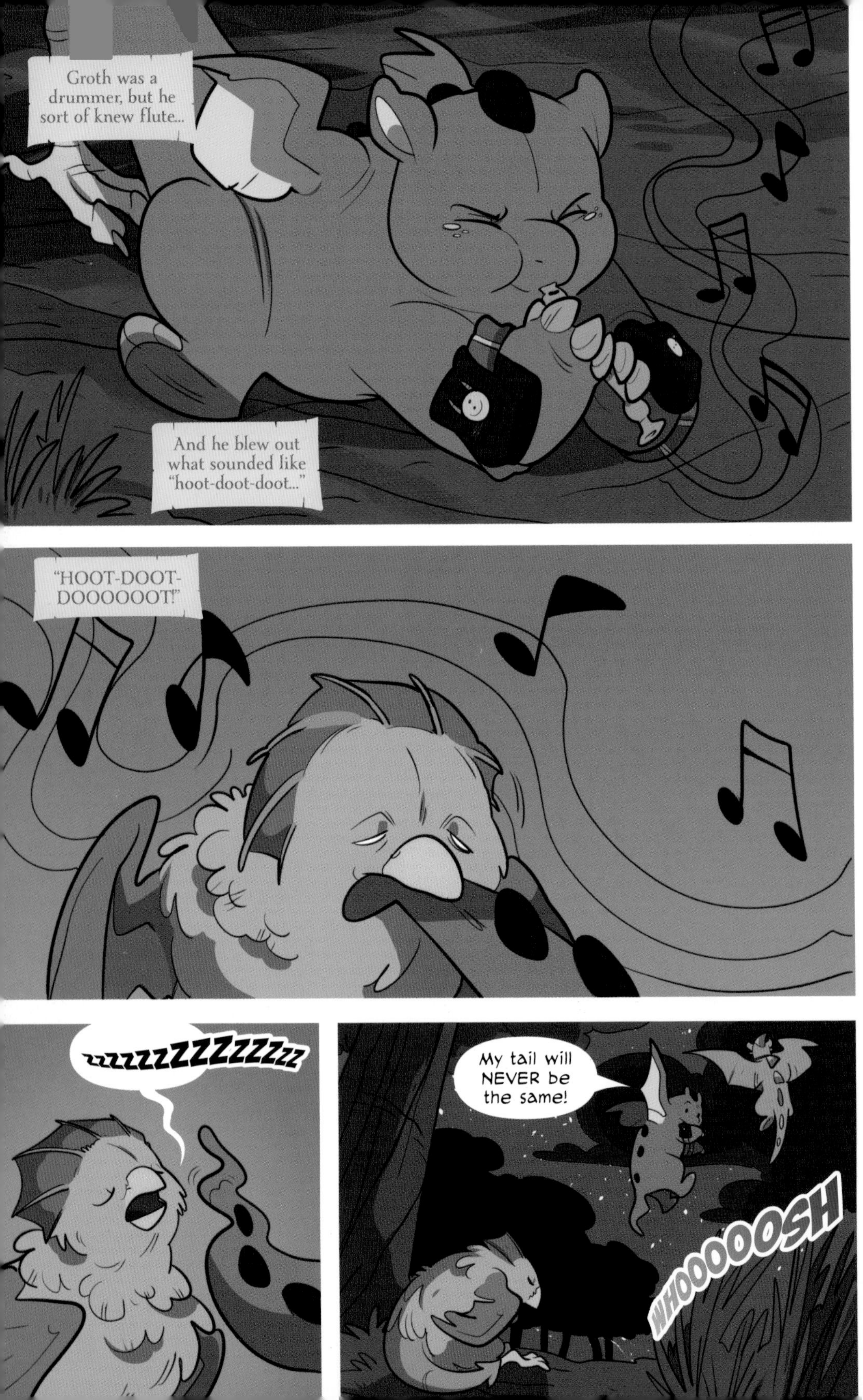

Groth was a drummer, but he sort of knew flute...
And he blew out what sounded like "hoot-doot-doot..."
"HOOT-DOOT-DOOOOOOT!"
zzzzzzZZZZzzzz
My tail will NEVER be the same!
WHOOOOOOSH

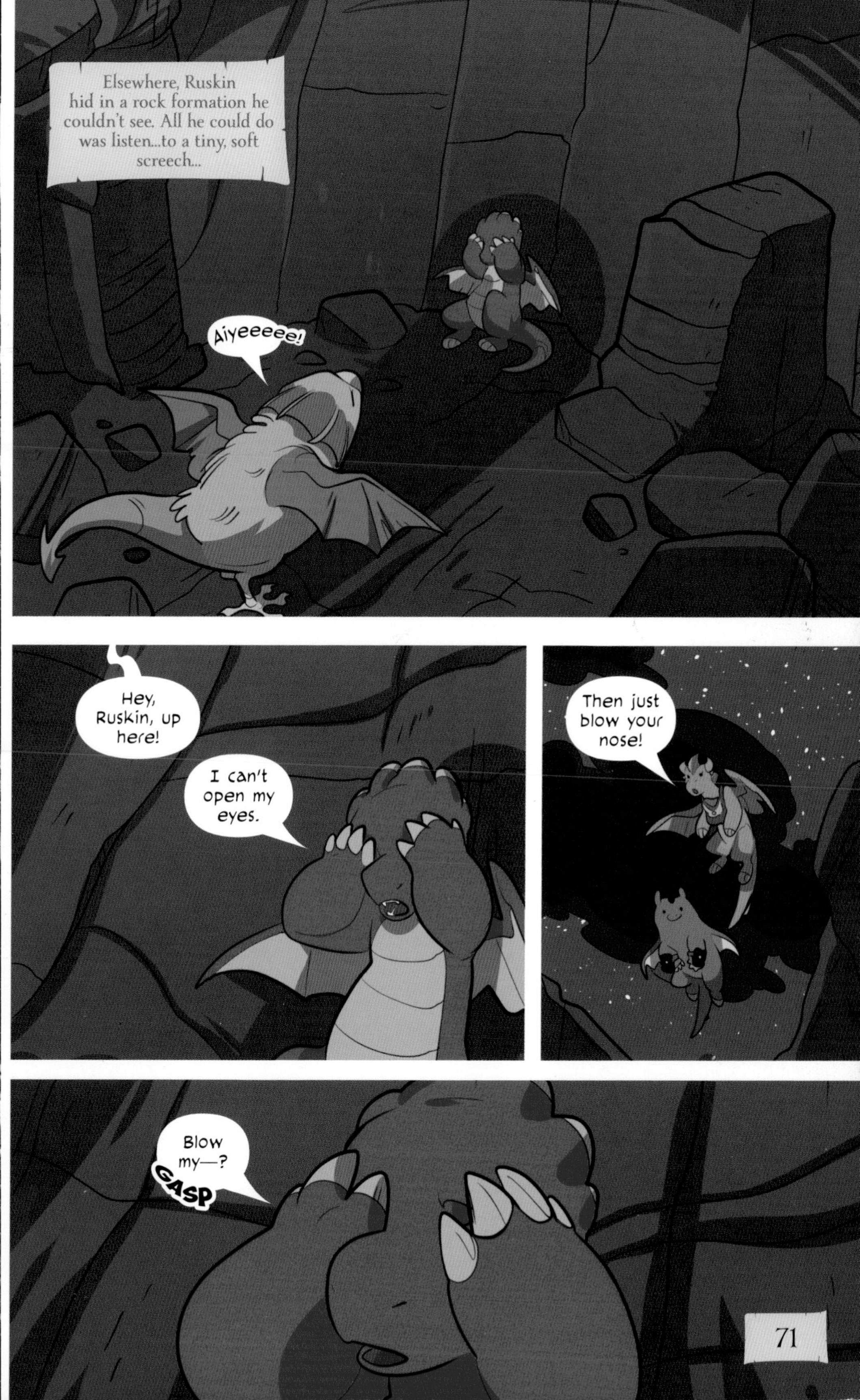
Elsewhere, Ruskin hid in a rock formation he couldn't see. All he could do was listen...to a tiny, soft screech...
Aiyeeeee!
Hey, Ruskin, up here!
I can't open my eyes.
Then just blow your nose!
Blow my—?
GASP

And where is that disgusting-looking basilisk?

Probably somewhere licking its feathers.

This place isn't that spooky.

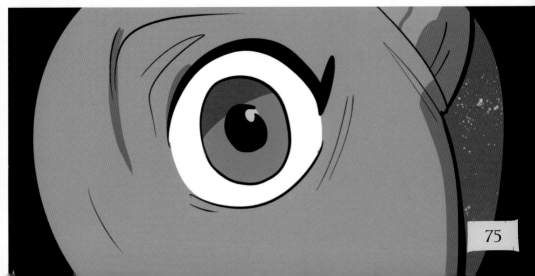

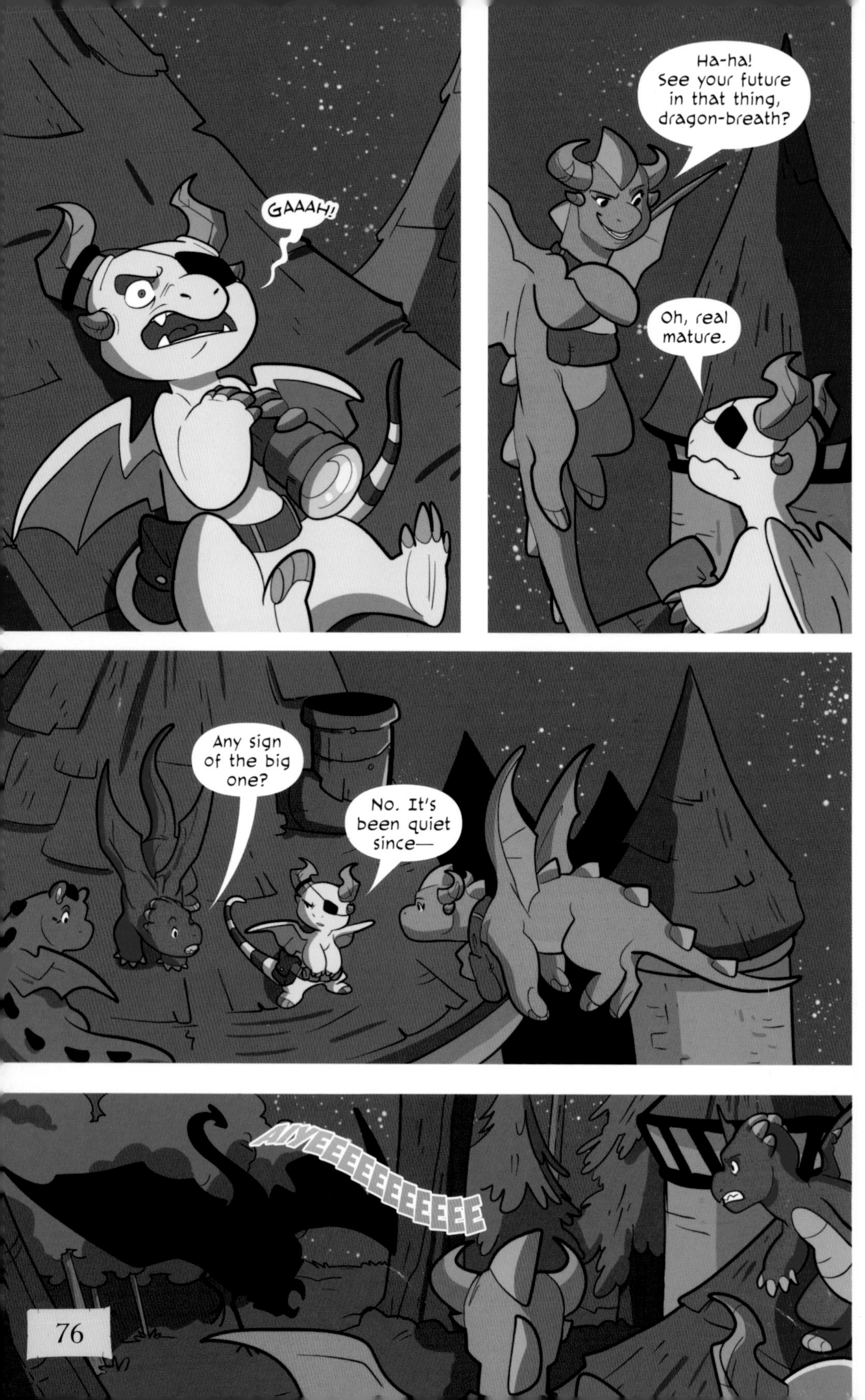
GAAAH!
Ha-ha! See your future in that thing, dragon-breath?
Oh, real mature.
Any sign of the big one?
No. It's been quiet since—
AIYEEEEEEEEEEEE

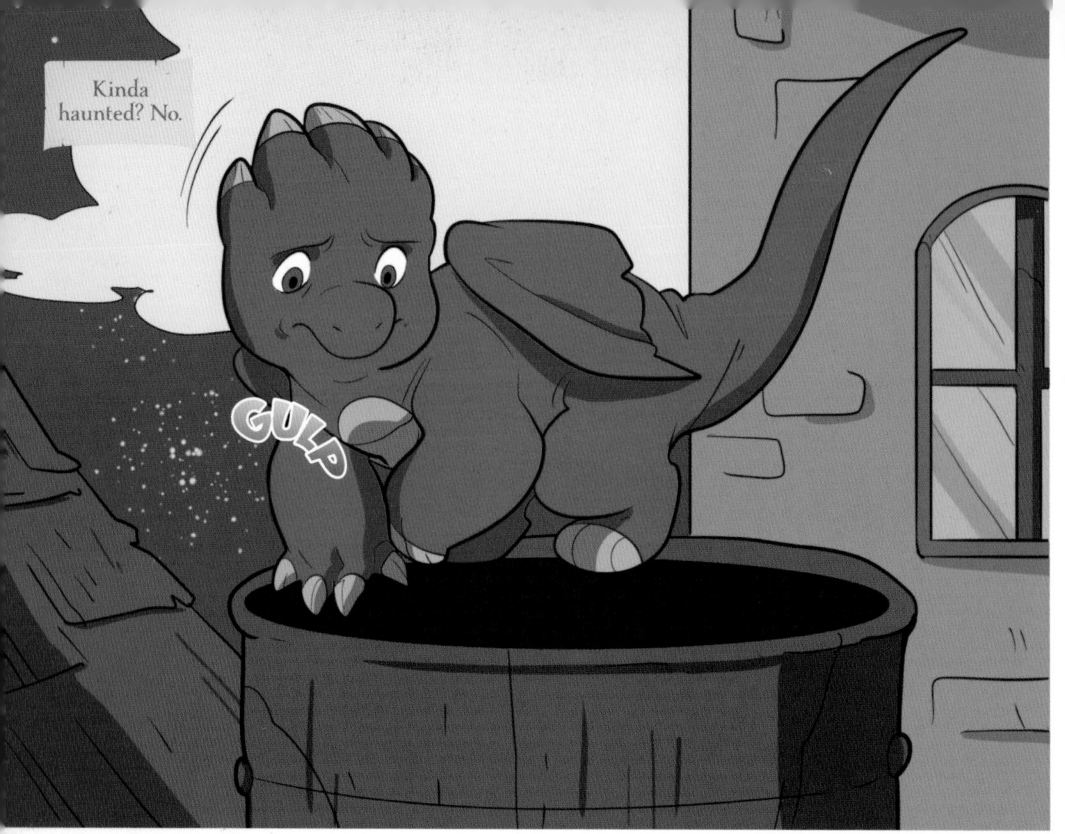
Kinda haunted? No.
GULP

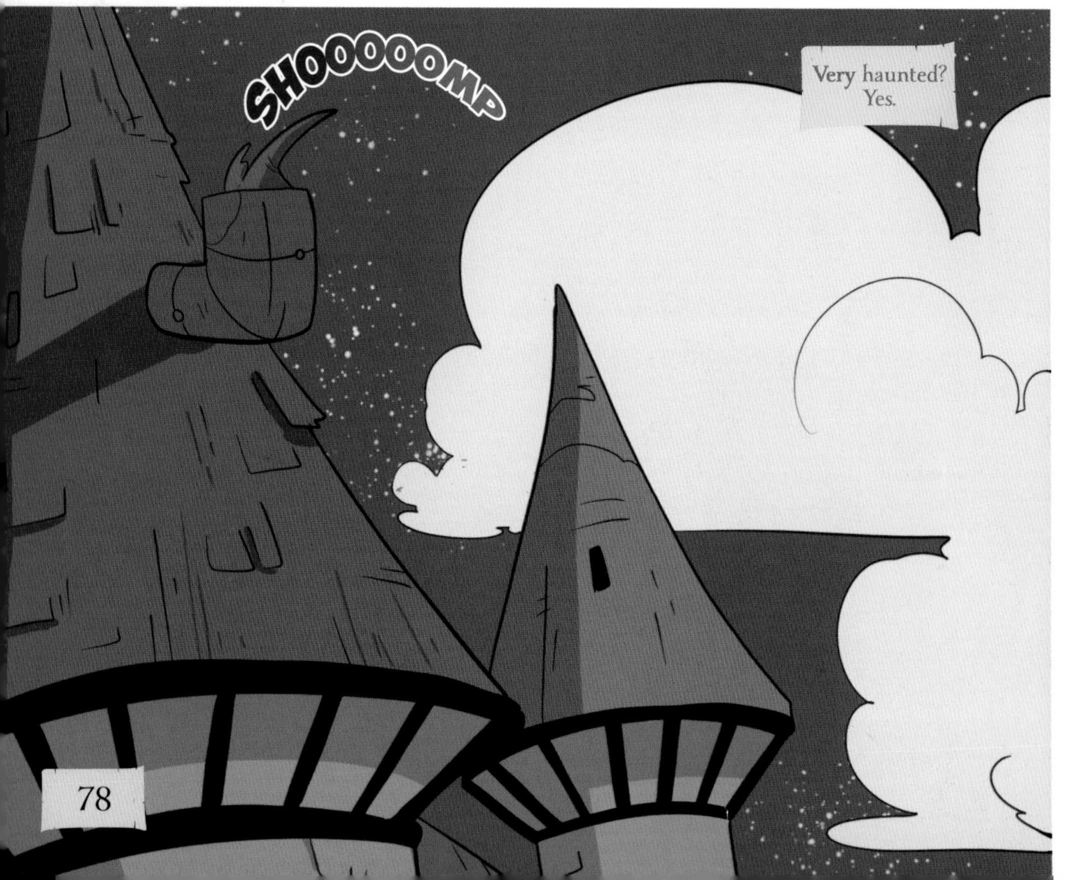
SHOOOOOOMP
Very haunted? Yes.

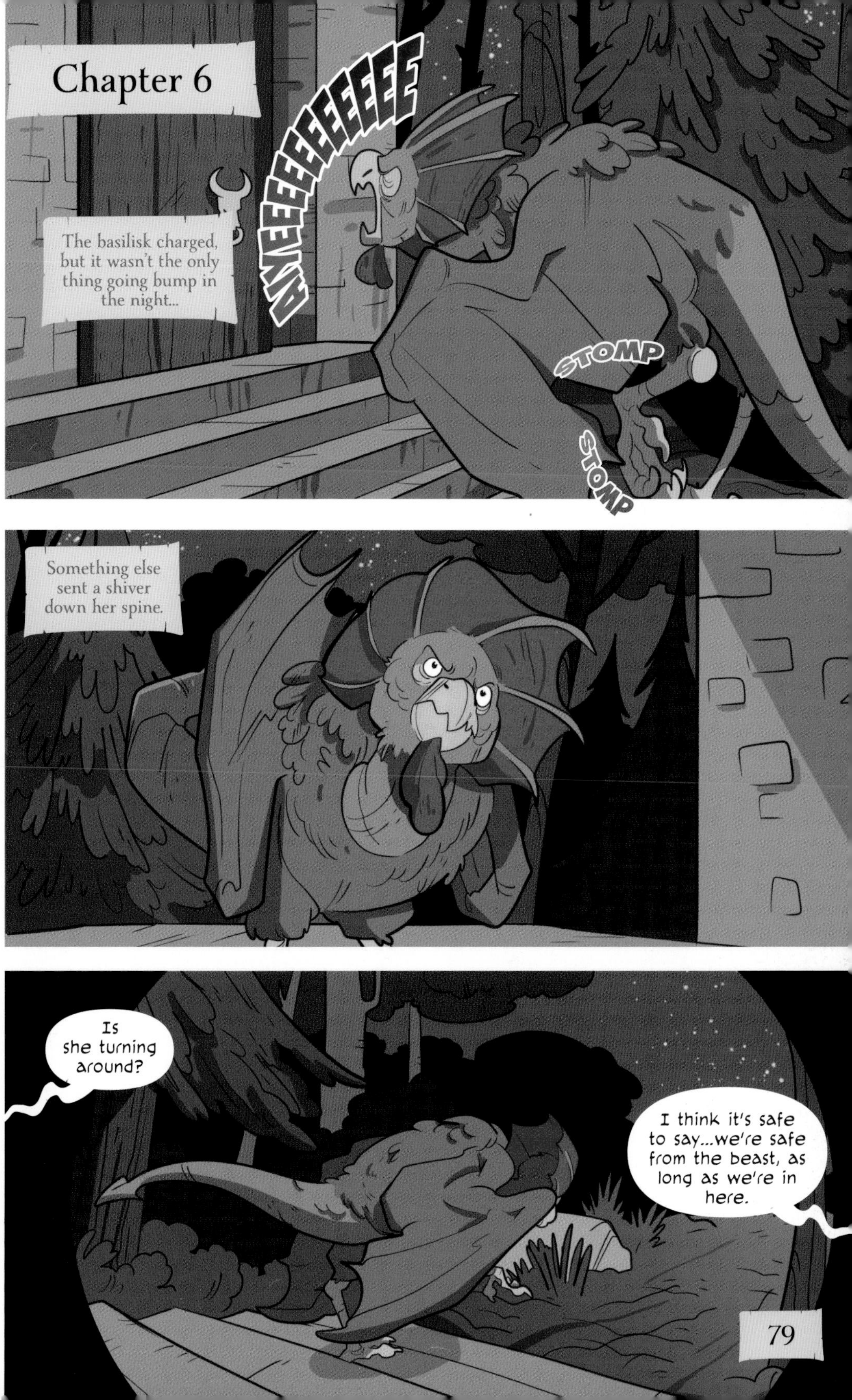
Chapter 6
The basilisk charged, but it wasn't the only thing going bump in the night...
SKWEEEEEEEEEEE
STOMP
STOMP
Something else sent a shiver down her spine.
Is she turning around?
I think it's safe to say...we're safe from the beast, as long as we're in here.

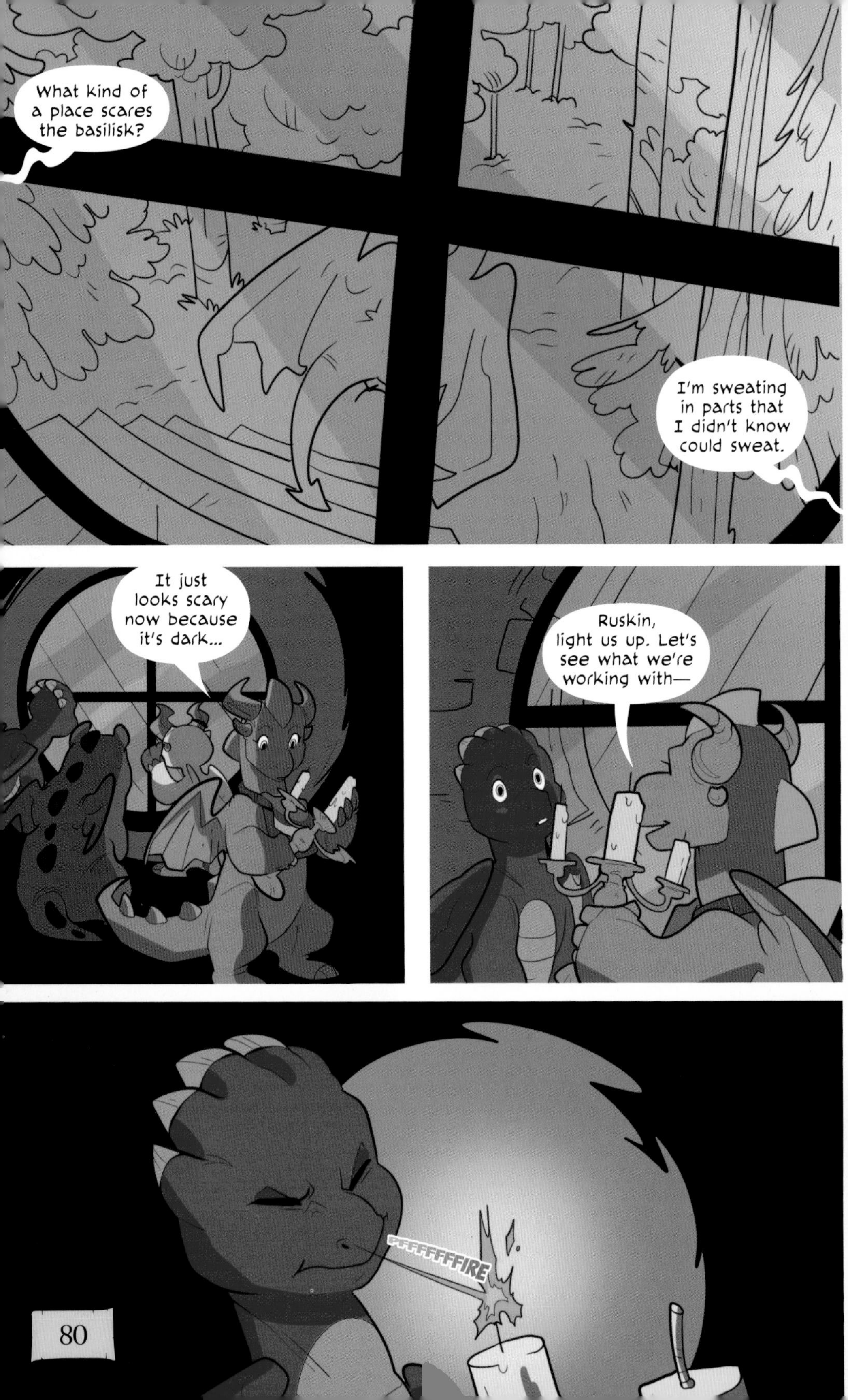
What kind of a place scares the basilisk?
I'm sweating in parts that I didn't know could sweat.
It just looks scary now because it's dark...
Ruskin, light us up. Let's see what we're working with—
PFFFFFFFFIRE

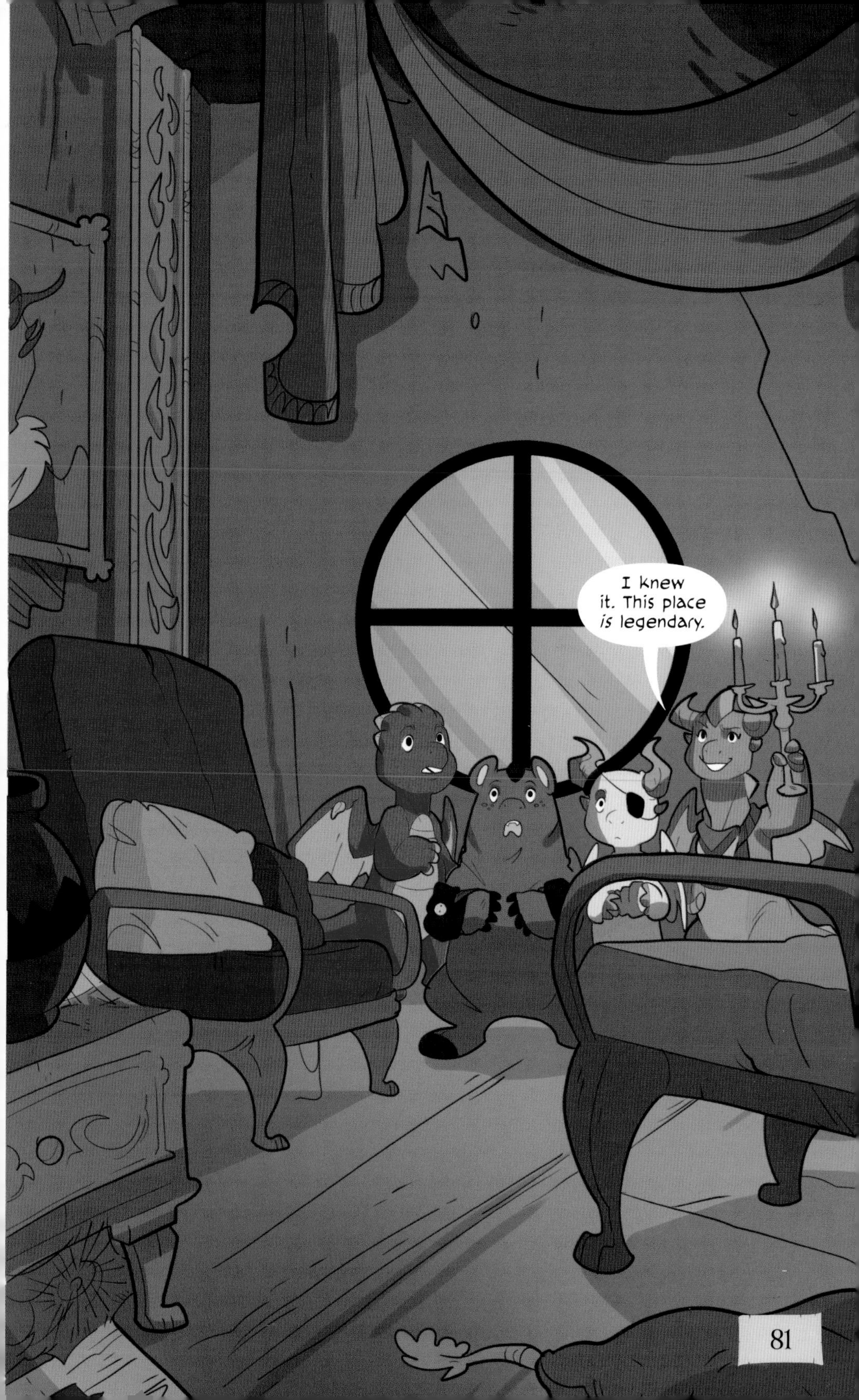
I knew it. This place *is* legendary.

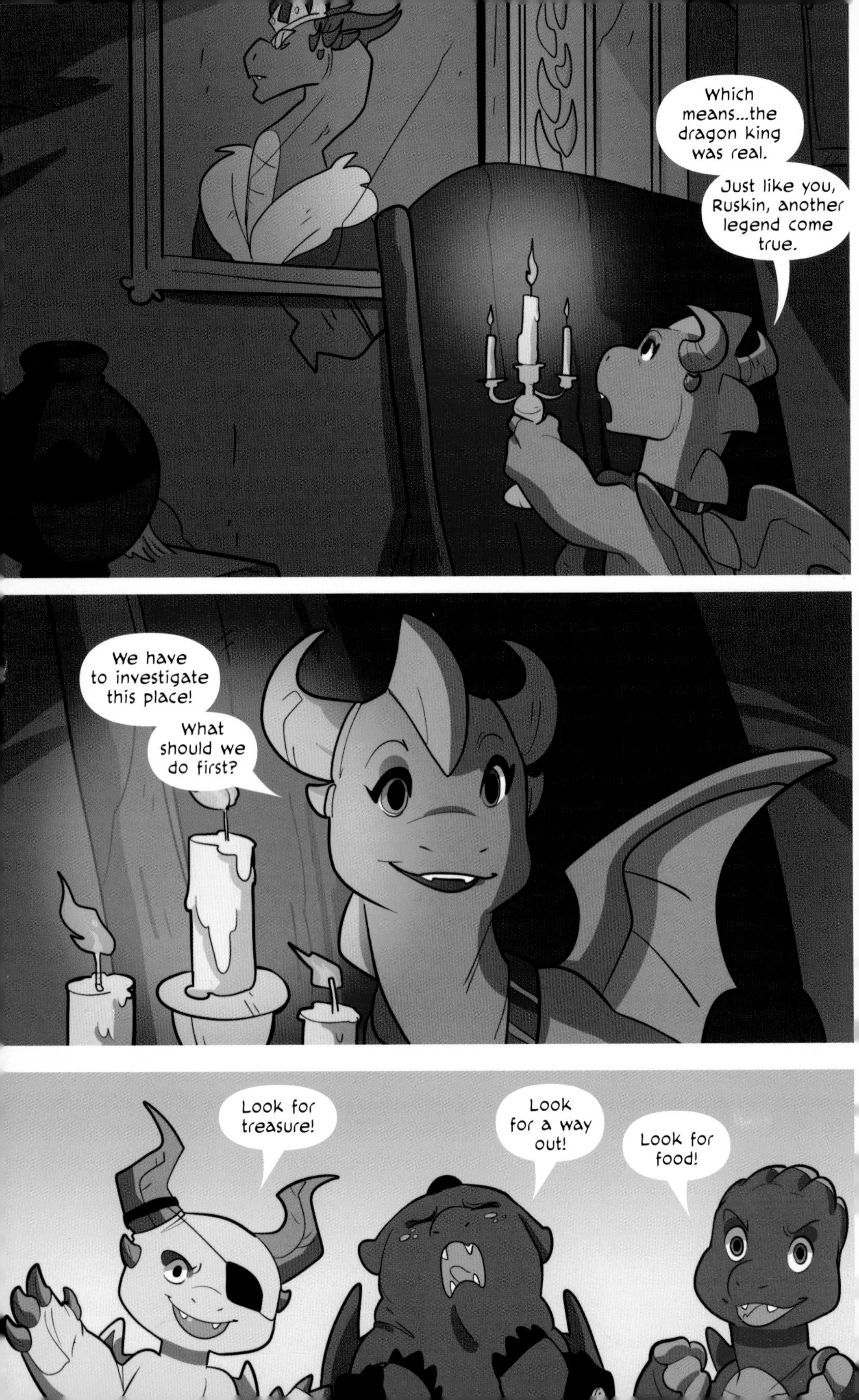
Which means...the dragon king was real.
Just like you, Ruskin, another legend come true.
We have to investigate this place!
What should we do first?
Look for treasure!
Look for a way out!
Look for food!

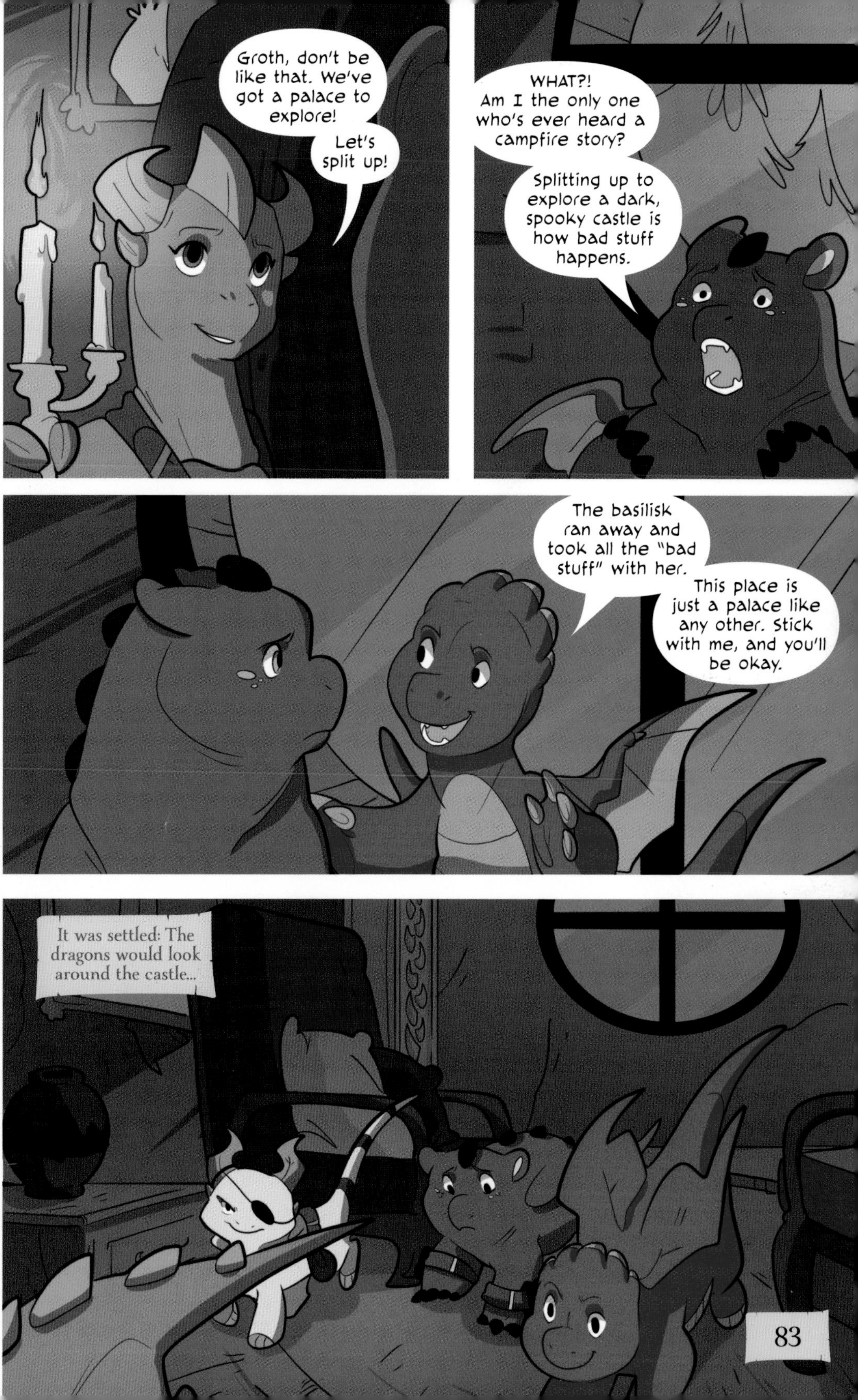

Groth, don't be like that. We've got a palace to explore!
Let's split up!
WHAT?! Am I the only one who's ever heard a campfire story?
Splitting up to explore a dark, spooky castle is how bad stuff happens.
The basilisk ran away and took all the "bad stuff" with her.
This place is just a palace like any other. Stick with me, and you'll be okay.
It was settled: The dragons would look around the castle...

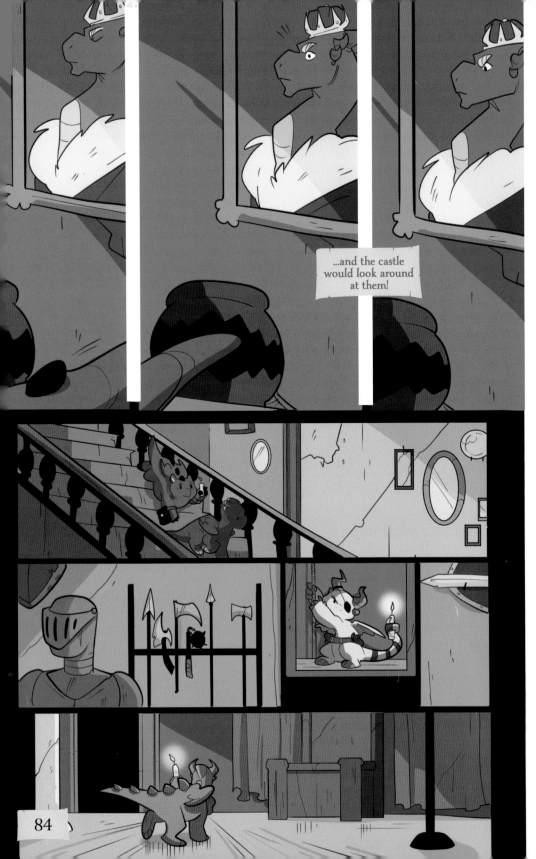

...and the castle
would look around
at them!

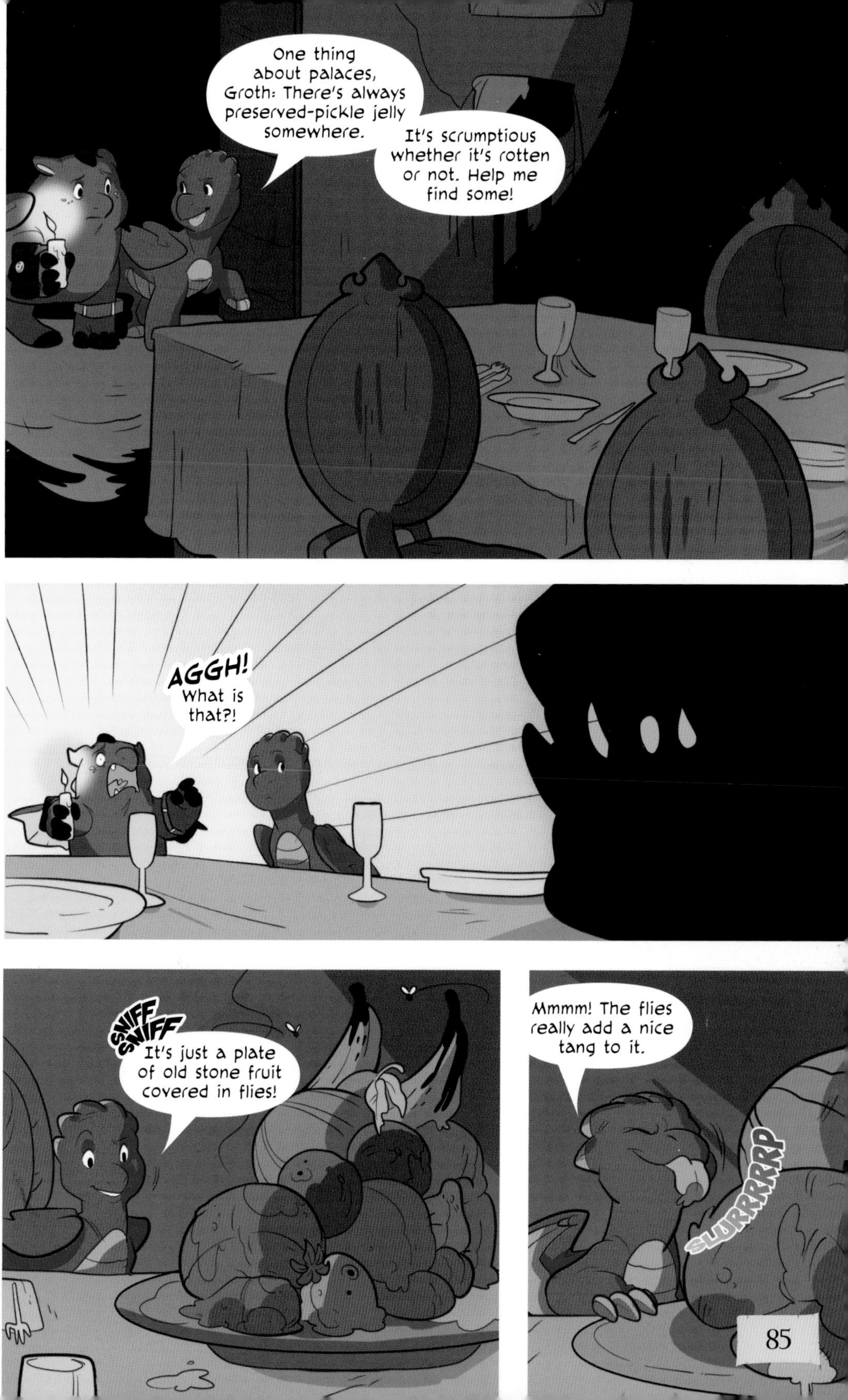
One thing about palaces, Groth: There's always preserved-pickle jelly somewhere.
It's scrumptious whether it's rotten or not. Help me find some!
AGGH! What is that?!
SNIFF SNIFF
It's just a plate of old stone fruit covered in flies!
Mmmm! The flies really add a nice tang to it.
SLURRRRRP

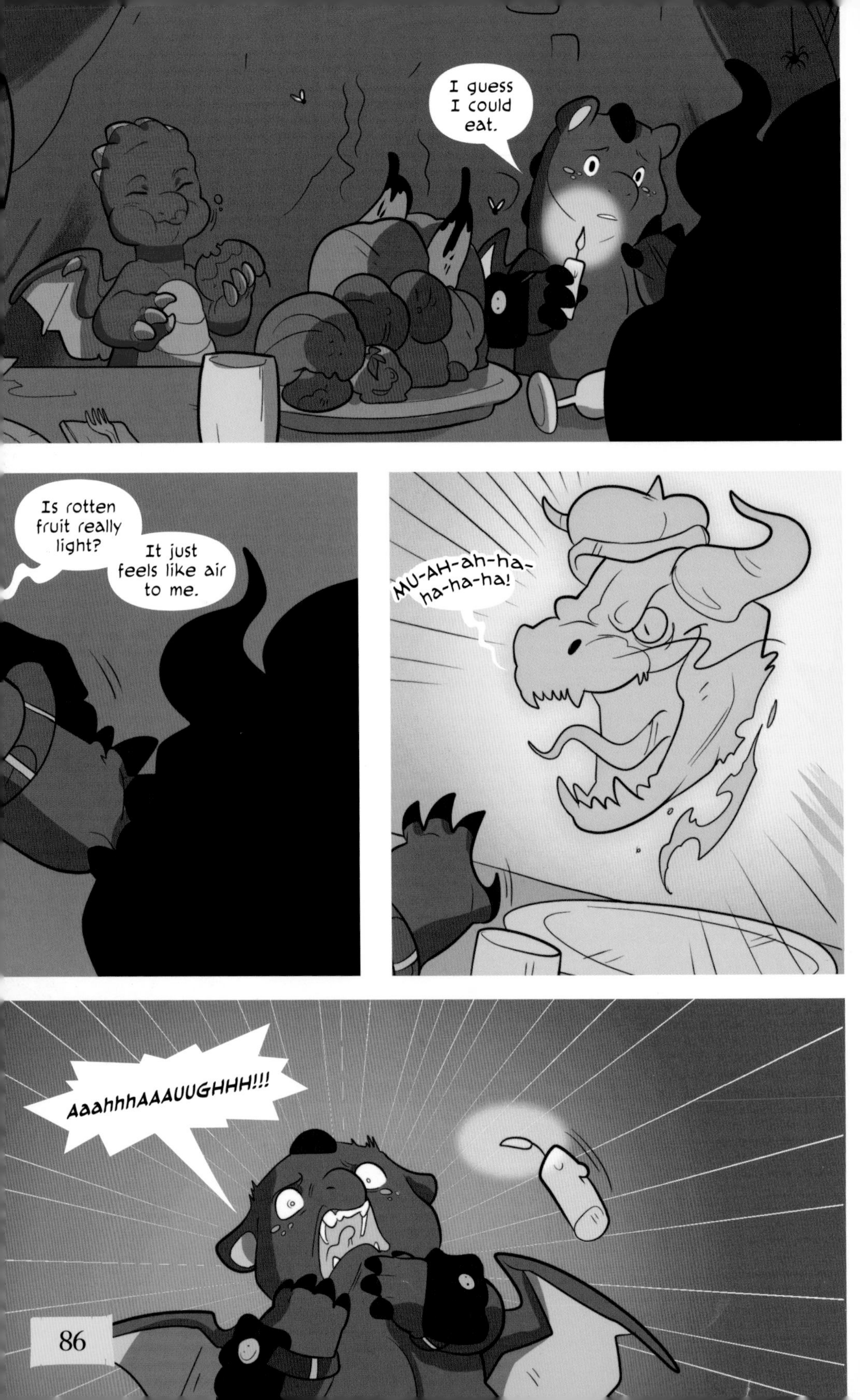
I guess I could eat.
Is rotten fruit really light?
It just feels like air to me.
MU-AH-ah-ha-ha-ha-ha!
AaahhhAAAUUGHHH!!!

87

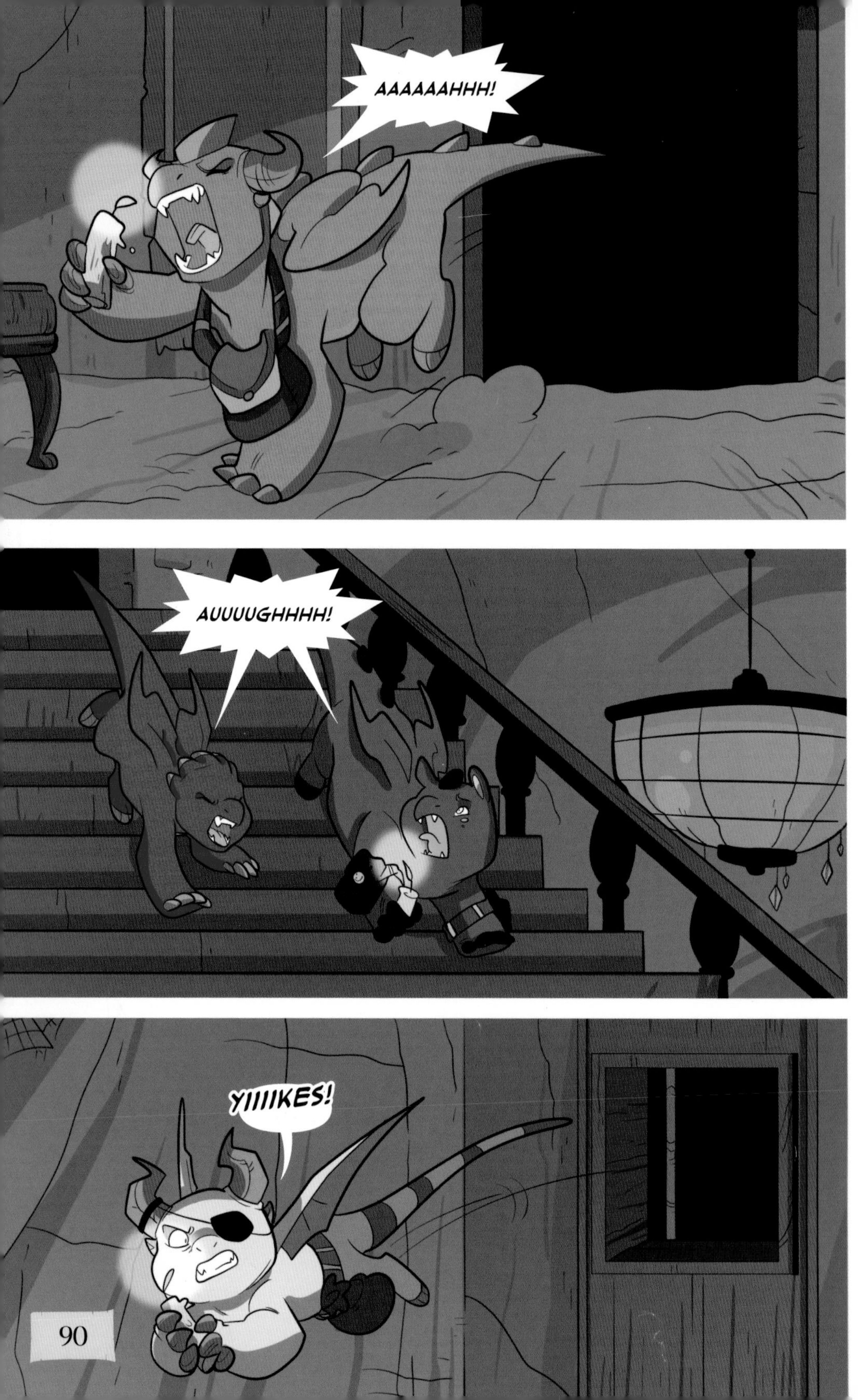
AAAAAAHHH!
AUUUUGHHHH!
YIIIIKES!

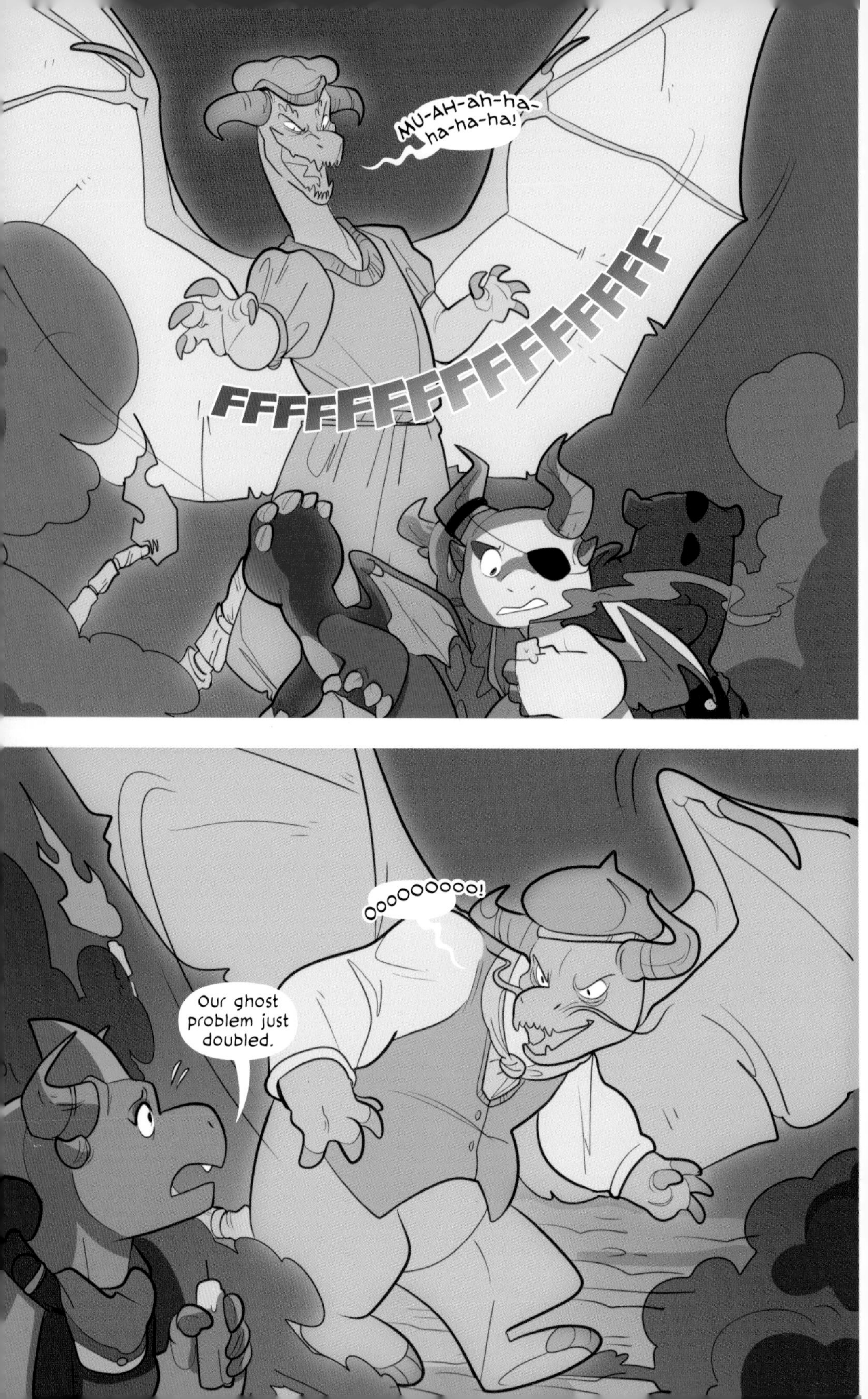
MU-AH-ah-ha-ha-ha-ha!
FFFFFFFFFFFFFF
OOOOOOOOO!
Our ghost problem just doubled.

Chapter 7

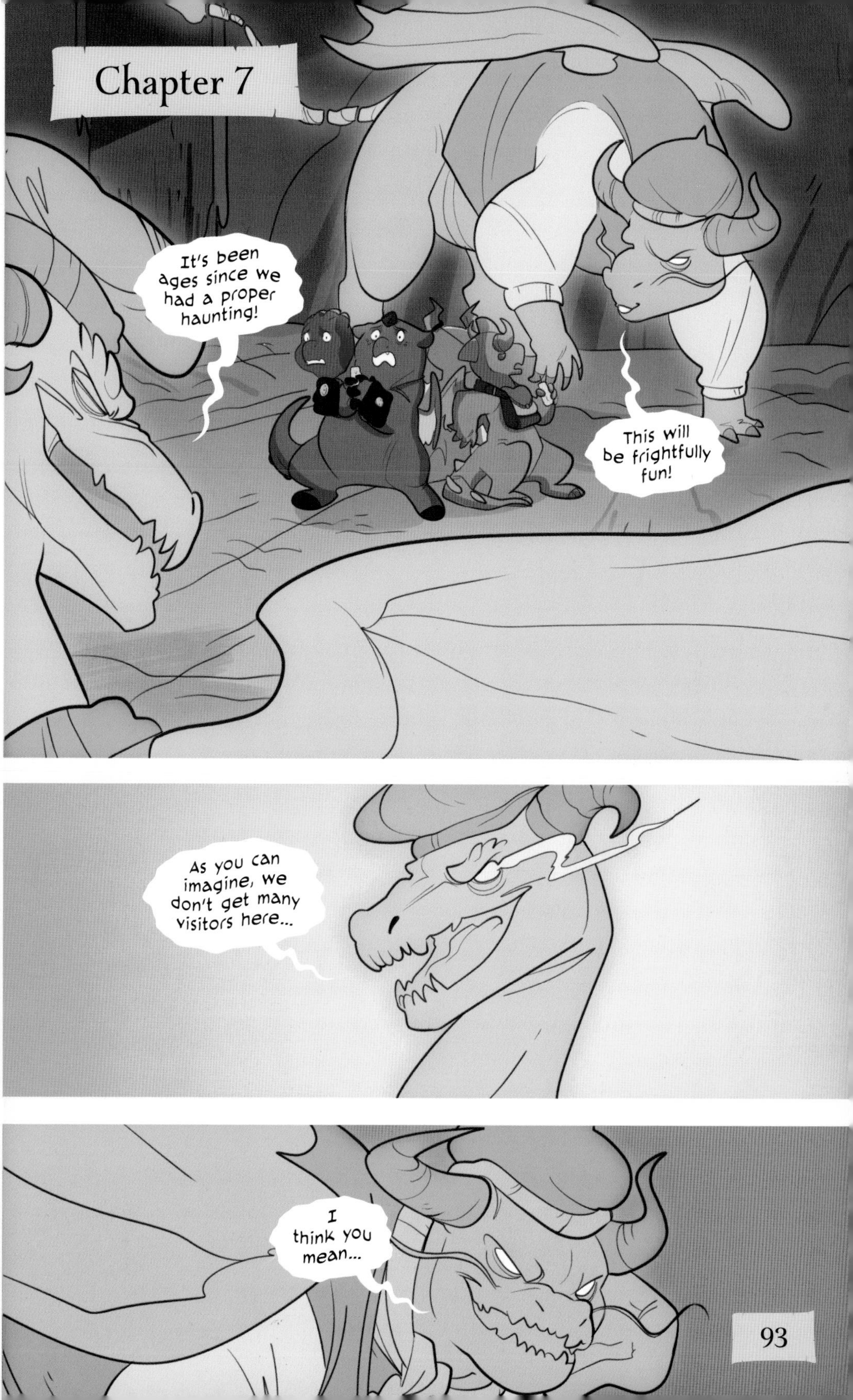
It's been ages since we had a proper haunting!
This will be frightfully fun!
As you can imagine, we don't get many visitors here...
I think you mean...

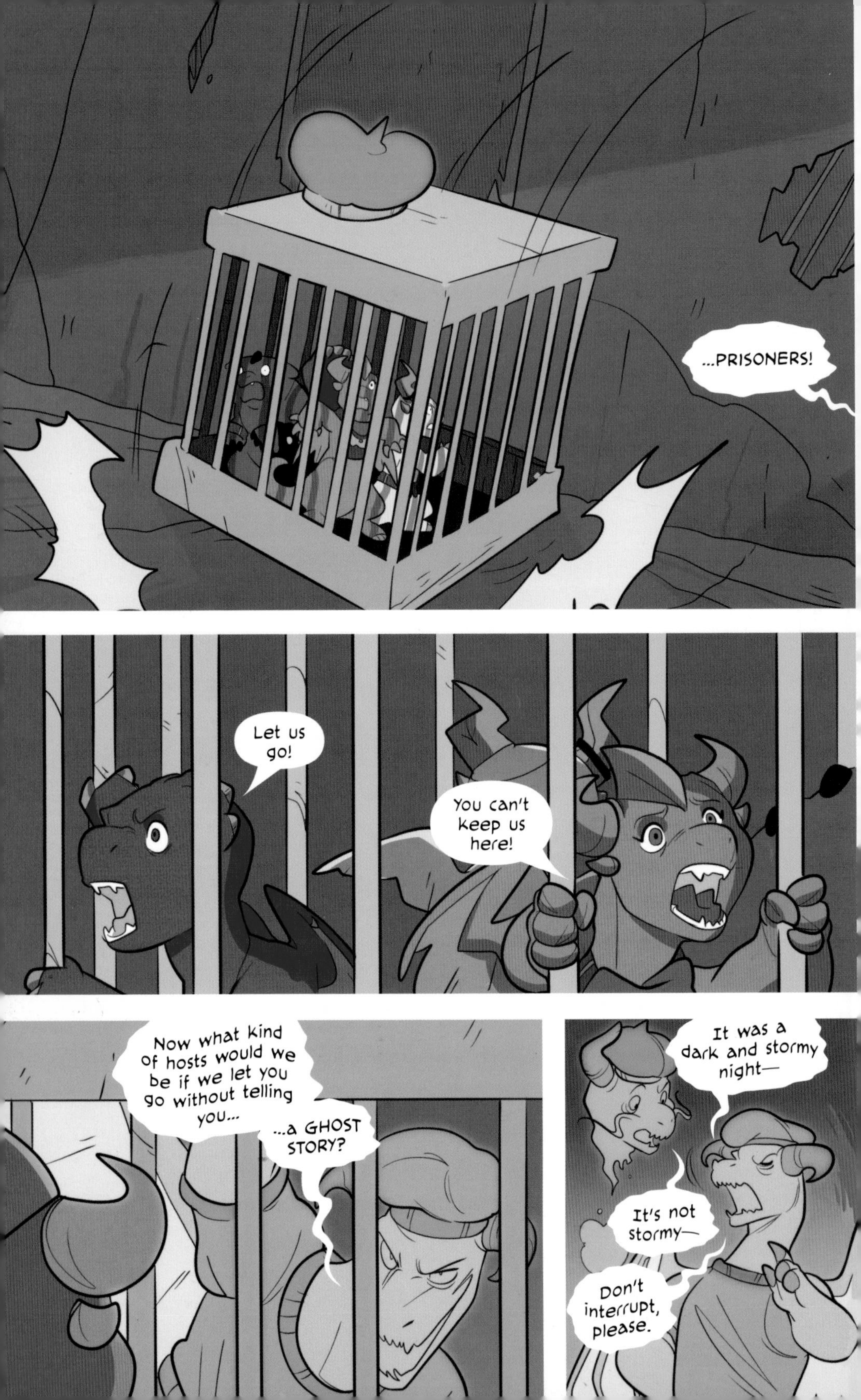
...PRISONERS!
Let us go!
You can't keep us here!
Now what kind of hosts would we be if we let you go without telling you...
...a GHOST STORY?
It was a dark and stormy night—
It's not stormy—
Don't interrupt, please.

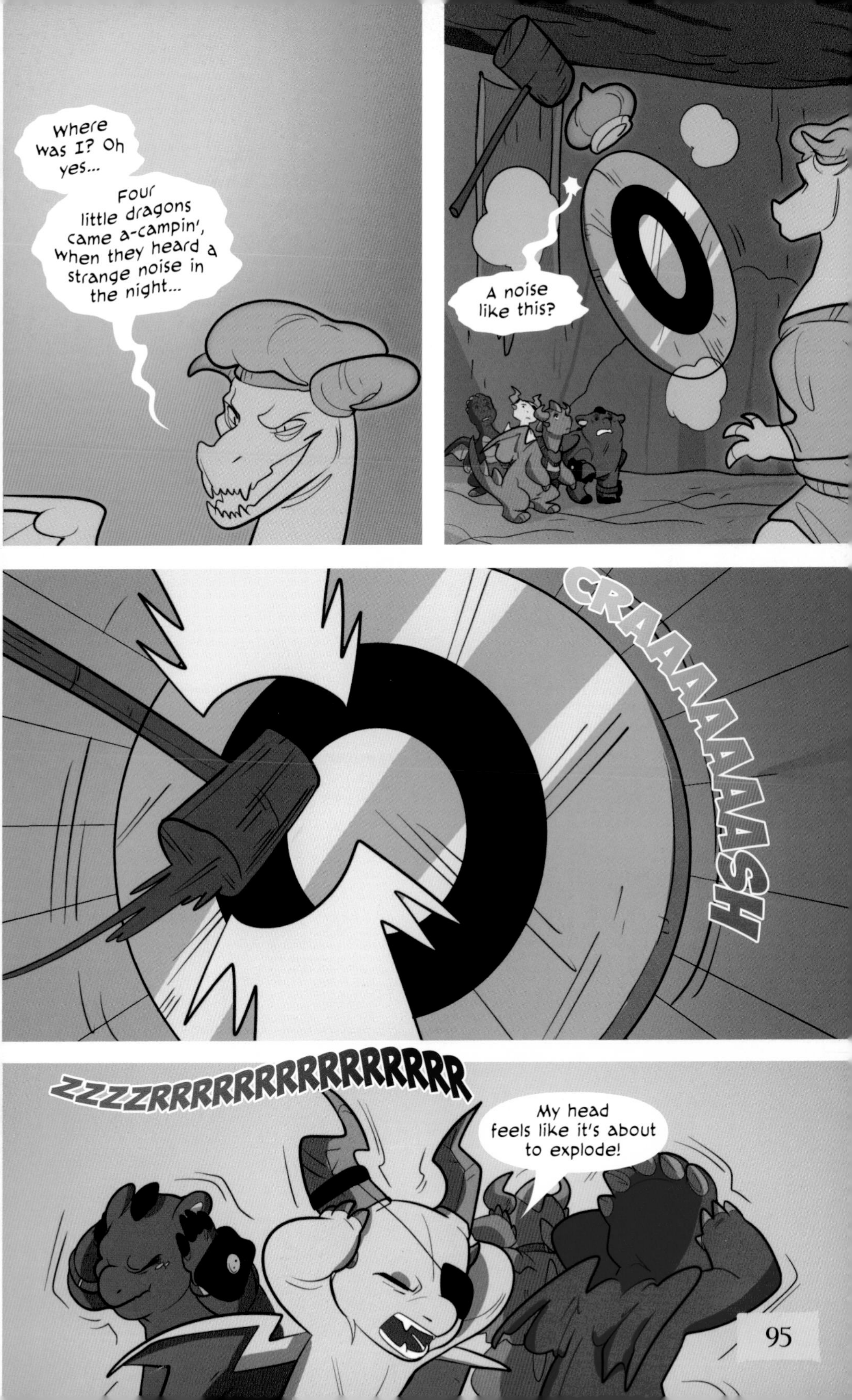

Where was I? Oh yes...
Four little dragons came a-campin', when they heard a strange noise in the night...
A noise like this?
CRAAAAAAASH
ZZZZRRRRRRRRRRRRRRR
My head feels like it's about to explode!

96

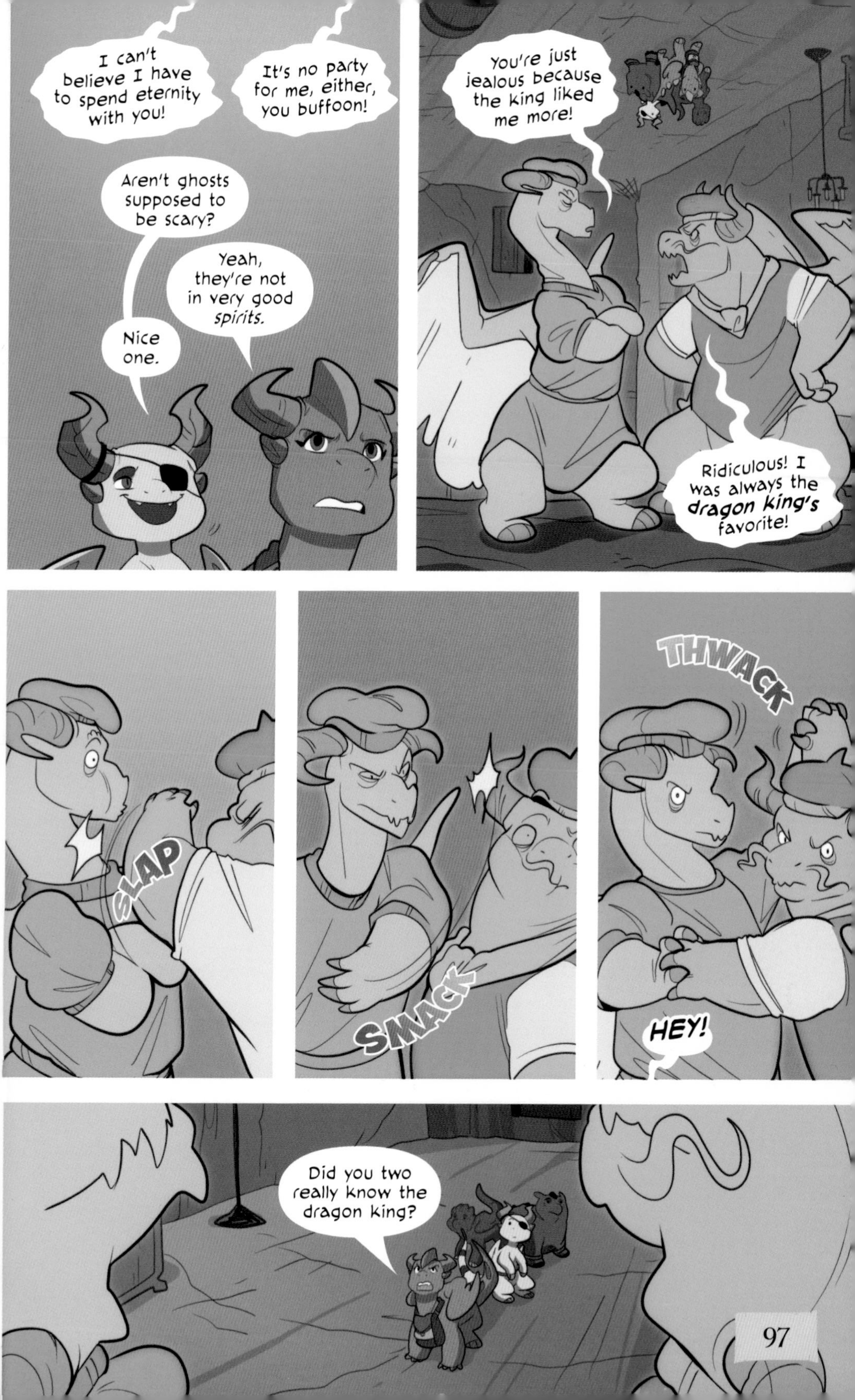
I can't believe I have to spend eternity with you!
It's no party for me, either, you buffoon!
Aren't ghosts supposed to be scary?
Yeah, they're not in very good *spirits.*
Nice one.
You're just jealous because the king liked me more!
Ridiculous! I was always the **dragon king's** favorite!
SLAP
SMACK
THWACK
HEY!
Did you two really know the dragon king?

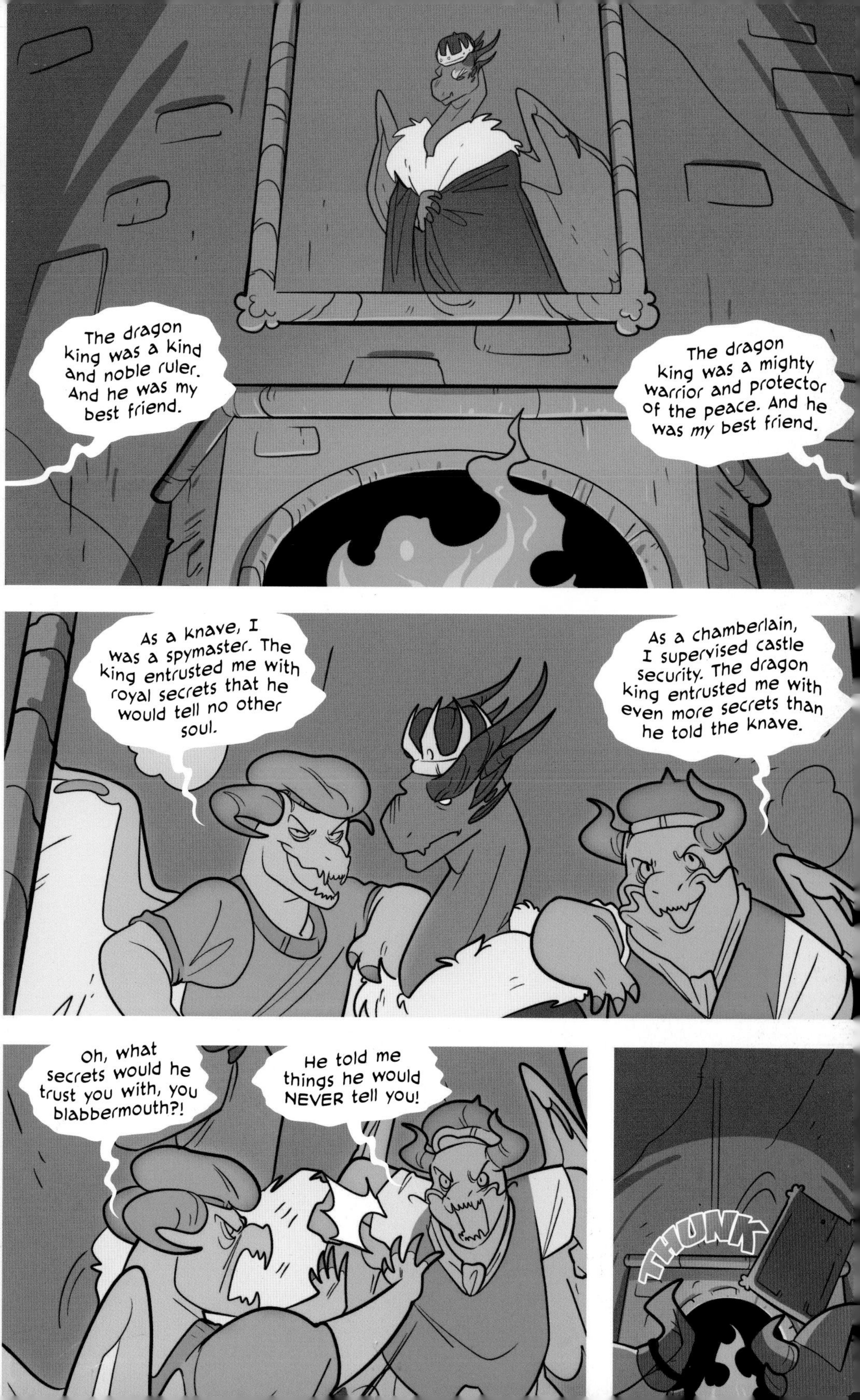
The dragon king was a kind and noble ruler. And he was my best friend.
The dragon king was a mighty warrior and protector of the peace. And he was *my* best friend.
As a knave, I was a spymaster. The king entrusted me with royal secrets that he would tell no other soul.
As a chamberlain, I supervised castle security. The dragon king entrusted me with even more secrets than he told the knave.
Oh, what secrets would he trust you with, you blabbermouth?!
He told me things he would NEVER tell you!
THUNK

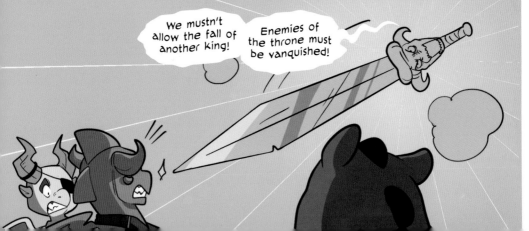

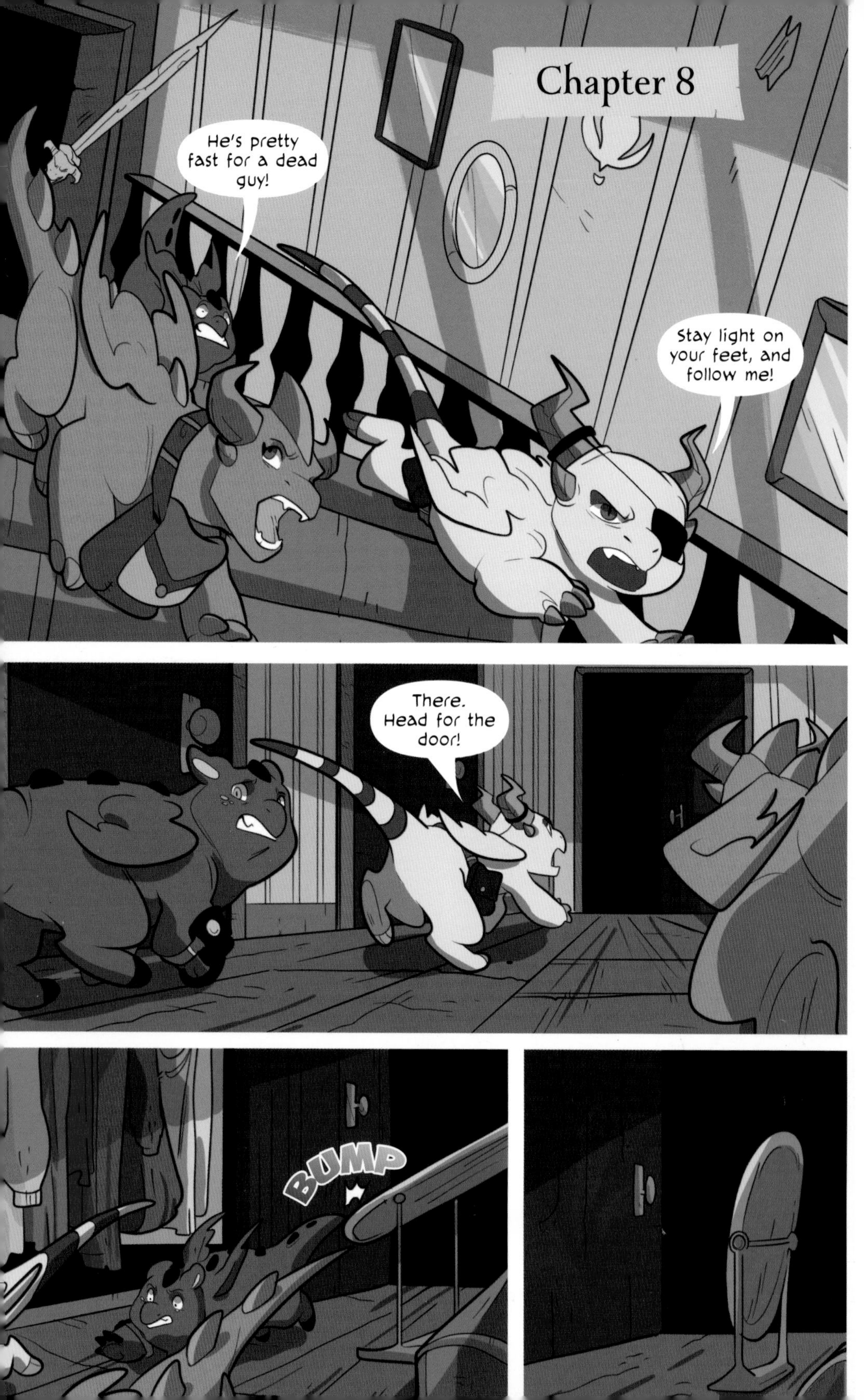
Chapter 8
He's pretty fast for a dead guy!
Stay light on your feet, and follow me!
There. Head for the door!
BUMP

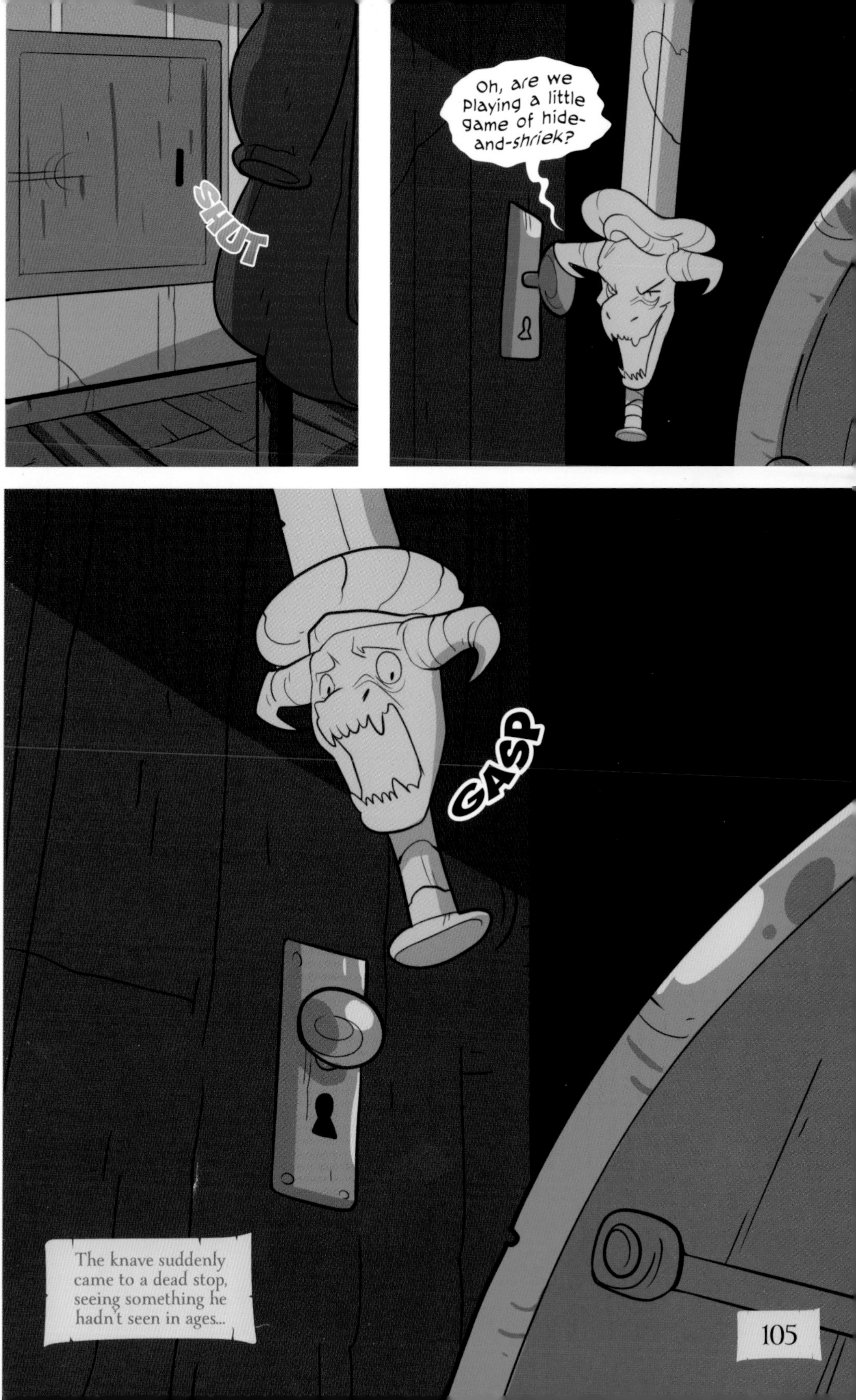
SHUT
Oh, are we playing a little game of hide-and-*shriek*?
GASP
The knave suddenly came to a dead stop, seeing something he hadn't seen in ages...

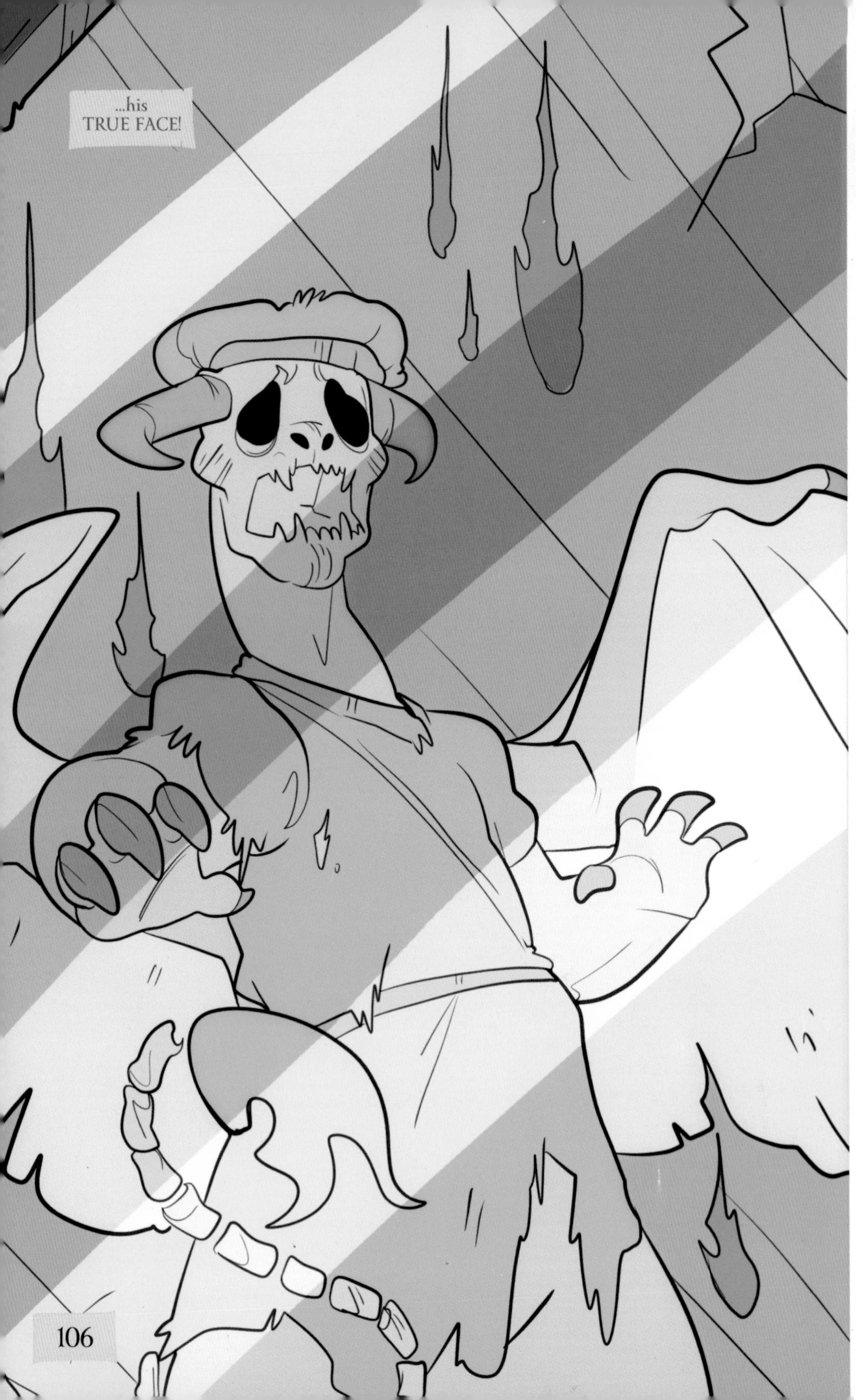
...his
TRUE FACE!

107

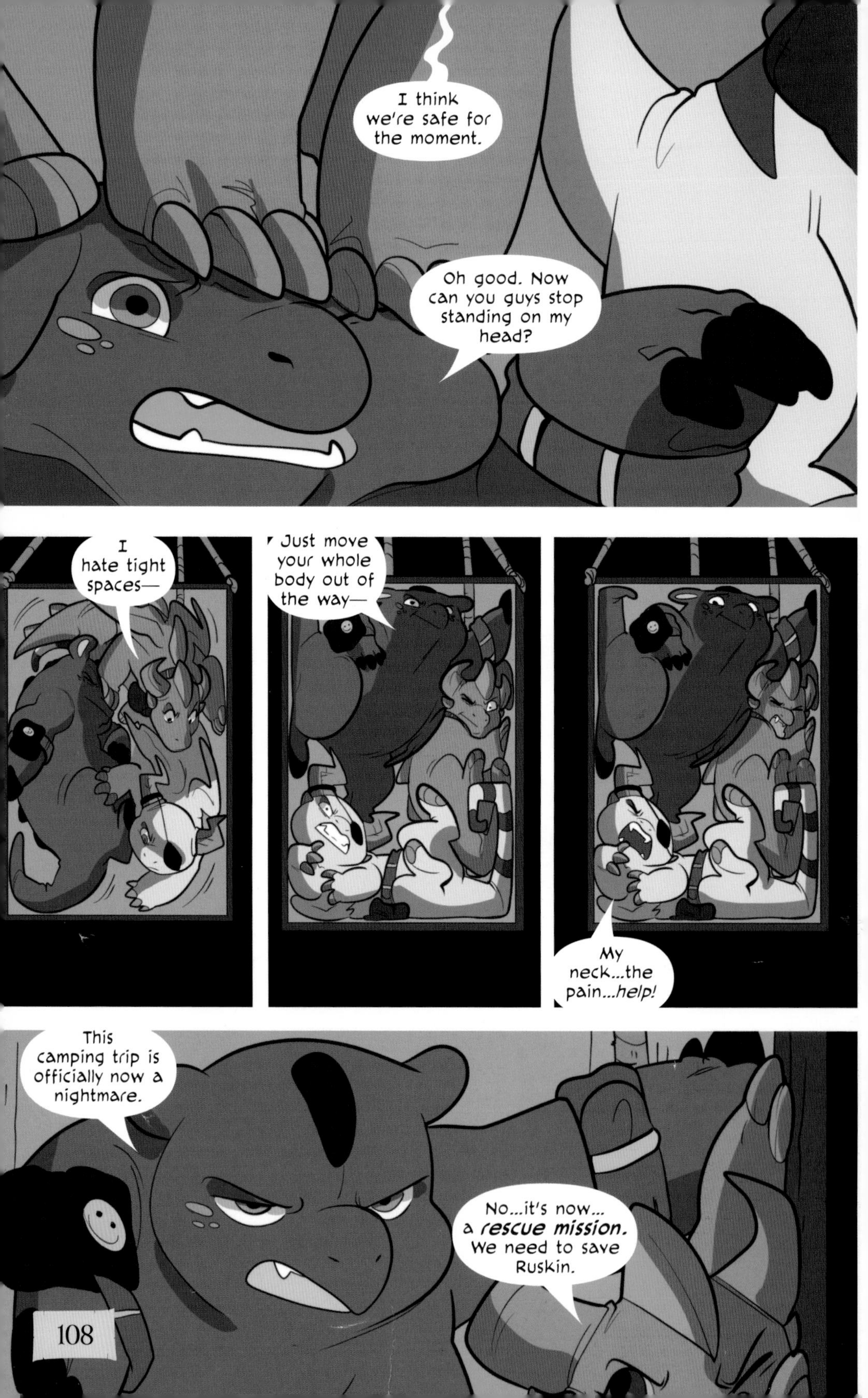
I think we're safe for the moment.
Oh good. Now can you guys stop standing on my head?
I hate tight spaces—
Just move your whole body out of the way—
My neck...the pain...*help!*
This camping trip is officially now a nightmare.
No...it's now... a ***rescue mission.*** We need to save Ruskin.

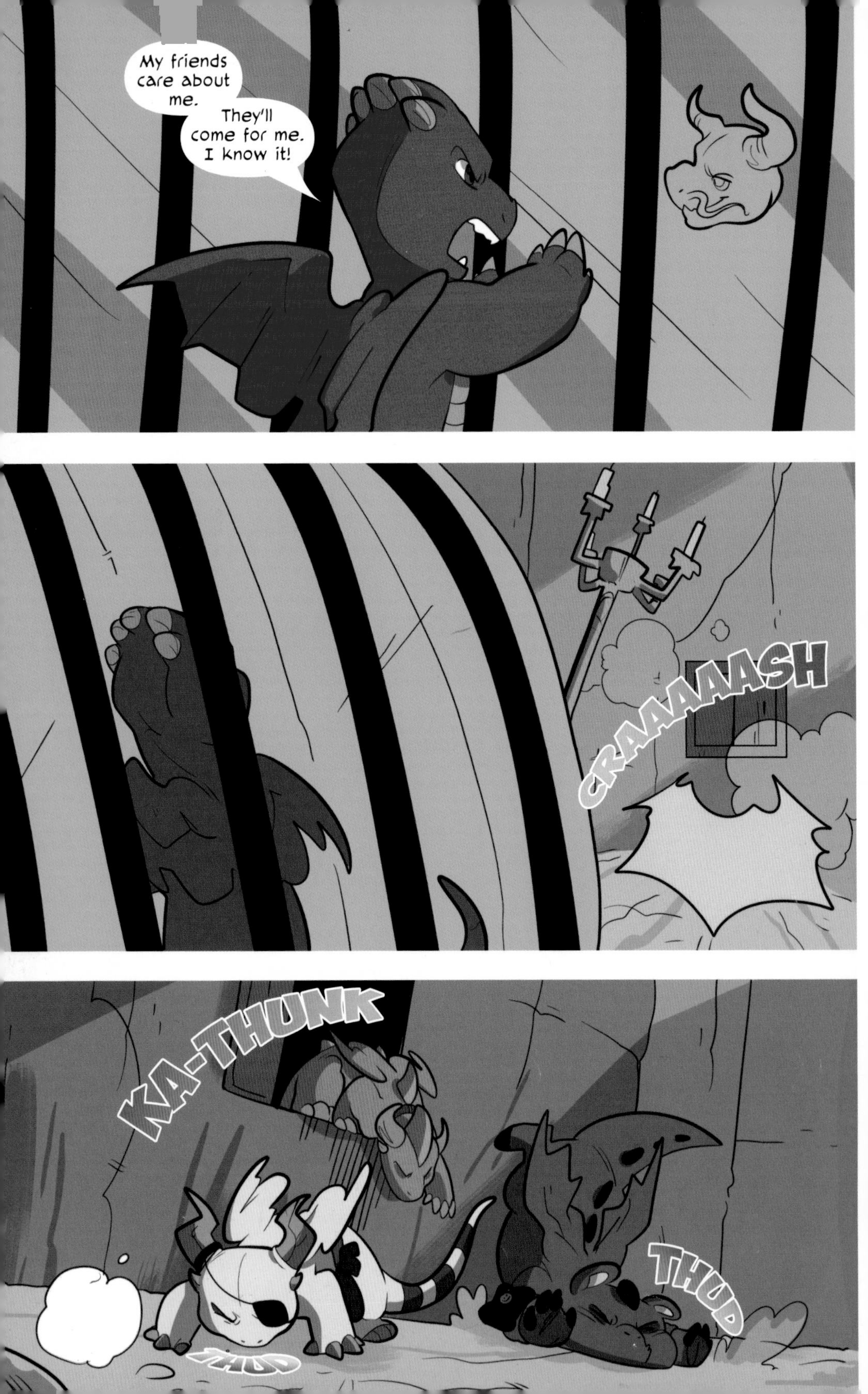
My friends care about me.
They'll come for me. I know it!
CRAAAAASH
KA-THUNK
THUD
THUD

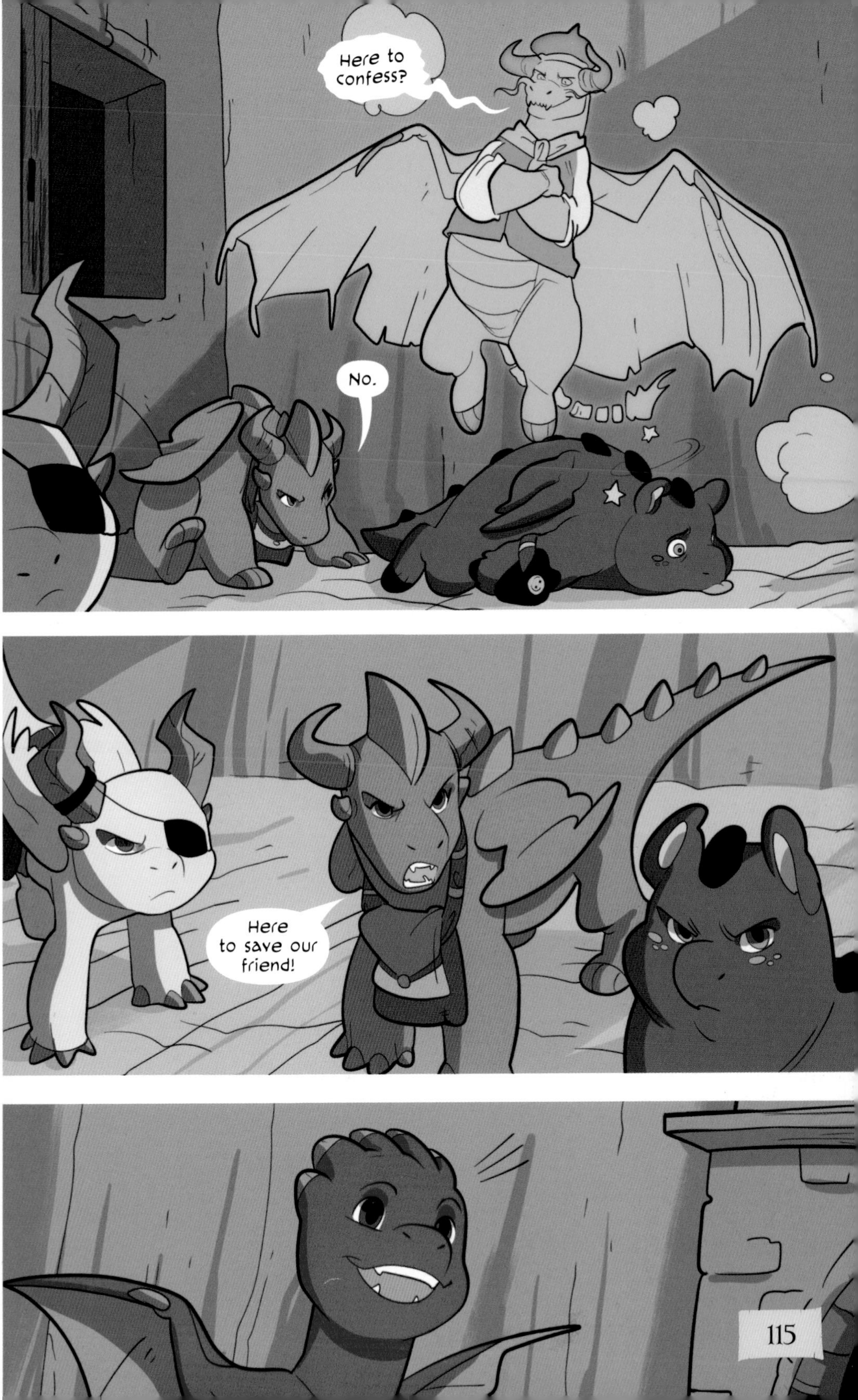
Here to confess?
No.
Here to save our friend!

Chapter 9

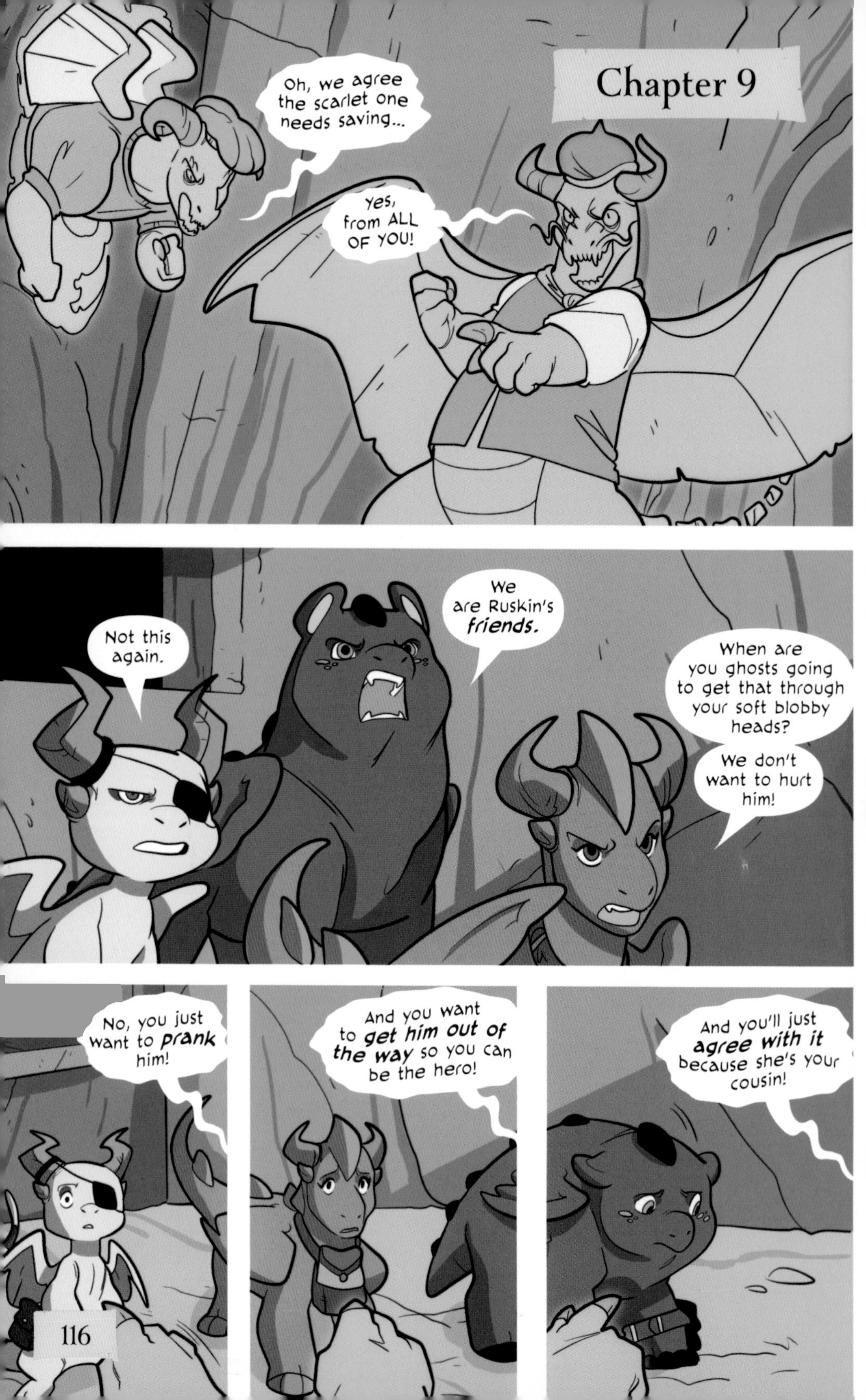
Oh, we agree the scarlet one needs saving...
Yes, from ALL OF YOU!
Not this again.
We are Ruskin's *friends.*
When are you ghosts going to get that through your soft blobby heads?
We don't want to hurt him!
No, you just want to *prank* him!
And you want to *get him out of the way* so you can be the hero!
And you'll just *agree with it* because she's your cousin!

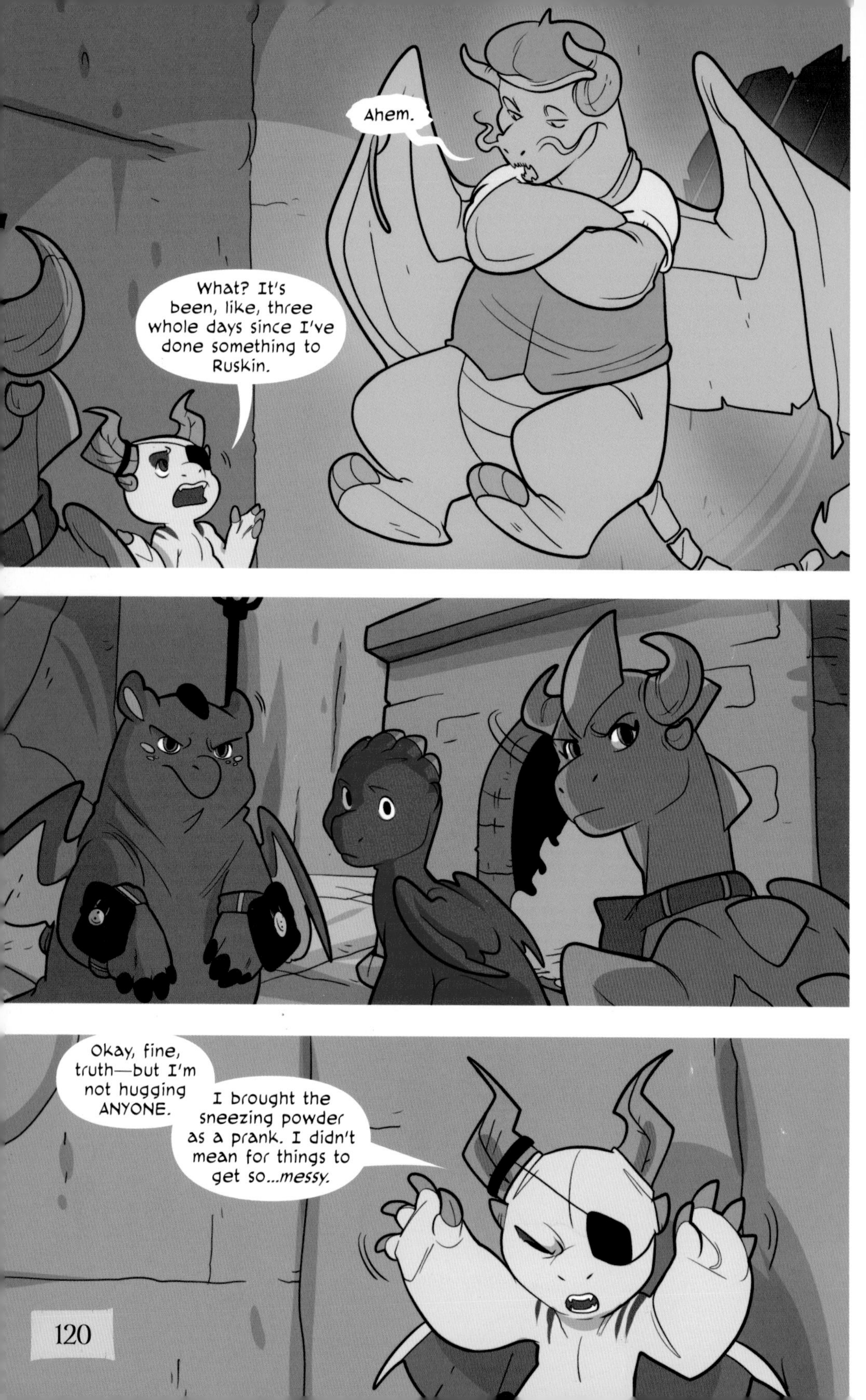
Ahem.
What? It's been, like, three whole days since I've done something to Ruskin.
Okay, fine, truth—but I'm not hugging ANYONE.
I brought the sneezing powder as a prank. I didn't mean for things to get so...*messy.*

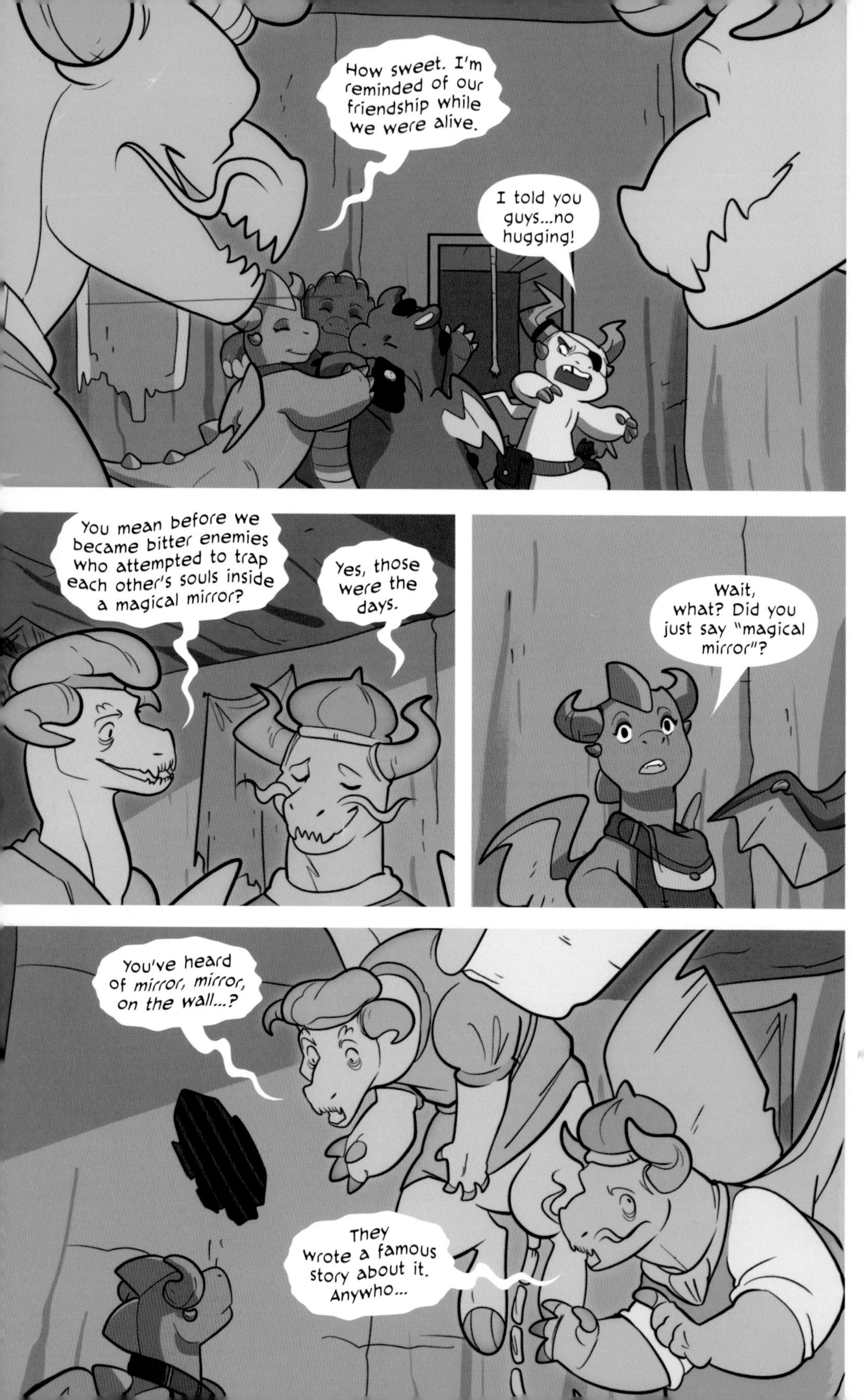
How sweet. I'm reminded of our friendship while we were alive.
I told you guys...no hugging!
You mean before we became bitter enemies who attempted to trap each other's souls inside a magical mirror?
Yes, those were the days.
Wait, what? Did you just say "magical mirror"?
You've heard of *mirror, mirror, on the wall*...?
They wrote a famous story about it. Anywho...

125

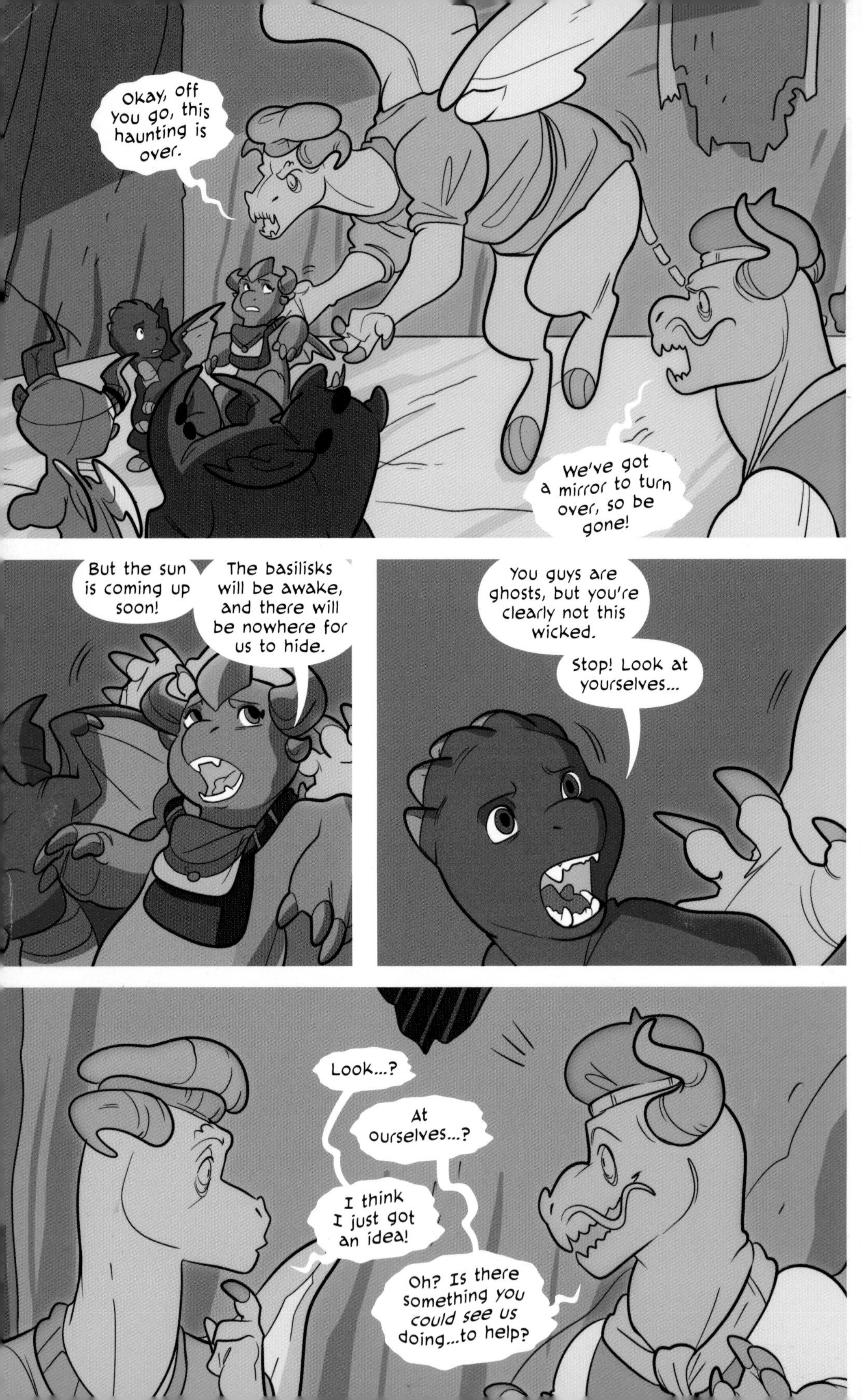
Okay, off you go, this haunting is over.
We've got a mirror to turn over, so be gone!
But the sun is coming up soon!
The basilisks will be awake, and there will be nowhere for us to hide.
You guys are ghosts, but you're clearly not this wicked.
Stop! Look at yourselves...
Look...?
At ourselves...?
I think I just got an idea!
Oh? Is there something *you* could see us doing...to help?

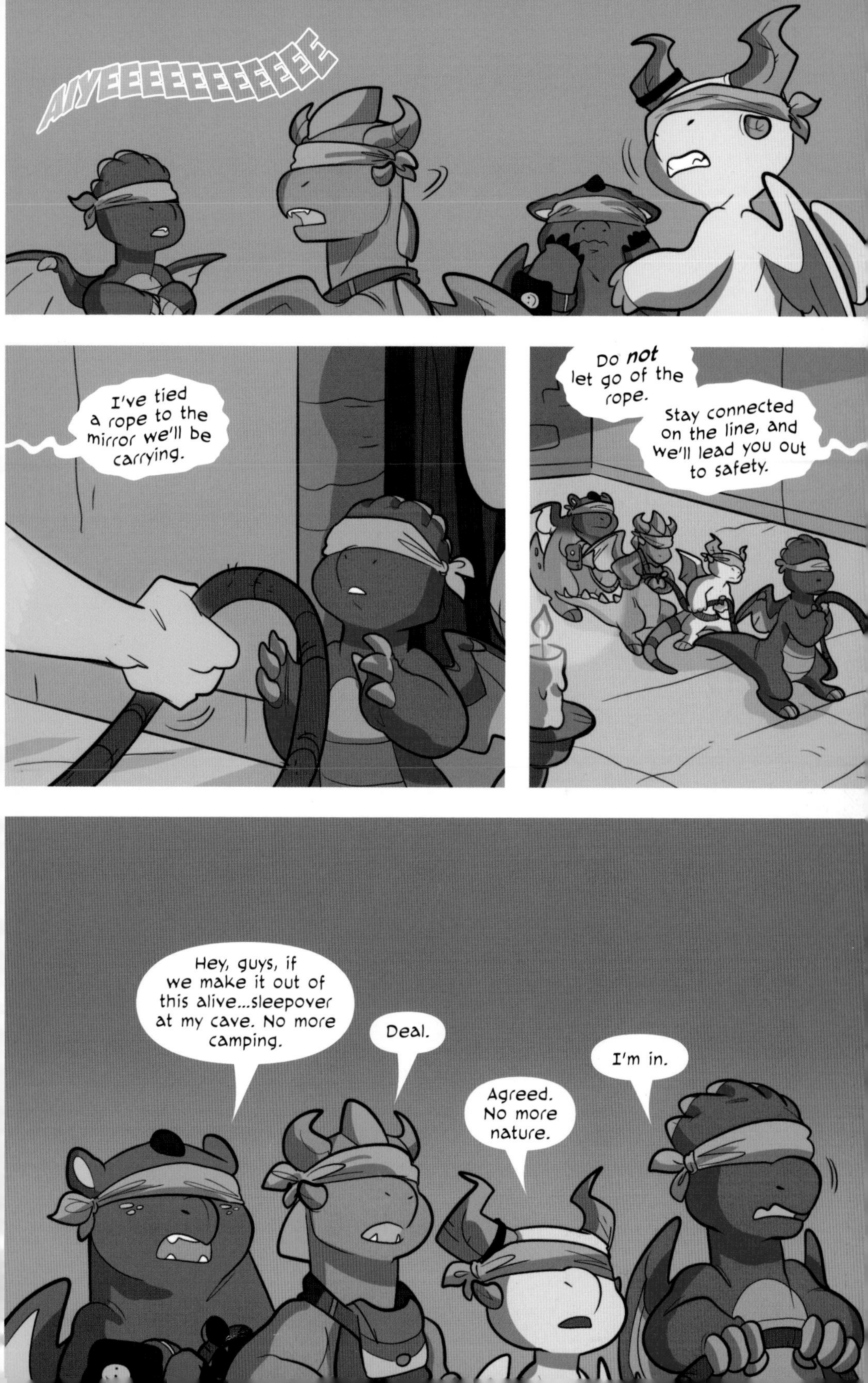
AIYEEEEEEEEEEEE
I've tied a rope to the mirror we'll be carrying.
Do not let go of the rope.
Stay connected on the line, and we'll lead you out to safety.
Hey, guys, if we make it out of this alive...sleepover at my cave. No more camping.
Deal.
Agreed. No more nature.
I'm in.

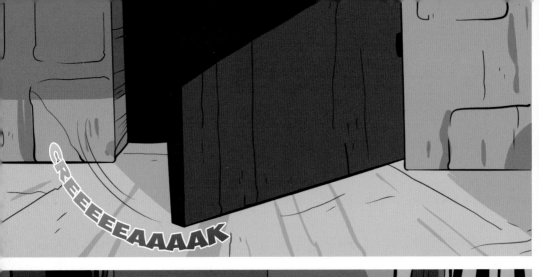

CREEEEEAAAAK

Remind me why we're not just flying away right now? We have wings.

So do basilisks. They may not see well at night, but they're ace fliers during the day.

Those things can fly?!

Shhhh!

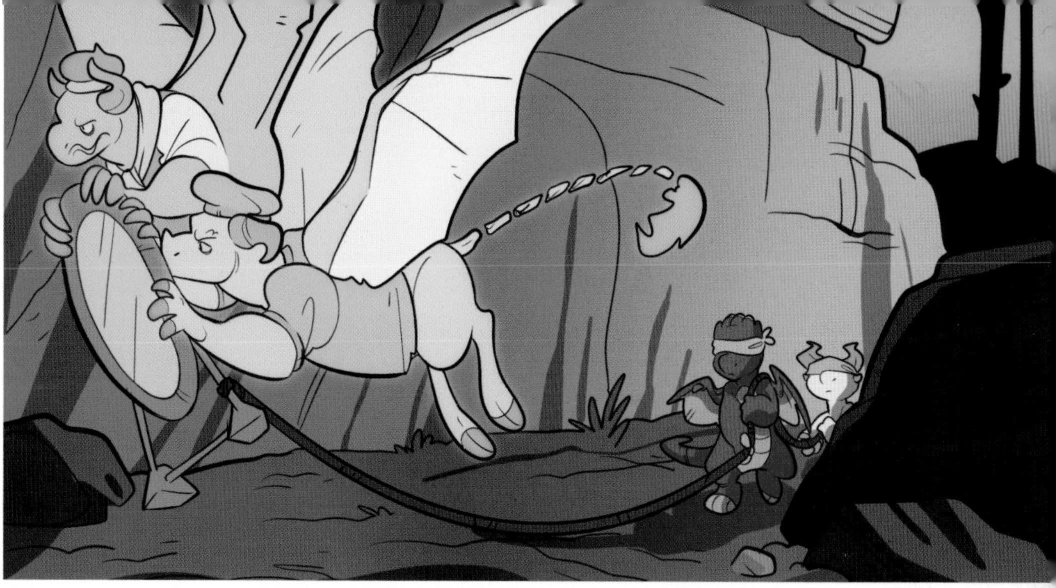

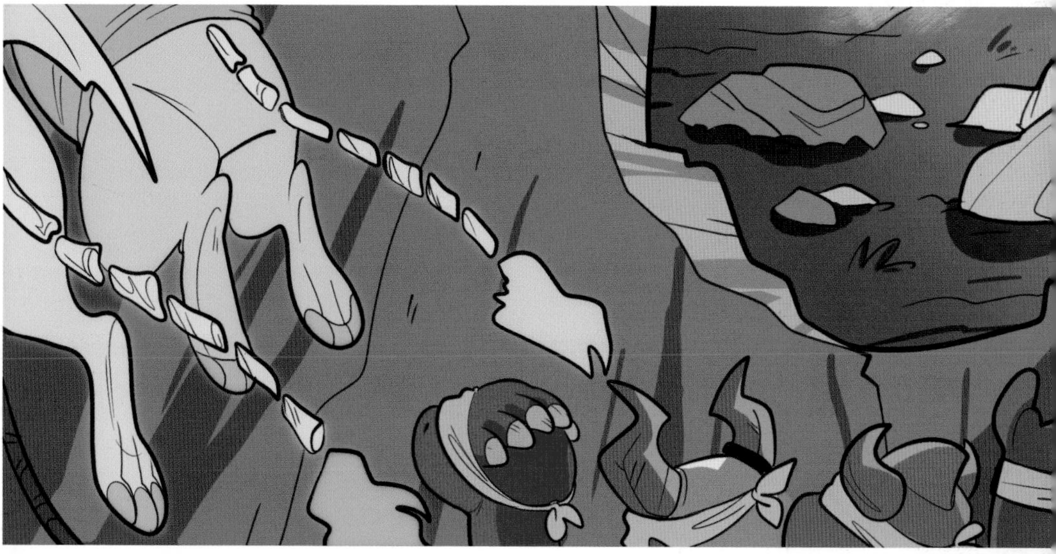

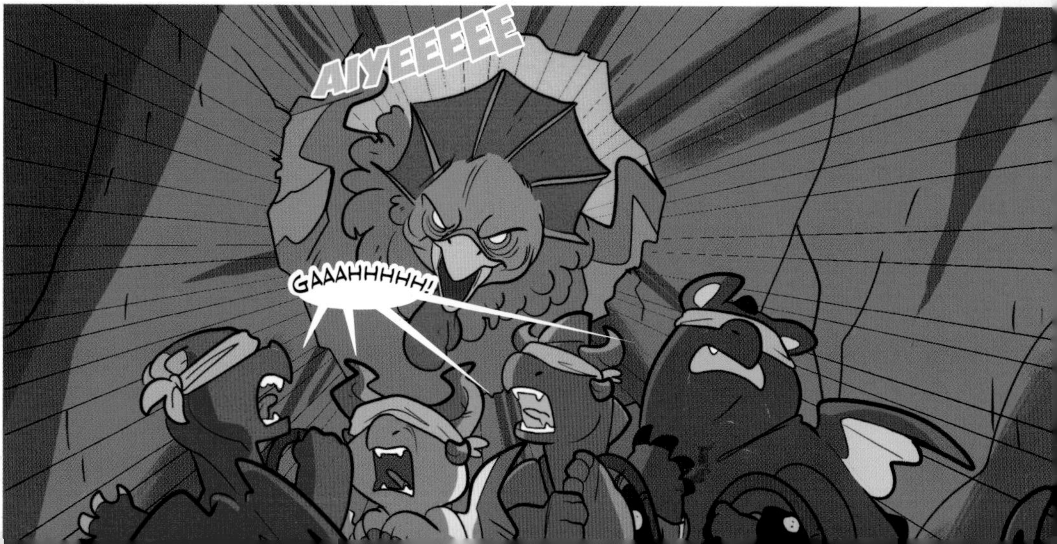
AIYEEEEE
GAAAHHHHH!

What's happening?

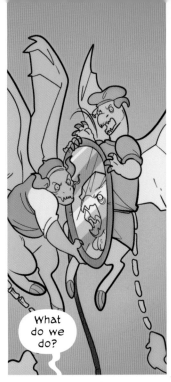

What do we do?

AIYNN

SHIIIING

RUN!

We stunned her!

You mean I stunned her!

THUD

This stinks! We're in an epic high-speed escape, and we can't watch it!

Groth, keep your blindfold on and use your imagination!

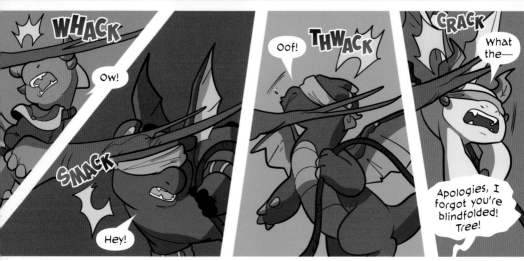

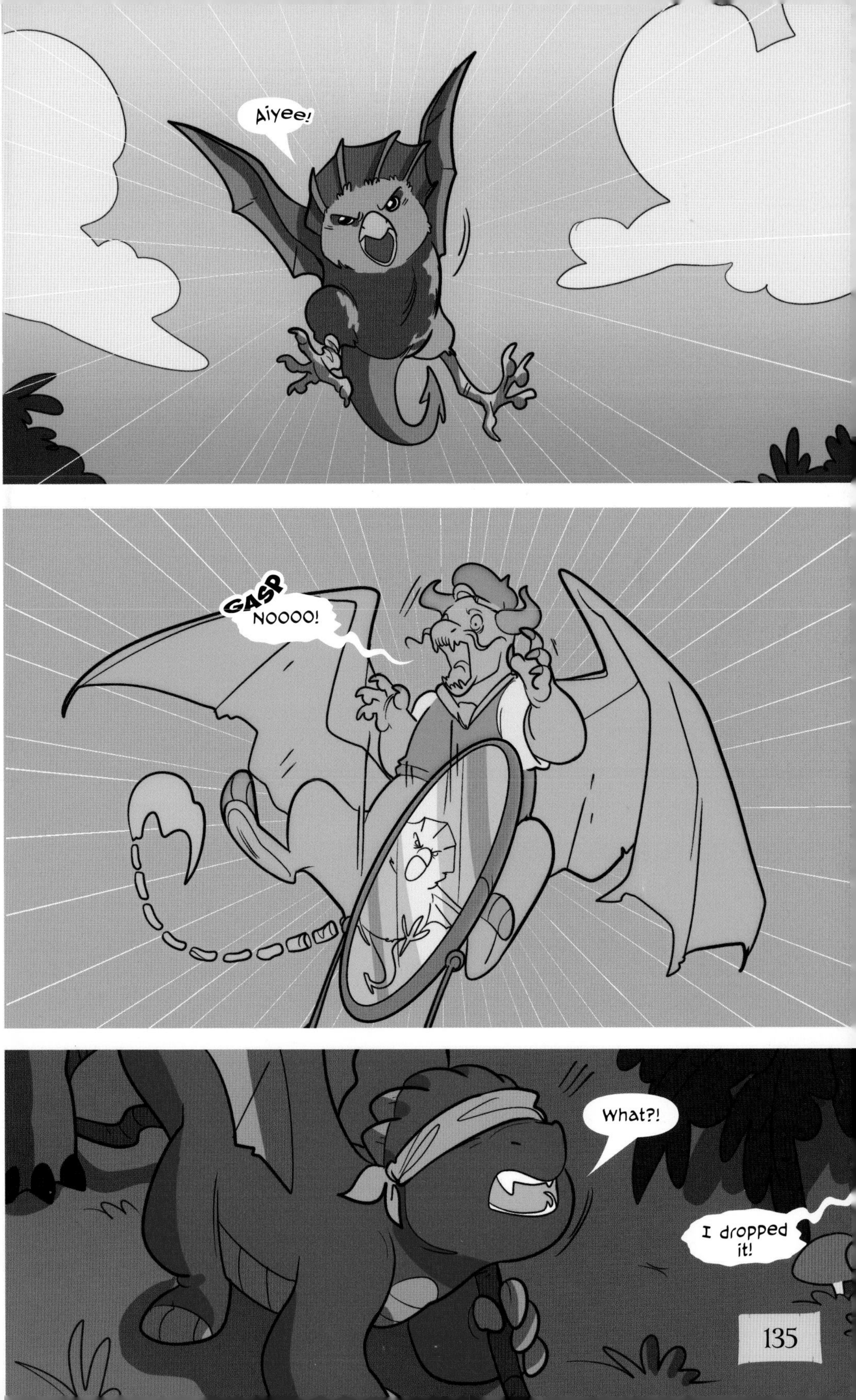
Aiyee!
GASP
NOOOO!
What?!
I dropped it!

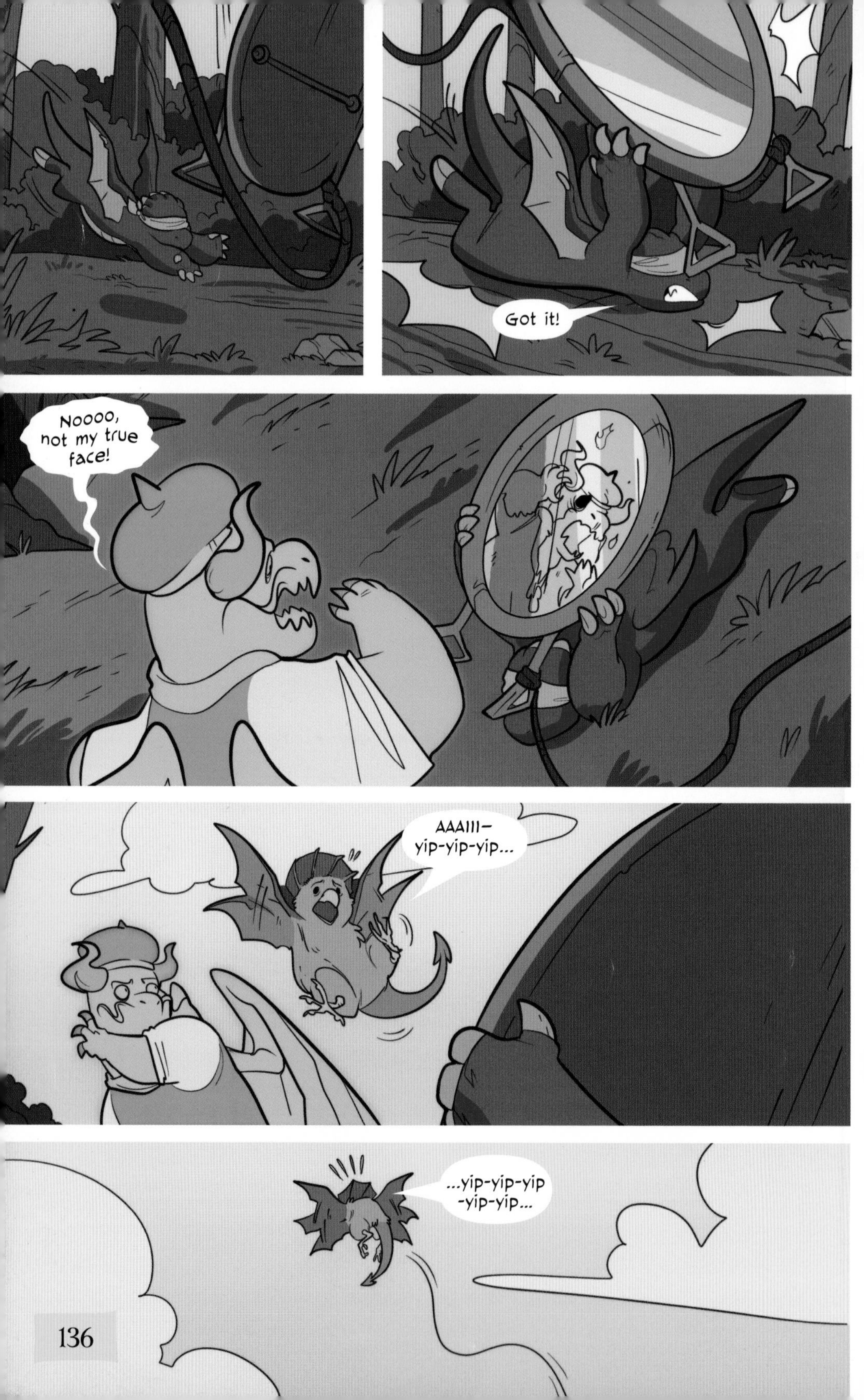
Got it!
Noooo, not my true face!
AAAIII—yip-yip-yip...
...yip-yip-yip -yip-yip...

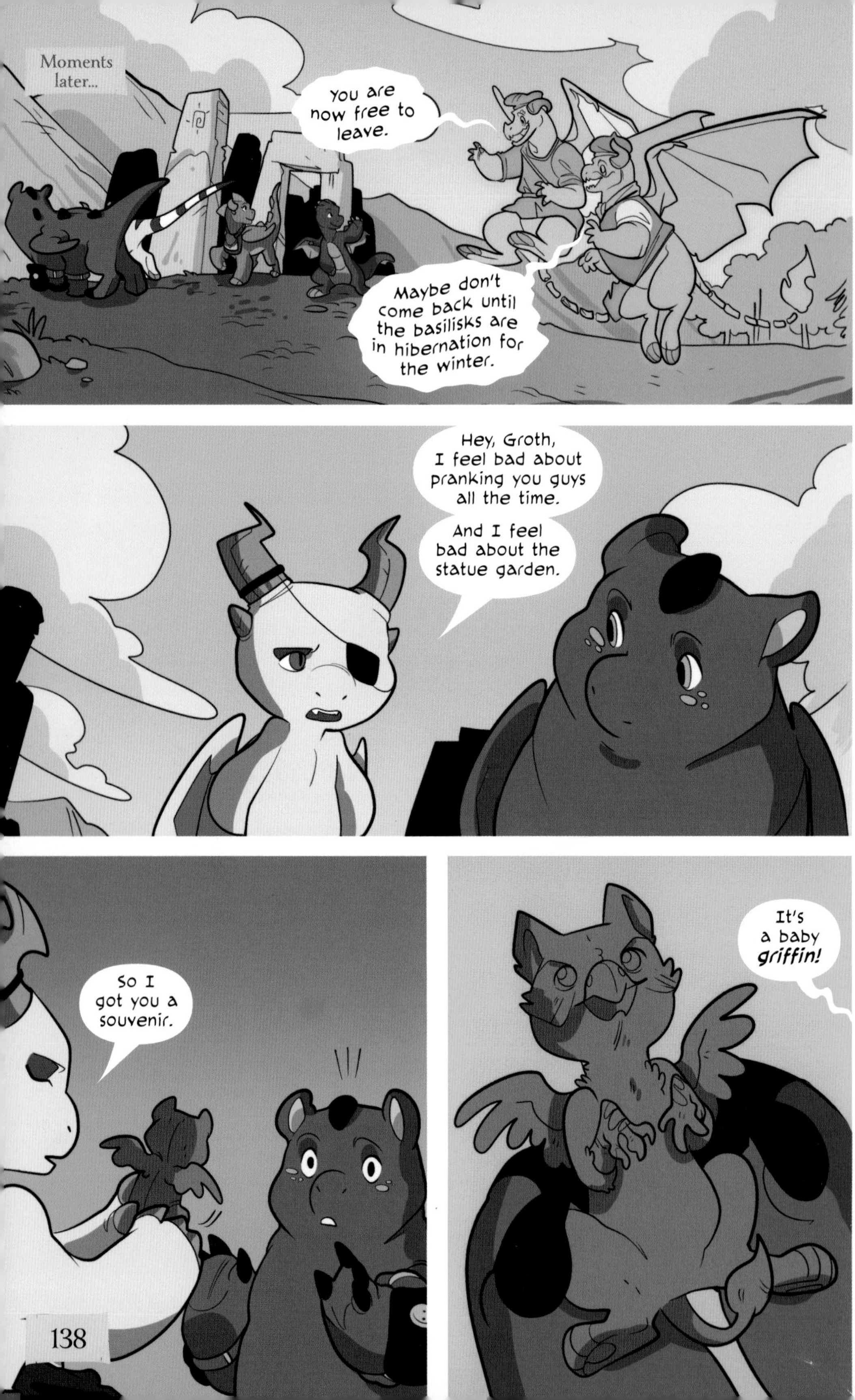
Moments later...
You are now free to leave.
Maybe don't come back until the basilisks are in hibernation for the winter.
Hey, Groth, I feel bad about pranking you guys all the time.
And I feel bad about the statue garden.
So I got you a souvenir.
It's a baby *griffin!*

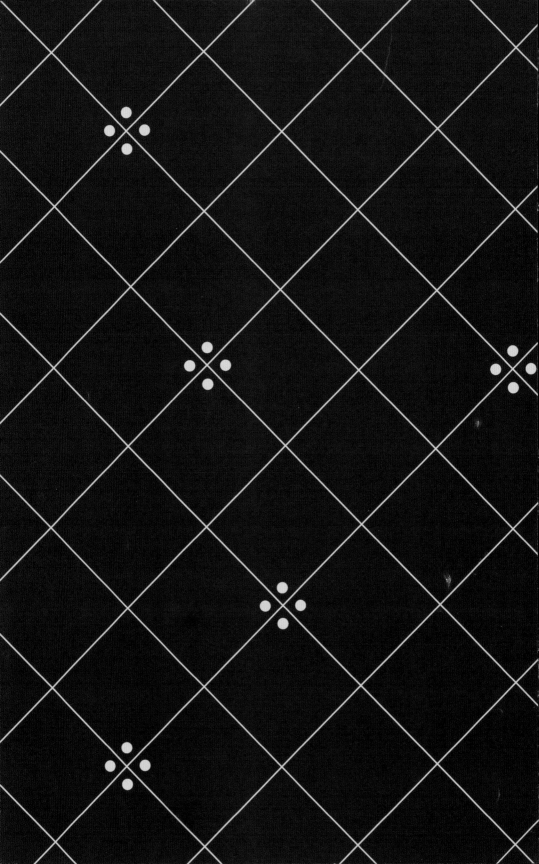

What's in store for Ruskin and his friends next? Find out in . . .

Graphic Novel
DRAGON KINGDOM
of Wrenly
INFERNO NEW YEAR

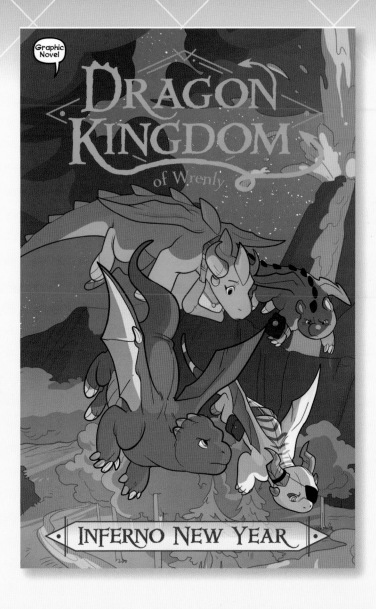

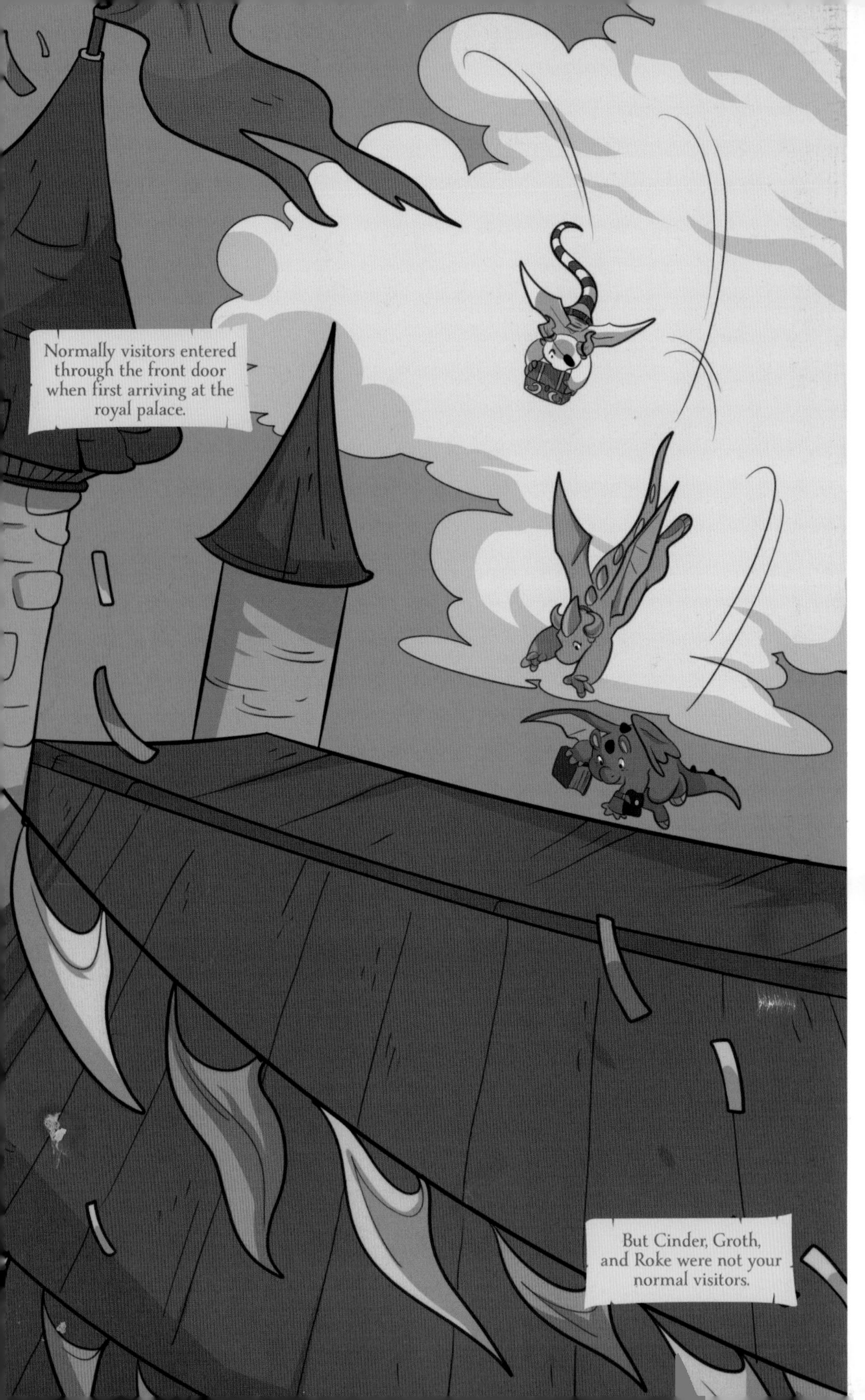
Normally visitors entered through the front door when first arriving at the royal palace.
But Cinder, Groth, and Roke were not your normal visitors.

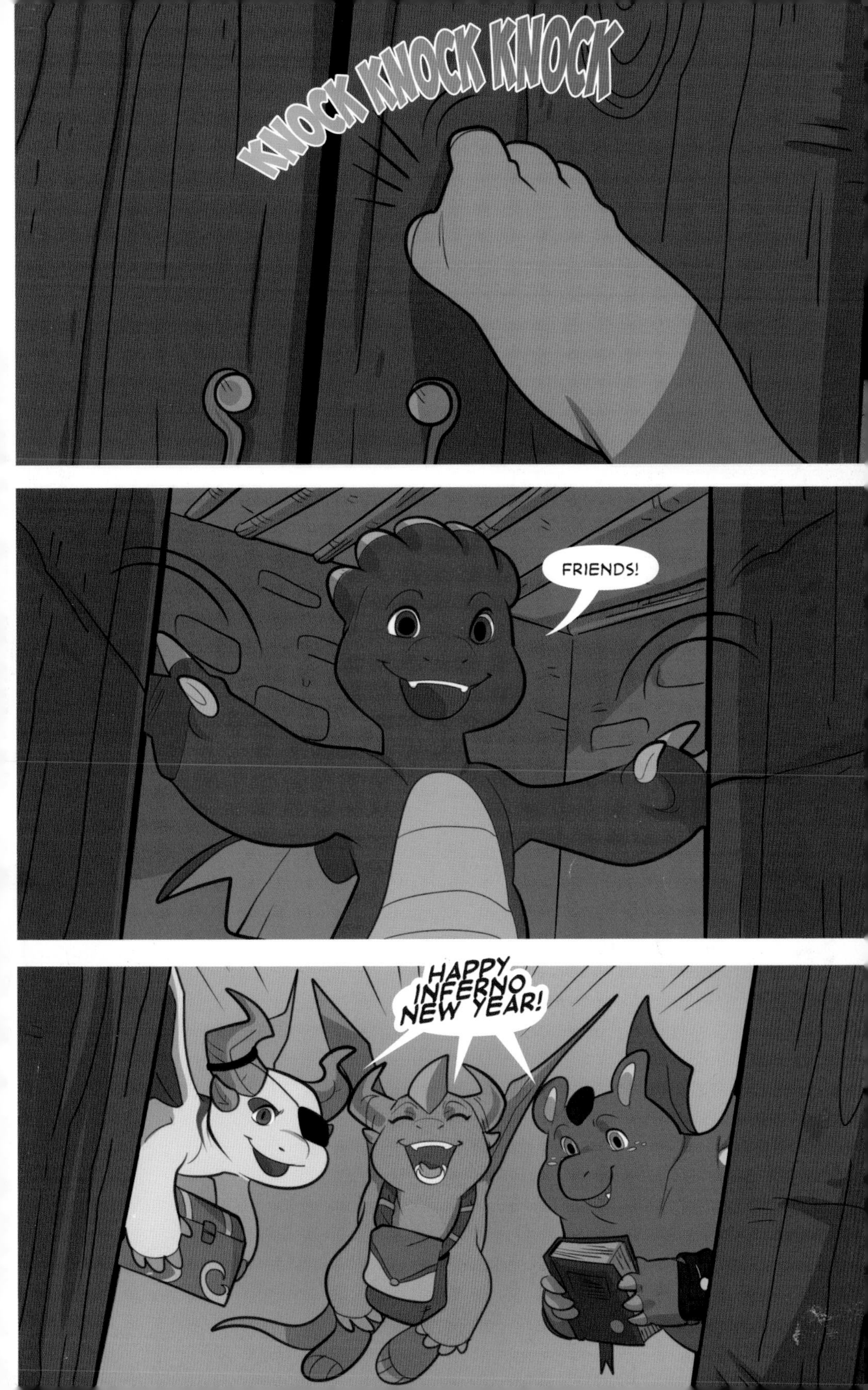
KNOCK KNOCK KNOCK
FRIENDS!
HAPPY INFERNO NEW YEAR!

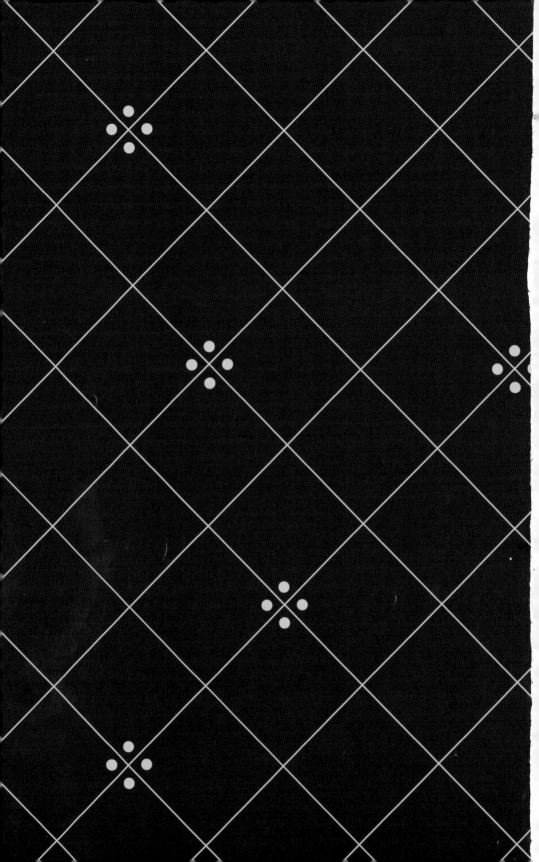